BEAUTY'S ROSE

SHONNA SLAYTON

D1566952

AMARETTO PRESS

"Banish Fear" poem from *La Belle et la Bête* by Jeanne-Marie Leprince de Beaumont, © 1796, now in public domain.

PRINT ISBN: **978-1-947736-51-1**

EBOOK ISBN: **978-1-947736-50-4**

To: Fairy-tale fans.

*Beauty's Rose is inspired by the 1796 version of La Belle et la Bête by
Jeanne-Marie Leprince de Beaumont*

PROLOGUE

*T*hyme fluttered from one cypress tree to the next as she waited for the others.

This isn't good. Never in my life.

She glanced down to the other side of the wall. *Oh, dear. It's really happening.*

Here came her fellow fairies now. Clove with her short, spiky hair and matching attitude, and Sage, the oldest of them all, normally calm, but today showing signs of concern around her eyes.

Thyme turned her ire on Clove. "What did you do?"

Clove sputtered. "Why are you attacking me?"

Thyme pointed over the brick wall, and the other two fluttered over the garden to see what the fuss was about.

Immediately, Sage reached for Clove's hand. "Oh, dear."

Clove stared at the young man transforming into a beast below them. "I wouldn't. I mean, I didn't." She turned to Thyme. "Did I?"

Sage fluttered around the scene, her tiny forehead wrinkled in thought. "You did."

Thyme shook her head. And they thought *she* was the one

who needed supervision. She so wanted to point this out to bossy Clove, but it was obvious from Clove's expression that the fairy was in enough pain.

Clove slapped her tiny thighs in frustration. "I don't know how this happened. I never made it a generational test. It was only for the prince, and when he passed the test using the second chance, the test should have been over. My place in his story ended when he and Beauty fell in love."

"You were quite critical of the prince," Sage pointed out. "Are you sure you didn't accidentally make it harsher than you intended? Maybe you had the thought in the back of your mind?"

"I might have." Clove bit a fingernail. "Does it work that way?"

"He's the first boy born into the family line," Sage pointed out. "It's been girls for generations. Surely it wouldn't lie dormant for so long."

The three fairies stared at one another. This was something new. The curse had transferred to the offspring.

How were they going to fix it?

CHAPTER 1

*M*argot shoved her Walkman into her carry-on luggage before dabbing at the perm solution dripping into her ear. Her friend Amy had tied her hair up in a plastic bag, and now her skin was tingling, bordering on burning, along her forehead. She shouldn't have left her perm to the last minute, but here she was in a rush to get ready for her summer trip and things sort of piled up.

"This stuff reeks," Margot said. "I feel sorry for the person who sits next to me on the plane tomorrow."

"I wouldn't mind the smell if I could go with you to France," Amy said. She stood, hands on hips, examining Margot's Arthur Rackham print of Sleeping Beauty tacked up on the bedroom wall. The print was one of seven fairy tales that Margot had framed and put on display.

"Why do you still have fairy tales on your walls?"

Margot ignored the derision in her voice. Last week, Amy had plastered her bedroom walls with INXS and Bryan Adams posters. Next month it would be something else.

"I like them."

"So did I. When I was five." Amy spun around and sat on the unmade bed. "I've moved on."

Margot's gaze landed on the scene of the princess reaching out with her finger toward the spindle. A spine-chilling image of the moment before tragedy was about to strike. It was one of her favorite scenes.

"When I was five," Margot said, "I dropped a penny into a well in the Rose Garden at Butchart Gardens in Victoria and wished I could *be* in a fairy tale. My sister made fun, but Mom told me it was a wonderful wish. My posters keep the dream alive, so don't spoil it for me."

Amy frowned in sympathy before she wrinkled her nose. "Of course, you made a wish like that." She tapped Margot on the head.

"Watch it. The plastic bag will fall off." Margot patted her tingling head to make sure nothing had slipped. This was the worst part of getting a perm.

Margot hadn't known, but their trip to the famous gardens would be the last family trip they would take with Mom. Margot was too young to realize the significance of the wheelchair her father pushed, other than she got to ride on her mom's lap when her little legs were too tired. But her mother was dying, and the gardens were where she wanted to go one last time. They'd all made wishes in that well, but none had come true.

"Promise me you'll not stay cooped up inside your aunt's castle reading all day. You can waste your time doing that here in Bellingham."

"Technically, I'm only living within the walls of the old city, not the castle itself because it's a museum, not a B&B. But my aunt's apartment is close enough to the castle that I'm sure I'll be able to see it from whichever window nook I've tucked myself into," Margot said with a grin.

Dad tapped the side of the door frame, interrupting Amy's retort. "You girls about done?"

"Almost. Amy needs to rinse me."

"Good. I'm getting hungry. The gang is meeting us at six for dinner. They all want to say goodbye."

"I'll have her ready by five," Amy said, shoving Margot toward the door. She stopped at Margot's desk. "Is this it?" She picked up the invitation from the heritage society.

The family had gotten the invitation to the town reunion in the spring. It came in an embossed envelope, and printed on thick cream paper, it read:

CALLING ALL DESCENDANTS OF
THE MEDIEVAL TOWN OF CHAPAIS
Join us for our first annual celebration of our unique heritage.
Festival, Food, and Revelry
Kids: petting zoo and pony rides
Teens: dress to compete in our Beauty and the Beast contest.
(Prizes for best costumes)
Adults: discounted rates for descendants of townsfolk
Contact the heritage committee for more details.
You do not want to miss this historic event!

"YEAH, FANCY ISN'T IT?"

Mom's family had come from Chapais, and she would likely have talked them all into going, were she still alive. As the family stood now, Margot's older sister was off and married, and her brother had also moved out of the house to start his career. Neither of them wanted to go all the way to France for a town reunion. And Dad was coaching a championship ball team over the summer, so he couldn't go either.

Then Great-Aunt Suzette sent a personal invitation asking them to come:

"You can all stay in my apartment above the bookshop. You are the last of my family, and I'd hate to sit at a reunion table alone."

How could Dad say no to such a plea? They all agreed that Margot should go to represent the family. They even pitched in to buy her plane ticket.

Margot had never thought of herself as representing. She was the odd duck. The only reader in a family of sports fanatics. If she hadn't looked so much like the photographs of her mom— same heart-shaped face and wide-set hazel eyes, she would have sworn the stork dropped her off at the wrong house.

Then it was a rush to get Margot's passport, and the next thing she knew, she was getting a perm while Amy helped pack her suitcase and teased her about her obsession with fairy tales.

"You're a daydreamer, Margot. You live in your head too much. Go experience real life. Be spontaneous while you're over there."

"Agreed. I plan to spontaneously read through every book in the medieval history section at my aunt's bookshop." Margot smiled cheekily.

"That's not what I mean, and you know it." Amy suddenly looked serious. "And don't worry so much about what everyone thinks of you or your accent. Just talk." She pointed to the posters on the wall. "French is a romance language, so get swept up in it like you get swept up in your fairy tales."

Margot struggled at speaking French. She thought learning to speak it would be easy because of her roots, but it turned out, that wasn't the case. This summer was her chance to get fluent so she could earn a scholarship to a college in France that was *literally* in a castle. Dad wouldn't let her go next year if she didn't speak the language enough to get by.

Margot shook her head. "I don't get swept up in anything. I know the difference between real life and fairy tales. Besides, books are in my blood. I come from a long line of bookish people."

Dad clicked on the TV in the living room and the sound of a ball game added background noise. "Well, at least the book gene got to me. My dad's sports gene dominated in my siblings but weakened by the time I came along."

Amy laughed. "Let's get you rinsed."

Margot followed Amy to the end of the hall. "Finally. My scalp is on fire." She held a towel up to her forehead to protect her face, then stuck her head under the faucet in the tub. When the plastic bag came off, a fresh burst of ammonia stung her nostrils.

"Close your eyes," Amy said.

The cool water cascaded over her head and brought relief from both the burning sensation and the sharp odor. "My brother and sister won't show tonight. They never do. Once they left home, they never looked back."

"Does it matter?" Amy turned off the water. She took a fresh towel and began to press it against the curlers, jabbing the hard pink plastic into Margot's skull.

"I can't change them," Margot said.

She moved to the sink, and Amy squirted on the neutralizing solution. When she started unrolling the curlers, Margot added, "It would be nice for Dad if they would check in with him now and then, you know?"

"Don't worry about them. Or your dad. It'll bring you down when you should be enjoying an amazing summer trip."

Margot turned slightly, hair still in Amy's grip. "Thanks. Same goes for you. Ignore your family drama and enjoy working at Expo 86."

Finally, the curlers were out. Another rinse under the tap, and Amy handed her the towel to scrunch-dry her own hair as they returned to Margot's bedroom and half-empty suitcase.

"Here, pack this to remember me by." Amy pulled a cassette tape out of her bucket bag, a drawstring purse. "I made us a summer of '86 tape so we'll always remember this summer...even if we're spending it apart."

"Thanks." Margot did a quick scan of the titles. "These are great. 'If She Knew What She Wants' by The Bangles, 'Take My Breath Away' from Berlin. We never did see that movie, did we?"

"No, but I'm going to *Karate Kid II* this weekend."

"Without me?"

"Mr. Miyagi waits for no one."

"Fine." Margot continued scanning the tape. "This is a good one. 'Something About You'—Level 42, and my favorite, 'Mad About You'—Belinda Carlisle, thank you." Margot wiggled the tape. "Uh, you put a lot of love songs on here."

"It's the summer of love," Amy said. "I'm calling it right now. If you don't come back with a French boyfriend, I don't know what I'll do with you."

"You can't make these things happen."

"Oh, but you can. You've got no reputation over there. What's the town's name again?"

"Chapais." She voiced the *s* on the end.

"*Chapais.*" Amy corrected her in a proper French accent, no *s*. She had no trouble in French but was a terrible tutor. "In Chapais no one knows you're a wallflower. You can pretend you're popular."

"Gee, thanks. I didn't know I was unpopular." Margot tossed a pillow at Amy's head.

"You know what I mean. If you think you're popular, you'll act popular. You'll get the *garçon*."

"Get my waiter? Maybe it was a good thing you never taught me French. At least I know that one."

Amy wrinkled her brow, then shook her head. "Garçon means boy."

"Right."

Amy laughed. "Doesn't matter. It's happening. You'll find a French boyfriend, and I'll meet someone from Sweden at the

Swatch exhibit, and we'll exchange Swatches along with our undying love."

Margot laughed. Sometimes Amy could be so cheesy. "I think you mean from Switzerland."

"What did I say?"

"Sweden."

"Oh, well, same diff. Besides, I also put that friends are friends forever song on there. I know you like that one."

"I saw. Thank you. I am going to miss you."

They were each going off on their summer adventures. If nothing else, the summer of '86 would be different and memorable. With her going to France for this town reunion, and Amy off to work in her uncle's Cantonese restaurant near the World's Expo in Vancouver, something interesting was bound to happen. Amy thought it was all about boys, but Margot was hoping for something longer lasting and life changing.

"Well, Mr. Tremblay? What do you think?" Amy paraded Margot into the living room.

He glanced up from the baseball stats in front of him. "As beautiful as ever."

"Told you I have skills," Amy said smugly. "Just give it a little back comb at the sides and—for me—please use hair spray. Now, about your wardrobe…"

Margot held up her hands. "I'm good, thanks." Amy was all designer; Margot was curl up and read. Comfy all the way. "Be happy you talked me into the perm."

"Speaking of wardrobe," Dad said, "your sister gave you her costume. It's hanging in the hall closet."

"Costume?" Amy scooted out to the hall.

"Oh. I don't think I'll enter the dress-up contest. That's not really my thing."

Amy squealed and came back with the outfit. "You must. This is perfect!"

She held up a long, burgundy skirt, an ecru peasant blouse,

and a white apron with ruffles. A blue patterned scarf was draped around the hanger.

A warm memory tugged at Margot. "Is that Mom's?" Margot asked, reaching for the scarf.

"Yeah. Yeah, that was her favorite. I'm surprised your sister is letting you take it with you."

"Me, too." Margot fingered the soft material, letting it drop as Amy ran off to pack it.

Dad put down his pen and leaned back in the chair. "You remind me of her."

"Mom?"

"Neither of you enjoyed hanging out at all our ball games. And your mother even preferred the TV to be set to another channel. The two of you would have gone off and had your fun while we spent hours at the field."

Margot didn't know her dad had noticed how out of sync she felt with the family.

"She would have been thrilled you were taking this trip. She loved Chapais so much she almost lived there."

"What stopped her?"

Dad grinned. "She met me. Couldn't resist the guns." He flexed his arms, and Margot rolled her eyes.

"You sure you'll be all right while I'm gone?" She frowned at the corn chips and pop bottle on the table. "I stocked the freezer with meals for you, but you've got to remember to take them out."

"I'll be fine. Bring me back the tackiest souvenir you can find."

Margot smiled. "You got it."

Amy headed for the front door. "Well, I better get home and let you finish up." She turned around. "Oh, one more gift. I almost forgot." She pulled out a small, clear tube. "Kissing Potion lip gloss. In bubble gum."

"*Yum*, with the roller ball?"

"In case you meet someone."

Margot shook her head while taking the ultra-shiny lip gloss. "Let me remind you of my summer goals. One: survive meeting a bunch of strangers. Two: learn to speak French. Three: experience France. So, unless the *someone* is a fairy-tale prince, any guy I meet will be low down on my priority list."

CHAPTER 2

*B*ienvenue.

Margot stared at the sign welcoming her to France.

Bienvenue.

Bienvenue, Aunty Suzette…where are you?

Ever since Margot had cleared customs, she'd been standing with her luggage examining every elderly woman who walked by, hoping to lock eyes with someone looking for a teenager from America. Her plane had been delayed several hours in Chicago, but surely her aunt would have waited for her.

Margot pulled off her headphones and stuffed her Walkman back into her carry-on bag. She'd worn out her second set of batteries, and the replacements lay in the bottom of her large suitcase. She didn't want to open it up and dig to the bottom, scattering her unmentionables all over such a public place.

She'd do another sweep of the airport, call her aunt from the pay phone one more time, and then if those came up empty, she'd have to call home in the hopes that Dad was awake. It would be something close to four o'clock in the morning for him.

Margot picked up her bags and began to wander around the

airport, keeping her ears pricked for anyone speaking English. A teenage boy looking as lost as she was zipped past the newsstand in front of her. He was cute, brown feathered hair a little on the long side and wore a T-shirt with a blazer over top and jeans. They had cute boys in France. *Nice.*

He held a small sign at his side, one of those that drivers used to find the people they are picking up. She tilted her head to read it as he swung it in time with his gait. *Did that say Margot?*

She quickly adjusted her bags and chased after him. Her aunt could have sent a driver for her. She followed him until she confirmed it was her name. Margot Tremblay.

"Hey," she called, sudden relief making her bold. "Stop. *Arrêt!* I'm here. You're looking for me."

The guy glanced over his shoulder and saw her frantic movements. He stopped and turned around. "Margot?" he asked, looking hopeful while he held up the sign.

Now, there was an authentic French accent. Nice, deep, with a perfectly rolled *r*, even though Amy says the French don't roll their *r*'s.

She nodded.

"You're late." He said abruptly. He spoke in thickly accented English, but it was English!

"Oh. Yeah," she said, taken aback. "Sorry, but my plane was late."

He said something in French, but all she could do was shrug her ignorance.

"I don't speak French that well," she said with an awkward laugh, wondering how much English he knew. "I was worried I'd be left here all alone and have to draw pictures to ask for a hotel."

He let out a breath and indicated with a wave that she should follow him.

She hesitated for half a second. Her aunt wouldn't send a serial killer to pick her up, would she?

The hurried boy didn't wait to see if she was following, and he walked fast. Like *fast*-fast. He was already halfway down the corridor before she'd decided to go with him.

Margot hiked up her carry-on bag and chased after him again with her big suitcase banging against her leg.

Amy would think this was funny. Margot reviewed how she would write this scene down in a letter to make her friend laugh. She'd talk about how she had to dodge little old French women and groups of American tourists—hey! English speakers! A little late, as she didn't need their help now.

She followed the boy out into the final wisps of a glorious sunset. The patches of clear sky had been hidden from her inside the building, and she was glad the clouds were going away. She paused a moment to take in her first full view of France. The deep orange light turned the trees golden and warmed her heart.

"And so it begins," she said to herself. Because she couldn't say it to the guy who was now halfway across the parking lot. She was losing sight of his broad shoulders. "Wait up!" *I guess chivalry is dead.*

It had been a long day, and she had expected to meet her aunt and be showered with long-lost-relative love, so she was disappointed at this abrupt departure.

"Wait up!" She burst after the boy before he could disappear on her.

By the time she reached his car—a surprisingly cute blue(ish) old convertible that had seen better days—he had it running, the motor not exactly purring, but at least working.

She stood beside the back of the car wondering if he expected her to toss her bags into the small back seat and hop in.

He got out, pulling on leather driving gloves and then opened the tiny trunk. She hefted her luggage in and let him squeeze it into the space.

When he slid into the driver's side, she said, "Thank you. Merci." *Ha, I'll be fluent by the end of summer at this rate.*

The boy responded with a slew of French that didn't make a

lick of sense. But it sure sounded good coming from him. Margot wanted to know who he was and how he knew her aunt. As in, was this drive a favor for her aunt, or did he expect her to pay him like a taxi driver? He may have been explaining all those things to her, but she'd never know.

She smiled at him, hoping he didn't need any information from her.

He frowned and shook his head at her silence. Then he slipped sunglasses over his stormy gray eyes and drove out of the parking lot, music blasting.

Now that she had been picked up from the airport and was on to her next destination, Margot should be able to relax and enjoy the scenery. For one thing, the sunset here stretched out into a golden twilight made for a movie set.

Although, if by *relaxed*, that meant she still held on to her house keys in case she needed to punch the guy beside her, then yes, she was relaxed. All these years of being careful around strangers and suddenly she'd ditched all her training and was riding alone in a car, as far away from home as she could get, with a complete stranger. She'd end up on the news yet.

"What happened to my aunt Suzette? I thought she was picking me up."

"You're late," he said again.

"So…she sent you instead?" Margot was going for clarification, not a lecture. It wasn't her fault the plane had a problem.

"I pick up tourists all day long. You are last. I come back for you."

"Oh. I'm glad you did."

Conversation killer. She glanced at him as he stared straight ahead. *That's okay. Eyes on the road.* She focused her attention back to the French countryside. Any normal person would be having a great time right now: in a convertible with the top down, a sunset over the vineyards in France, and a handsome stranger with a wicked accent in the driver's seat. It all sounded good for a novel, but in reality, it made her a tad nervous.

"You need to get out of your head," Amy always said. "Life is what is happening right now, not in your imagination."

They'd had this same discussion whenever her friend was trying to talk her into going somewhere. Margot would rather curl up with a good book than go out to a party. At least in a novel, she knew the ending would be a happy one. And if the character got caught in the rain, Margot could enjoy the sensation without actually getting cold and wet. And where else but in a book could you go back in time and experience a medieval castle? Okay, well, this summer was all about experiencing a medieval castle, albeit with a modern twist.

She scanned the distant hills, eager for her first glimpse at the walled city of Chapais where she'd be staying. *I'm going to live in a medieval city.* If nothing else good happened this summer, she didn't care. She was going to live near a castle.

All these thoughts flew as fast as the car flew down the road. However, she must have fallen asleep at some point, because she woke to a gentle nudge.

"Chapais," said a deep voice.

She realized her driver was pointing to something in the distance. She sat up and took in a sharp breath. A storybook castle rose above the twinkling lights of a small town. Larger spotlights illuminated the outer wall like it was a movie set. "That's where I get to stay?"

She sat up straight in her seat, not wanting to miss a thing. She glanced at the driver, and though it was getting dark, got the impression he was appraising her reaction. *Do I pass inspection?*

She counted at least thirty-two small guard towers along the wall and, at the back, several larger towers, which were likely part of the castle proper.

"Nothing in my town is very old compared to this. The oldest building was built in 1858, and it's the oldest brick building in all of Washington state. That was like yesterday compared to this."

The driver grunted, and Margot tried not to interpret it as anything, but she couldn't help think he was judging her. For what? Her giddiness at seeing a castle? Her lack of a proper history in her hometown?

No matter. The fairy tale fan in her couldn't be happier. As she studied the crenellated walls, she imagined the surrounding fields ripe with summer wheat and dotted with peasant huts.

Back to reality, the car pulled into a dirt parking lot beside the ancient wall. The boy shut off the engine and hopped out.

Margot followed, gaping at the thick limestone wall rising above the earthen bank. If she was nervous before, now she felt only pure excitement. She dove into her carry-on to dig out her slim Kodak disc camera.

Meanwhile, the boy took out her luggage and dropped it to the ground.

Margot waved her camera at him, indicating she'd like a picture. He shrugged and waited while she framed his convertible and the castle...and, surreptitiously, him. The lighting wasn't the best, but that didn't matter. She just needed a shot of this guy and his car to send to Amy.

"Thanks," she said as he rubbed his eyes from the bright flash.

She followed her chauffeur (hey, another French word) as he carried her large suitcase up to an iron gate which was open. She paused on the threshold before stepping onto the ancient streets inside the wall. She didn't mean to be dramatic, but it was her attempt to *experience* the moment.

Electric lamps shone pools of light onto the cobblestones, but even that modern touch didn't take away from the ancient feel of the place. Second-story houses hung over the streets, their windows cheerily lit behind their curtains. So, folks still lived above their shops, just like in medieval times. Given the liberal use of electricity, she hoped that also meant other modern conveniences...like plumbing. Maybe even TV? She was all for studying history, but she wouldn't want to live without recent inventions.

Far-off music played from what she guessed was a pub farther down the street. All the shops they were walking past were closed, including the one her driver stopped in front of.

The wooden sign, which hung out over the road, was decorated with a carving of three books, two stacked horizontally with a third upright and slightly opened to reveal its pages. Small, paned windows allowed a darkened glimpse into a book display.

I'm here!

CHAPTER 3

The driver walked past the bookstore door and into a narrow alley. An even narrower set of stone stairs went up the side of the building. He dropped her luggage at the bottom and pointed to the door at the top.

"Great. Thanks for the ride, er, merci." She grabbed her bags and quickly ascended, hoping he wouldn't stop her and ask for money. She had no idea how much a trip from the airport should cost. Nor did she know how French money worked yet.

At the top, she glanced down and was relieved to see him waiting at the bottom of the stairs, even if he stood with his arms crossed impatiently. Aunty Suzette would know what to do with him.

She knocked on the door and prayed that her great-aunt was inside. When no one answered, she felt the chill of the night air bring up more worry. She'd not been able to get in touch with her aunt since landing at the airport. What if something had happened to her? Surely the driver would have said something. Or given her a key?

She checked under the mat, but there was no key left for her.

She skimmed the top of the door frame. No key. She pounded on the door one more time.

"Hello?" She called out, not wanting to disturb the neighbors, but worried she'd have to fend for herself tonight. The only sound was the thrumming of the rock music coming from the pub. *How odd. They should be playing a dulcimer or a lute or something.*

Margot called to the boy at the bottom of the stairs. "She's not here."

"Leave your bag," he said. "Follow me."

"But all my stuff is in here."

"Come," he said, leaving no room for argument.

Margot shoved her suitcase into the darkest corner and descended the stairs. "Where are we going?"

"She is already there. We're late," he said.

"What—" she started to ask for clarification, but he cut her off.

"The welcome dinner. They want us all to go."

Margot followed the irritated boy to the source of the music. Down the darkened lane and a few twists and turns later, they were at the town square. A wide, open space surrounded by ancient buildings and the castle proper just beyond. String lights hung crisscross over the square to provide dim lighting, and a mishmash of square and round tables covered with white tablecloths were crammed into the space.

Up at the front, a middle-aged king and queen presided at the head table along with several others dressed up as royalty. The queen wore a modest crown and a green gown trimmed in gold. She smiled often at the bearded king who wore a doublet matched to her dress.

"Margot?" A gray-haired woman seated near the fountain got up and came her way. "*Bonjour,* Margot!" she said in a sprightly voice, followed by a quick flow of French and a kiss on the cheek.

"Aunty, I mean, *Tante* Suzette?" Relief flooded her veins. "So good to see you. You do speak English?" Margot asked hopefully, looking eye level with her aunt. "From your letters, I assumed."

"Yes, yes, dear. English. I speak English. Your father said you needed to learn French, so I was obliging." Her accent was only slight. Perhaps working in a tourist town gave her lots of practice speaking English. "I was saying how much you look like your mother."

"Thank you. I'm told that a lot."

Suzette looked around the square. "Where is Burke?"

"Was he the driver?" Margot searched the square for the only familiar face she knew. "There. He's leaning against the wall."

Suzette called out in French, waving a hand at an empty chair at her table. He shook his head and remained where he was. Suzette's countenance fell. "I wish he would let me thank him properly for fetching you. I had to stay behind and help with the dinner. How did you like him? Was he a gentleman?"

"He was…" Margot searched for the right word. "Efficient."

"Yes. That's a good description of him. Let's sit." Suzette led the way to her table. "Ladies, this is my great-niece from America." Suzette introduced three other older women sitting at their table. When she reached the last lady, a woman in a bright flowered dress with pinkish hair under her straw hat, she said, "And this is Thyme, one of the heritage committee members. She organized this welcome dinner."

Thyme stood and embraced Margot like a long-lost friend. She smelled of peaches.

"Oh, hello," Margot said in surprise at the warm welcome.

"What do you think of our little town? Your aunt tells us you've never had the pleasure to be here." Thyme also spoke in clear English, her accent lilting like a song.

Margot took in the buildings made from stone, their cozy square-paned windows and medieval styles. Not to mention the actors at the head table creating a vision of the past. "I love it. Thanks for inviting me."

Thyme looked pleased. "Chapais is one of my favorite historic places in France. Almost perfectly preserved from the old days. I know you just got here, but you must meet the other committee members." She waved, trying to get the attention of another woman seated in the middle of the square. "We're all wearing the same hat so we're easy to spot," she said. "Oh, bother. They're not looking my way. That's Clove, with the short, spiky hair talking to the young lady in the sundress. And Sage with the gray hair is over there at that long table. You'll meet them before the weekend is over. We're three peas in a pod, as they say."

Once they were all seated, Thyme called over a waitress dressed in a peasant blouse and skirt and asked her to bring Margot a dinner plate. The other diners had already moved on to dessert, some chocolate and raspberry concoction.

"You're just in time for our Trivial Pursuit game. Are you familiar?"

"Yes, I've played."

"Good. Ours will be different, but similar."

The music stopped, and one of the women from the heritage committee took hold of a microphone and tapped it to make sure it was on. She began with a few pleasantries, followed by instructions on how to play the game, dividing everyone by table. She spoke in French, but Suzette translated for Margot and another woman at the table.

"They've taken five of the categories and made them specific to Chapais, so the History category is medieval history, Art and Literature is fairy tales, Geography will be about France, jousting is our Sport, and French gardens for Science and Nature." Suzette turned to Burke again, inviting him to join their team. "He is an expert on Chapais. We'd win for certain. Not that I'm competitive."

He held up his hand in a stop motion and shook his head. He was still wearing the leather driving gloves like he was just waiting for an opportunity to slip back out to the car.

"Burke can't play," Thyme said. "He helped us write the questions. Besides, the game is more for our visitors."

"Of course. But the locals can help?" Suzette seemed eager to play.

"Yes. We want everyone to get to know one another and the town better."

The emcee asked the first question about the name of the river that flowed near the town. The table closest to her answered before Suzette had finished translating. The emcee gave them a blue ribbon. The first table to collect all five colors would win.

Game play continued at a fast clip until they reached a question about an obscure fairy tale.

"What was inside the iron stove in the forest?" Suzette translated.

Each table had already launched into a discussion over it, but Margot knew right away.

"An enchanted prince."

Suzette stood and shouted the answer in French.

"Correct."

"Well done, Margot. That was exciting." Suzette sat down.

When the emcee held up the brown ribbon for Art and Literature, Suzette nudged Margot to go get it. Everyone clapped for her as she wound her way around the tables.

"What is your name, child?" the emcee held tight to the ribbon, her green eyes sparkling as Margot reached out for the award.

"Margot."

"Well done, Margot." The emcee led the crowd in another round of applause while Margot worked her way back to the table.

She held the ribbon high for her teammates to see. Burke was also clapping and looking at her with...what? Not approval. That would be going too far. Admiration? She wondered if he thought he'd stump everyone on that. She smiled widely at him. He had no idea what it would take to challenge her on a fairy tale.

In the end, the table at the front collected all the colors first and won. No one at Margot's table could answer any of the sports questions. "Maybe one of us could take up jousting before next year," Margot joked.

"You have an interest in fairy tales?" Thyme asked. "Will you be taking part in the costume contest tomorrow night?"

Margot shook her head. "I don't think so."

"Why not? We've fewer young ladies here than I'd hoped for. It wouldn't do for someone as old as me to enter. If you'd like, I can get you a costume." She raised her eyebrows expectantly and simultaneously waved Burke over.

"No. Thank you. I actually have a medieval costume. My sister's."

"Ah, then you'll do it? Burke?" She extended a hand to him. "We're talking about the costume contest tomorrow night. You're entering, aren't you? Encourage this girl to join in the fun." She spoke in a mix of French and English such that Margot could follow the conversation.

"*Non.* I will not enter." Burke crossed his arms, making himself look more irritated than when he was at the airport.

The waitress shot him a look as she approached the table. "He thinks he is too good for us." She plastered a smile on her face. "Are you ready for your dessert, *mademoiselle*?"

"Yes, please." Margot tried not to look shocked at the boldness of the waitress in front of one of the organizers. But Margot could see her point. Burke had an air of disdain about him.

The waitress bent down and whispered in Margot's ear, "He'd win as beast without a costume."

Burke took a step back like he was about to leave.

"Thank you anyway," Thyme said. "You'll see how much fun everyone has tomorrow, and you'll wish you had joined." She gave Margot's arm a squeeze. "Right, Margot?" Her expression was so earnest, Margot didn't know what came over her.

"Sure. I'll dress up." *What am I saying? I don't want to compete in a costume contest.*

Thyme beamed at her and nodded at Burke. "That's the spirit."

It wasn't spirit, rather a combination of feeling bad that Thyme had gone to so much effort and Margot's defenses being down after a long day of travel. She'd regret it in the morning. Dress up as Beauty in front of all these people?

"Ready to go back to the apartment?" Suzette asked. "You look about to fall asleep on the spot."

"Oh, do stay for the dancing," Thyme said.

"Margot really should get settled." Suzette stood. "And she needs to call her dad to let him know she arrived."

Margot nodded and said tentatively in French, "It was nice to meet you all."

"She's a pushy one," Suzette whispered as they left. "They all are on the committee, but they mean well. We've talked for years about an event like this, but it took those three ladies descending on the town to make it happen."

Margot turned around and caught Burke watching them leave. She started to lift her hand in a wave, but he looked away and joined Thyme at their table. *Oh, so now he sits.*

Suzette retraced the route Margot had taken with Burke, down the narrow, cobbled streets until they reached the bookshop. The storefront was maybe fourteen feet across, like the other shops they had passed, nothing like shopping at the mall with the large department stores. Quaint was the word that came to mind.

"The family legacy," Suzette said with pride. "You'll be able to see it better in the morning."

She slowly worked her way up the stairs and opened the door. Margot retrieved her suitcase from the shadows and followed Suzette in.

Like the storefront below, the apartment was also narrow, consisting of a small living space next to an even smaller kitchen. A hallway presumably led to the bedrooms and bathroom. The furnishings looked to be antiques from the Victorian era, overstuffed chairs with spindly legs. Flowered wallpaper plastered the living room and painted French landscapes hung at eye level. And the books! Books filled every flat surface from coffee table to side tables and kitchen counter. They leaned against walls and formed piles in the corners.

The stacks of books reminded Margot of her room back home. One never had enough bookcases to hold all the books.

"Your room is through there and the washroom beside."

Margot found her room and plopped her suitcase on the small daybed which was covered with a crocheted afghan. There was a small wardrobe painted white, and voile curtains fluttered with a slight breeze coming through the open window.

When she returned to the kitchen, Suzette had put the kettle on. "It's not much, given the old style, but it's cozy," Suzette said.

"No, this is great. Thank you. Merci." How long would she go on saying thank you twice?

"Here's the phone. Better call before we forget."

Margot took the handset and called home collect. Classic code for *I got here safely, but you don't need to spend the money to hear me say it.* Her dad refused the charge. Code for *message received; I love you.*

"I'm surprised I caught him at home."

"He wanted to know you were safe."

Suzette poured water into the teapot. "Chamomile? It helps me sleep after some excitement."

"Probably a good idea. I slept on the plane, so I'm off schedule."

"I'm sorry I wasn't the one to pick you up at the airport. But I understand Burke has a convertible, so I thought a young person might like that more than my Fuego.

Margot took the mugs and followed Suzette to the table. "His convertible is pretty cool. I didn't mind that part at all."

"Burke can come off a little intense; I hope that didn't put you off. You'll see him again tomorrow and get a chance to know him."

"How so?"

"He is helping me set up a computer in the bookshop. I didn't think I needed one, but he talked me into it. He can be as convincing as those heritage women."

Margot let out a breath. Burke was nice to look at, but was as arrogant a boy as she'd ever met. It would be best if she steered clear of him while she was in town.

CHAPTER 4

$\mathcal{L}$ ate the next day, Margot woke to the sound of tourists milling about the town. The people at street level weren't loud, but they created a general sense of movement. Margot lay for a moment, putting her thoughts in order, her sheets twisted from the dreams she'd had.

Several times during the night, she'd woken in a sweat with a vague memory of running through a forest, something dark and brooding chasing her. The dreams felt so real they set her pulse to racing. Each time she woke, she had to get up and turn the light on to reassure herself she was in a bedroom and that nothing was after her.

Sometimes having an active imagination was a dangerous thing. Fortunately, her fear of the dream quickly faded in the light of the summer sun pouring through her window.

Margot slipped out of bed and padded out to the living room which had a window overlooking the street. Immediately across from her was another apartment, sun shining on an abundance of ferns in the window. And down below, sure enough, vacationers meandered over the cobblestones, entering and exiting the bookshop below. For someone who was used to waking up to the drone of a lawn mower in a quiet neighborhood, Margot found it a little unnerving to have strangers carrying out their daily business so near to where she was sleeping unawares.

How late is it?

Leaving the tourists to do what tourists do, Margot looked for a clock to see how long she'd slept in. She found one in the kitchen. It was ten already. Margot snagged an orange out of the fruit bowl and then cut it into wedges. She'd once read that Louis XIV had a thing for oranges. Had them growing all over the Palace of Versailles, even inside. Fun facts she'd picked up before her trip.

After one look at the shower—was that a shower? It was just a hand-held device attached to the bathroom wall and there was no curtain. She decided she'd better wait for instructions before soaking the entire bathroom. Instead, she pulled out a pair of acid wash jeans and her favorite *I believe in 398.2* T-shirt, the Dewey decimal call number for fairy tales.

After making her bed, she unpacked the rest of her clothes. Her mother's scarf shot her with a pang of homesickness. Would Dad be all right without her this summer? He'd never been alone since Mom died. And he couldn't rely on her siblings to help him out at all.

A shout came from outside. "Bonjour!" Followed by an excited conversation below her. All right. She'd dawdled long enough. She should go down to the bookshop and check in with Suzette. It was time to start her summer vacation. A once-in-a-lifetime summer. The summer of love.

She exited the apartment, studying the ancient buildings of Chapais. Here she was, a simple peasant girl sent out on an errand to procure breakfast at the local bakery. Never mind that if she really were a peasant girl, she would probably be the one making the bread, having risen before dawn. Still, she was poor and hungry and maybe would need to beg alms from the travelers passing by the alley.

The travelers in T-shirts and ball caps.

Sigh. Imagination could only take a girl so far.

Margot stepped out of the alley as a customer was leaving, carrying a bag of books and a plastic sword. Margot waited for him to clear the door before she stepped inside. A delightful brass bell jingled as the door shut.

The room was amusingly haphazard with shelves forming rooms and alcoves for customers to explore. The scent of old books and fresh lavender rose up to welcome her, and she breathed in deeply. Books smelled good in any country.

Suzette's voice rose above the couple speaking German near the postcards at the entrance. She sat at the till, ringing up a sale. She wore a white peasant blouse covered by a red apron. The cash register was another relic from the past, a silver model with fancy scrollwork and tabs that popped up with the dollar amounts.

"Margot." Suzette called her over as the man left. "What do you think of the little bookshop?" Suzette asked.

"It's...amazing." Margot scanned the clustered and busy bookshelves. Little Christmas tree lights draped around the alcoves adding a firefly touch.

"I baby it. Never had children, so I fuss over this. Why don't you go explore the town this morning? Burke will show you around. He's in the back."

Margot's stomach dropped at Burke's name. She self-consciously tucked her hair behind her ear. "Are you sure he wants to show me around? I won't be imposing?" The waitress's comment came back to her, *He thinks he's too good for us.* "I'm perfectly happy exploring on my own."

"Don't be shy. He's lived here his whole life and can show you the best of the place. Go on back. He's expecting you."

So, he had to be talked into it? This was going to be fun.

Margot headed to the back of the store where she found a small storeroom filled with boxes and an office about the size of a closet. Burke sat at the desk in the cramped space typing two-fingered into a computer. He wore one of those long-sleeved white cotton shirts that boys wore at the beach at night and track pants.

The flashing green cursor made its way slowly across the screen as he went back and forth between looking at a stack of papers and at the keyboard. Margot might not know very much about computers, but she took typing this past year and knew she could touch-type faster than he could. She'd be able to help with inventory or whatever he was doing.

She cleared her throat, and he looked up, a pained expression on his face. Based on his awkward typing, she attributed the look to the job, not the interruption.

"Suzette said you were going to show me around town. Is now a good time?" When he didn't answer right away, she added, "Do you understand what I'm saying? I'm not sure how much English you know."

He looked back at the computer. "Enough." Then he marked his place on the list he was typing. The screen flipped to a screen saver, elongating geometric patterns bouncing around the monitor.

"Great." She stepped back into the hallway. *So not great.*

He stood and read her T-shirt, raising a curious eyebrow. Normally, she would explain the fairy tale connection, but today she left him wondering. If he was as good as he thought he was, he'd figure it out.

When they wound their way back through the shop, Suzette called Burke over and handed him some cash from the till. She whispered something, and he glanced at Margot before taking the money and nodding.

Margot opened her eyes wide. Was Suzette telling him to show her a good time? *Kill me now.* She pretended to be really interested in the row of new and used novels in front of her. She pulled one out, a romance novel with a bosomy woman locked in a heated embrace with a muscular man with an opened shirt. She quickly put it back on the shelf.

Burke touched her shoulder on his way to the door. She smiled and waved goodbye to her aunt. She hoped he didn't see the cover. Her friends—Amy—might be boy crazy, but she was still kind of embarrassed and naïve about the whole romance thing. Sure, she liked looking at boys from a distance, but she wouldn't know what to do with a boy if one ever actually paid attention to her. *In that way.* Book romances were so much easier to navigate.

Margot squinted and held her hand above her eyes while adjusting to the sun. Burke turned to the right and led her past a series of touristy shops selling everything from T-shirts to Eiffel Tower salt and pepper shakers. *What would the people living back then think of us today with our touristy things? Making money off the history of their lives. I can't imagine anyone doing that with my life.*

She moved past the tchotchkes and focused on the fact that she was actually walking the same streets that a girl her age would have walked hundreds of years ago. It was as close to time travel as she'd ever get. Like *Back to the Future,* her favorite movie from last summer. If she ignored the tourists, or better yet, imagined them in medieval costumes, she could totally pretend she was back in time.

"Excuse me," she said as she bumped into a tourist wearing a straw hat and aviator sunglasses.

Well, she could almost pretend. She couldn't imagine away that man's bulky camera that had to have cost a fortune. Her brother would totally know what kind of camera that was.

Burke set a fast pace again. A man on a mission. Maybe he was eager to get back to his typing. He sort of grunted and pointed as they dodged people who were out for a more leisurely stroll than they apparently were. At one point, Margot stopped to watch a candymaker dressed in a linen tunic forming intricate shapes with just two sticks, and she lost Burke.

She headed in the last direction she'd seen him and found herself back in the center square from last night. All the tables had been pulled back to the cafés they'd been taken from, leaving open cobblestones and room for carts displaying toys and T-shirts and flowers.

Ah, there he was. Talking to a pretty girl at the flower stall. She wore a ring of pink flowers in her long black hair and a salwar kameez, long tunic and pants, instead of a medieval peasant dress. Behind them was the castle proper, its parapets piercing the sky. A line had formed where the entrance area was roped off, funneling tourists in groups through the door. Curious, Margot tucked herself near a bench where two older ladies sat eating chocolate ice cream. She had a clear shot to watch the drama play out between Burke and the girl. The flower seller put her hands on her hips and shook her head. She didn't look happy. Burke grabbed a bunch of yellow and red tulips from her stall and shoved money at her before stalking off.

Like, wow. What was that about?

He scanned the courtyard until he found Margot. She waved, and he headed her way. His expression gave nothing away regarding the flower girl. He handed the flowers to Margot with a slight bow.

Margot grinned. "Merci," she said with a tentative accent. She'd never had a boy buy her flowers before and even though Suzette put him up to it, she still thought it a kind gesture. He was cute, and she was only here for the reunion. Even if he was kind of pretentious, he gave her flowers, so he wasn't completely unaware.

The ladies with the ice cream gave each other winking glances and then made some comments that turned Burke's cheeks red.

Margot recognized one of the women. The shorter one had run the game last night. "What did they say?" she asked.

"Nothing." He stiffened. *"Allons-y? Ready to go?"*

"I thought we could see the castle?" She nodded at the long line.

"Everyone went inside yesterday before dinner. You were late."

That again.

He made a derisive face and picked up a candy wrapper off the ground, then tossed it in a trash can. "Tourists."

"Oh. Okay. Then, yes, let's go back to the bookshop."

She would come back on her own to visit the castle. Chapais was much smaller than she'd expected, more like a neighborhood than a town. Certainly nothing like a modern city. She could navigate on her own after this.

Before turning away, Margot glanced at the flower girl, who was still scowling at Burke. *Okay, then. They've got a history.*

Burke said one last thing to the ladies on the bench. They gave each other knowing looks and wiggled their fingers at Margot.

She smiled in return, sure they had completely misread the situation.

Meanwhile, Burke had already left, parting the crowd with his broad shoulders and deliberate walk. She followed, glancing back and seeing the flower girl watching.

"How well do you think it's going?" Clove scraped the last of the chocolate from her cup.

"It's promising." Sage tossed her empty cup into the trash. "He bought that one flowers and made the other one jealous for doing so." She retied her shoelace in preparation for scouting around the square.

"Yes, but that was prompted." Clove waved her spoon. "I don't know if we can count that for anything. It needs to come from his heart for this to work."

"Doesn't matter how it started. Girls still like to get flowers. I think it was a nice touch; a good way to break the ice. You should have thought of it." Sage gently rebuked Clove. "Maybe we should have enlisted the bookshop owner from the start."

Thyme came rushing at them from across the square, her clipboard waving. "Did you see that? He bought a girl flowers. He's never done that before."

Clove shifted her sunglasses to the top of her head. "The bookshop lady instigated it. Means nothing."

"Oh, no. That's not what I saw." Thyme liked to stay optimistic about such matters. She saw how curious the girl had been, watching Burke in the town square. How her face lit up at the flowers. "The girl who arrived last night is one to watch. There's something about her. She sat at my table, so I should know."

Sage shook her head. "You've been saying that about every girl who's arrived since Tuesday."

"No, no. I haven't. Not completely, anyway. Besides, Margot's the one who answered the obscure fairy tale question. That has to count for something. One less hurdle for her to overcome if she knows how fairy tales work." Thyme put down her clipboard and bent down beside the bench. "Here, kitty, kitty," she called out to the tabby slinking by.

Clove settled her sunglasses back on her nose. "I'm still watching the girl from Paris. She lives nearby. It'll be easier for them to fall in love. We'd have more time."

"No one said this would be easy," Thyme straightened. "If it was easy, it would have happened already. The poor boy has no problem getting attention. It's keeping it that's his problem. Besides, we don't have much time. Did you see his hair just now? He'll be cutting it twice a day at this rate."

Sage nodded. "The curse is accelerating, but I'm confident his salvation is here. A village girl is what we need, right Clove? Well, technically, the ones who have come for the reunion are descendants of the village girls from when you originally cursed the prince."

"Tested," Cloves said, a strained smile on her face. "It was a test. Not a curse."

Sage ignored Clove's correction and turned to Thyme. "What's next on the agenda?"

"The little kids are having their games in the jousting arena. It will be adorable. You should come watch."

"And what is Burke doing?" Sage asked.

"Not cooperating," said Clove. "He's determined to finish setting up everyone's computers this summer. I can't convince him to take these next few days off to help me host the reunion families. He's at the bookshop still, I think."

Thyme nodded smugly. "Where the latest girl is staying? I'd say for once that he's picked the best place for him to be."

Clove picked up her clipboard from the bench and shoved it at Thyme. "I don't need him getting distracted with her. Start without me." She stalked off in the bookshop's direction.

CHAPTER 5

*M*argot followed behind as Burke blew through the bookstore in a hurry. He likely would have retreated to the office if Suzette hadn't blocked his way when she came from behind the counter to gush over the flowers.

"These are lovely. Margot, why don't you put them in water and we'll keep them here on the counter? There must be a vase of some kind back there. Burke can help you." She then said something to him in French. His expression remained unreadable, leaving Margot to wonder if he'd rather get back to the computer.

"Okay," Margot said with false cheer. When Burke left, she whispered, "He doesn't seem to like tourists."

"You're not a tourist. You're family. Descendants of this town share a bond with the past. You'll see. He'll come around by the end of the reunion. Normally, we're a quiet little town, a backdrop for photos. We all take some time to adjust to the busy tourist season."

It was kind of Suzette to say Margot was more than a tourist, and Margot thought she understood what kind of bond her aunt was talking about. Margot had always felt connected to the history of a place, but she thought that was more a result of her imagination than anything real.

"How does this town work?" Margot asked, "I mean, can anyone move here and set up shop?" *Who wouldn't want to live in a medieval town?*

"Yes, and no. To live inside the walls, you must be a descendant of someone who lived here. The homes get passed down through the generations. You are related to a long, noble line of booksellers. All in this same bookshop. All in this same apartment. And as far as what it was like when it was first built, it was a fishing port. So, it smelled like bass and mackerel. Sometimes bluefish. No refrigeration back then. Think about it."

Margot laughed at Suzette's interpretation. She hadn't thought of those kinds of smells, just things like fresh bread baked daily for the king. "What happens if someone dies without an heir?"

"Like me? The living quarters are purchased by the town and converted to business or storage space. I think in the end, they'd like us all to be gone so it is easier to preserve the buildings as they once were." She pointed to the flowers. "You'd better go put those in water before they wilt."

Margot walked into the back, past freestanding stacks of old hardcover books, to the back door where Burke was waiting by a small white porcelain sink stained with rust spots.

She scanned the squat wooden shelf beside it for something she could use as a vase. *Ignore the cute but brooding French boy.* There was an empty mason jar that would do the trick. "I found something." Her aunt was trying so hard to make her feel welcomed, but in doing so, she was making Burke carry most of the hospitality.

Silently, Burke took a wrench from the windowsill before he bent down and twisted something on the pipe under the sink. Then he turned the water on for the tap.

Never would have figured that out. "Merci." Margot filled the jar.

After Burke turned off the water, he set the wrench back on the windowsill. He paused like he wanted to say something, but just looked at her with those rakish eyes of his. She smiled nervously. He nodded and then returned to his office job.

Margot sighed. That went well.

She wiped the bottom of the jar dry before breathing in the scent of the tulips. Not the most fragrant flower, but pretty. She brought the flowers up to the till.

"Look at those. Just lovely." Suzette picked up her papers and slid a stack of books to the end of the counter to make room. "Burke has an eye for flowers."

"Did you ask him to buy them for me?"

Suzette cocked her head. "I told him to get you something to make you feel welcome." She patted Margot's hand. "He came up with those all on his own."

Margot smiled. "Thank you. I do feel welcome. The town is wonderful. And you grew up here?"

"I did. A Sergeant has been running the bookshop and living in the apartment above for as far back as I know." She frowned. "But I've no children to pass it on to. I don't know what will happen to the place after I'm gone, but surely someone from the town will keep it going. Your mother expressed an interest once, but America seemed to suit her more."

"She enjoyed being a librarian. Taught me to love books, too."

"You are welcome to spend as much time here as you want. Take books upstairs or out to the café. I don't mind." She eased back onto her chair. "I'm too old to stand on my feet all day."

"Is there anything I can do to help? Shelve books for you?"

"I might take you up on that. Maybe after the reunion weekend? I want you to connect with your roots first."

"How long have you known Burke?" Margot asked casually, keeping an eye on the hallway to the back.

"Since he was a young thing."

"Is he always so...pompous?"

"He's very conscientious." Suzette shifted her gaze over Margot's shoulder to the front of the store. She shook her head slightly at the front window. "Speaking of being talked into things, here comes Clove. She and the heritage committee have turned this place upside down with all their plans."

The door opened in a whoosh; the bell hitting hard. In walked the woman from the heritage committee. "Burke *ici?*" she said.

"Bonjour," Suzette said with a smile. "Mademoiselle Clove, have you met my great-niece, Margot? She won a ribbon for answering one of those hard questions last night. Margot? Clove was the emcee last night."

Clove stopped looking around the store and focused on Margot. "Pleased to meet you formally," she said in clear English.

Margot smiled. "That was a fun game." *Was she the only one not fluent in more than one language?*

"Burke?" Clove repeated, dismissing Margot.

"He's in the back trying to modernize the store," Suzette said. "That newfangled machine back there is to keep track of inventory. Burke thinks I should track what sells best, but I can tell him that. Books about Chapais."

Clove barged past the counter and went into the back.

"Make yourself at home," Suzette said frowning. "See what I mean? When she's on a mission, there is no getting in her way."

Soon she was back, Burke in tow.

"Where are you going with my technician?" Suzette said with a wink to Margot.

"Reunion business," she said, shuffling Burke out the front door.

"I like to get my digs in where I can," Suzette said. "She may have done a lot to revitalize this town, but she's awfully bossy about it."

Clove seemed to have taken half the energy from the place when she took Burke with her. In fact, the store seemed quiet over all. Fewer customers browsed the shelves and fewer people walked past the door or looked in the window.

"Lunch time?" Margot asked, the scent of roasted meat filtering in from the street.

"Yes. Business thins when the smell of smoked turkey legs spreads out from the food court."

"I'll have to try one while I'm here. Shall I go out and bring some back for you?"

"I've had enough turkey legs to last me till I die, thank you. But you go ahead. Take your time. Maybe find out where Clove stole Burke off to and see if you can steal him back for me."

Margot laughed. "I'll see what I can do."

CHAPTER 6

*M*argot raced up the outside steps with the apartment key Suzette had given her. After grabbing her bucket bag, camera, and English-French dictionary, she followed her nose back to the town square and stood in line to buy a turkey leg. One needed the proper sustenance to explore a medieval town.

How fun was it that all the employees dressed like they were still in medieval times? While she waited, she watched a juggler toss leather balls in the air and then tried to sell them to families passing by. He spotted her, and he called out in French. She shrugged like she didn't understand but was pretty sure he said something to make her blush.

When she got to the front of the line, she parroted the words the person before her had said and was rewarded with a juicy roasted turkey leg and a drink. She handed over some money and received the change, trusting they'd given her the correct amount. "Merci." She added what she hoped was a French flair to her accent.

The large wooden gate beside the castle proper had been thrown open, and a barker stood on a hay bale shouting and waving people to come his way. The tourists were entering with their food, so Margot joined the crowd. She recognized the word *les enfants* to be *the children*.

Sure enough, children were being herded onto the dirt floor of the arena while their parents sat on the bleachers at one end. The space was set up like a rodeo arena back home, so this must be the jousting area. All this fit inside the walled city?

After last night, Margot knew jousting had started in France, by some guy whose name she'd already forgotten. And chivalry, the code of knightly conduct, came from the French word for horse, *cheval*. If she had to pick a sport, jousting seemed much more interesting to her than any of the ball sports her family was into. At least in jousting, people dressed up similarly to the way she imagined her fairy-tale characters would look.

She found a seat near the end of the bleachers and finished her lunch while everyone got organized. Clove and Thyme were there with their clipboards to line up the kids. Burke trotted out a tub filled with equipment, followed by a teen girl carrying a small bag. She looked like the girl wearing the sundress last night. A visitor, like herself, apparently from Paris, if she'd overheard correctly.

Margot's attention landed back on Burke. He was magnetic, that was for sure. His hair was longer than she remembered from before lunch. Seemed like it brushed the top of his collar when he was buying her flowers, but now it was a little past. *Buying her flowers!* Correction. Buying her flowers on behalf of Suzette. He might act chivalrous once or twice, but his arrogant vibe left a sour taste.

"Margot, would you like to help, too?" Thyme called up to her. "We've got lots of kids here today and we're missing one of our volunteers."

Margot cleared her thoughts about Burke. "Sure." She joined them in the arena. It was nice to be included as a local instead of a visitor. "What do you need me to do?"

Thyme took a step back. "Whatever Burke needs."

Burke looked over with a quizzical expression. *Oh, great. Now he thinks I'm following him.*

The girl from the flower stand rushed in, apologizing for being late, and something else Margot didn't understand.

"Do you still need me?" Margot asked, directing the question at Thyme.

"You can stay," Burke answered. "Help Tanvi."

Tanvi smiled. "Nice to meet you," she said in careful English. "What is your name?"

"Margot."

"You have French name, but you are American?"

"Yes. French on my mom's side of the family, but we don't speak it at home. I'm so glad you know English." *So much for French immersion. She avoided speaking it every chance she got.*

"This is a tourist town. Many of us know enough of two or three languages to make small talk."

Burke lined the children up for a sack race. He had the girl from Paris help him at the finish line while Margot and Tanvi handed out burlap bags to the hyper children.

"You're all just a bunch of jumping beans," Margot said. "Wait for him to say go."

After the children crossed the finish line, Burke handed out ribbons to the first five across. By then, the kids had noticed four knights walking toward them with buckets of plastic swords. Each knight wore a different color: yellow, blue, green, and red, and each had a unique family crest stitched to his surcoat.

The kids swarmed the knights, who were good-hearted enough to play along. Margot and the other girls went to help corral the kids while Burke cleaned up from the sack race. When the girl from Paris noticed Burke by himself, she went over and struck up a conversation.

Tanvi also noticed. "He always catches girls' attention at first. But is a lost cause. He never asks them out."

"Why not?"

"He is too high up? What is the word? A snob? Doesn't like the girls from town or the village. Maybe this girl from Paris will be good enough for him."

"Maybe." Margot turned her attention back to the poor knights trying to teach the kids how to play safely with the swords.

Tanvi introduced Margot to the youngest of the knights, dressed in yellow. "Meet Silvain. You should come and see him joust later."

"Help me," he said as a little boy tackled his legs. Silvain was tall and the little boy barely came up to the top of his thigh.

Margot pulled the boy off and gave him a plastic sword. "Here, try to hit the fence like the others are doing."

"So, you are from America?" Silvain asked, draping an arm across the top of the wooden fence.

"Yes, I'm here for the town reunion."

"What family?"

"The bookshop owner, Suzette Sergeant is my great-aunt."

"We have a bookshop?" he asked. "Must be down one of the smaller streets."

Two little boys started hitting each other with the swords, and she quickly intervened.

"How long you stay?" Silvain asked, focused on her and not the rambunctious children.

"A few weeks."

"Good. You will come out with us? Our group, me and Tanvi and some others. We go to beach and things."

"*Oui*, merci." Margot remembered to get some French in. She wanted them to talk to her more in their language. Everyone was being so nice to make sure she understood what was going on.

A piercing wail cut through their conversation as one of the boys lay facedown on the ground. Burke ran over and dusted the boy off. Blood seeped through the dirt on the boy's knee.

Burke carried the boy over to the supplies and then washed the wound using a water bottle. He said something in a "buck up" kind of voice and then stood, crossing his arms in dismissal. The little boy continued to wipe at his eyes and look at his wet knee.

"Here, I have a bandage." Margot dug through her bag and efficiently stuck it onto the boy's knee. He smiled through his tears and ran off to show his mom, who had made her way down the bleachers and onto the arena.

"You travel with the first aid kit?" Burke said, eyebrow raised.

"Girl Scout," Margot said.

After a few more games with the knights, Sage lined up the children along the fence.

"Parents, please meet us in the town square. We've a special show for you all."

Silvain followed beside Margot, and Burke shot him an irritated look. He said something in French and jutted his chin back in the arena's direction.

"I *am* entertaining the tourists," Silvain said and draped an arm around Margot.

Margot quickly sought to diffuse the situation and ducked out from under Silvain's arm. "If you've got something else to do, it's okay. I'll go with the children."

Silvain waggled his eyebrows at Burke and said something in French that made Burke glare at him. Then Silvain slugged him good-naturedly in the shoulder and continued escorting Margot to the town square. "You need a translator," he said. "I am happy to be at your service."

A large puppet theater filled a portion of the staging area. Once the children saw it, they dashed forward to get the best seats.

Miss Thyme took the microphone with gusto. "I hope you are enjoying our reunion weekend. We have quite the treat for you all today. A traveling puppet troupe has stopped by to tell us a story. Sit quietly children, so the puppets will come out and talk to us."

Clove stood near the back, always watching, like a bouncer ready to *shush* any child getting out of hand.

Thyme continued. "You will hear a local legend that has been passed down from father to daughter for centuries. Who knows, maybe one of you is a descendant of one of the characters. I give you *La Belle et la Bête, Beauty and the Beast,* as told by our narrator, Guignol."

"Bonjour les enfants!" a wooden hand puppet with molded black hair and little hands looking like mittens danced across the stage. The children responded with cheers.

A silhouette of a mansion popped up on the side of the theater, followed by a puppet of a young man wearing a crown walking toward it.

"Once upon a time," Guignol said, "a young prince was sent to the family's summer home in Chapais while his father and brothers went to war. A grand house was built on the hunting grounds for the king, a pleasure house way out in the countryside."

Silvain dutifully sat beside Margot, translating for her and a British couple who joined them after telling their son to settle down and watch the puppets.

"The prince is angry about being sent away to a remote area and spends his time moping in the orchards. Until one day he climbs a tree and sees *la jeune fille* on the other side of the orchard wall." Silvain smiled at Margot. "France is the most romantic place in the world, *n'est-ce pas?*"

She nodded, and when his attention returned to the puppet show, Margot stole a glance at Burke to see if he was watching the show or if he was still irritated with Silvain. He sat still on a bench, intently picking at something on his shoe. *Hmm. He's probably heard this before.*

Silvain continued. "The seeds of love are planted, but the

fairies living in the forest question the prince's character. One gives him a test that he, in his selfish mind, immediately fails. He is not worthy of the beauty across the wall who is pure of heart. As a consequence, the fairy turns him into a beast. Traps him in a world of his own destruction, but still gives him a second chance to grow into something else."

The silhouette of the beast came upon the scene and roared. Then Guignol came out with a rose silhouette and affixed it stage left.

The wind picked up at the same time a chill raised goose bumps on Margot's arms. She let herself get carried away in the story, leaning forward when the beast gave Belle the magic ring so she could go to her father one last time.

"When you want to come back to me," he said, "put the ring on the table beside your bed before you fall asleep."

The scene saddened Margot because she knew the girl would forget to return in a week and by then it would be too late for the beast. Until Belle's love was realized, and she told the beast she couldn't live without him.

"And that is the true story of *La Belle et la Bête*," Guignol concluded. The audience clapped enthusiastically and a bright-eyed girl stood with her hands on her hips, obviously annoyed.

"That can't be a true story," she said. "This castle is inside the walls with all the houses. There's no garden."

Silvain laughed when he translated, but Margot had already understood most of what she said.

"You are correct," Thyme said. "Back then, the houses didn't reach this far. The town grew up from the port and they extended the walls to where you see them now." She addressed the rest of the crowd. "That's all we have planned for today. Please join us tonight for another dinner in the town square. We've got some great entertainment prepared for you. Could we have the teenagers meet over at the fountain for five minutes? I'd like to go over tonight's plans with you."

Margot, Tanvi, Burke, and several others warily grouped together. What would these ladies have them do?

"Here is the sign-up sheet for the costume contest tomorrow." Thyme held it up. "As you can see, we only have one name here, for Beauty."

Margot's eyes widened. It was her name.

"Especially you locals, you have no excuse to not sign up. Perhaps you could get together with a visitor and help each other create your costumes? Anyone?"

Tanvi raised her hand.

"Excellent. Burke? Silvain? Anyone want to be the beast?"

Silvain shoved Burke forward. Nervous laughter followed, but Burke clenched his fists, his jaw set. Burke looked like he could down the guy in one punch, but he refrained. Margot let her breath go.

"Where's Jean Robert?" Thyme said, moving on. "Any of you visitors?" She glanced at the handful of teenage guys trying to avoid eye contact. "I thought this would be more popular. What if I tell you the prize is…" she consulted her clipboard. "An NES?"

At this announcement, the boys perked up.

Thyme leaned over to Clove and asked in a stage whisper, "What is this?"

Even Margot knew that one. It was a new gaming system. Several hands went up, and Thyme had her pick of potential beasts. Except for Burke.

Three other girls, also eager to win the game, added their names to the list for Beauty.

Thyme quickly ran through some instructions and then dismissed them.

"I didn't realize the town was so focused on *La Belle et la Bête,*" Margot said to Tanvi.

"For tourists. The town was in, *er*—how do you say—going down until the heritage committee started telling the story to bring people in." She looked at Margot, "Or back, like this reunion. The stores now sell fairy tale souvenirs. It's a big hit."

"Do you believe any of it? That the fairy tale originated here?"

Tanvi shrugged. "Does not matter if I believe. *Le conte de fée*, fairy tale, gives me a job for the summer. I am happy."

But wouldn't that be something if the fairy tale originated in this town? Margot looked over and caught Burke watching her. Her view was cut off when Silvain stepped in between them.

"New girl, what are you doing today?" he said. "Will you see me joust later?"

A sporting event? Nuh-uh. "Oh, I'm feeling the jet lag kick in. I should go back to the apartment and catch up on some sleep."

"I'll walk you back. You can show me where the bookshop is." When they started to leave, Burke called out to Silvain, jerking his head toward the tournament grounds.

Silvain answered with a dismissive wave. "I've got time." He took Margot by the elbow and directed her away from the square. "I get so tired of that guy."

CHAPTER 7

*B*urke stared at Silvain for a moment before shaking his head in obvious irritation. Then he stalked off on his own in the arena's direction.

"It's okay with me if you've got somewhere to be." Margot stopped walking with Silvain and stepped close to an outdoor display of plastic shields to get out of the way of the other tourists. "I can show you where the store is tomorrow."

"Don't let him get under your skin. He likes to tell everyone what to do. He is not the boss."

Changing to a more neutral subject as they continued down the street, Margot asked. "How are you going to dress up like the beast?"

"I have some ideas, but you will have to wait and see. Unless you want to come over and help me get ready."

Alone with Silvain? She didn't want to give him the wrong impression, so she quickly thought of an excuse. "It would be a better surprise if I don't see you ahead of time. Besides, I have to get ready myself."

They'd reached the bookshop by now and Silvain leaned against the wall with his arm above Margot's head. "We should win the contest tonight. You can be my Belle, and I'll be your Beast."

Heh. Margot ducked out from under his arm as the door to the bookshop opened and Suzette stepped out.

"Margot, there you are. I was beginning to wonder if you got lost." She turned her attention to Silvain.

"No, the puppet show just ended." Margot took another step away. "This is Silvain; he's one of the knights." *Obviously. He is wearing a knight's costume.*

"I see," said Suzette, with a slight smile.

Silvain politely bowed and said something about a beautiful woman. Likely one of his canned lines from his job.

He chucked Margot's chin. "Come watch me joust this weekend."

Mortified, Margot glanced at Suzette. *I'm not encouraging this* she tried to say with her wide eyes.

Silvain started walking backwards. He pounded his fist into his hand before turning around and strutting back toward the town center.

"New friend?" Suzette asked.

"Yes, I met several people today. He's the most...friendly."

Suzette chuckled. "Feel free to use me as an excuse if you ever need to get out of a situation."

"I think he's harmless, but I'll keep that in mind, merci. But I'm not into sports, so I'm sure he'll lose interest soon enough. I'm just the new girl, and he's bored."

"You sell yourself short. He's not the only boy who's noticed you since you've arrived."

That was news to her. "Oh?"

Suzette opened the door for a customer. "Us old folks enjoy watching the shenanigans you young people go through." She started to follow the customer inside but paused at the threshold.

"Is that all you're going to tell me?" Margot said.

"We've all been there." Suzette pointed at Silvain's retreating back. "Finding our way. This town, especially, seems to have a habit of repeating the past. I guess because it's a small town and families have stayed for generations. We pass on our customs and even our sins." She glanced at Margot. "Sorry, I'm getting philosophical in my old age."

Margot stepped out of the doorway. She didn't want to interrupt Suzette while she was working.

"I'll probably lay down and read for a bit. Is that okay with you?"

"Yes, I'll be in the shop if you need me. Sleep all you like. Don't feel like you have to go to all the events the committee has planned, but consider taking in the joust at least once while you're here. You'll enjoy it despite the knights…or maybe because of them."

Margot waved her goodbye and continued up to the apartment. She pulled a kid's book from one of Suzette's stacks. The text looked close to her level of French, so she took it to her cozy room. She settled into bed and began to study.

Her understanding had been bolstered from hearing the sounds all day and she happily realized that reading in French was fun. She returned to Suzette's stack for several more books and read until her eyes grew tired, and her gaze drifted off the page and out the window.

I'm in France. In a medieval city. This is so weird. Parts were very much like a fairy tale and others, quite modern. Most everyone had been friendly. Even Burke, despite his expediency at the airport, had moments of friendliness. She could see now that he was devoted to the town and trying to help the heritage committee to have a successful weekend. *Wonder which family he is descended from. I should have asked. And that Silvain. What a character. Not shy at all.* Margot closed her eyes as she continued to think about her visit. The puppet show was fun. Oh, but she got so distracted with events she still hadn't made it to the castle. As she thought about the castle, her thoughts of the beast puppet merged and grew until she slipped into a dream of a beast as a living thing hiding in the corner of the castle.

She quietly observed him, wondering what else would happen when he stirred and noticed her staring.

"Who are you?" he barked at her.

She jumped a little, realizing that he could see her. She took a step back, like she would back away from a bear.

"Why are you here?" he demanded.

"Where is here?" she said, continuing to back away. Now it no longer felt like a castle. There were thick trees on either side of her like in the last dream, and the creature was deep in the forest so she couldn't see him anymore. She wasn't as scared as the last time she was here...at least, she wasn't running this time.

He stepped forward, a large frightening beast wrapped in shadow so that his eyes glowed when he looked at her. "My nightmare."

She took another step back, shocked at the sight and the intensity of his voice.

"Wait, don't go," he said. "At least tell me your name."

Margot turned and jolted awake. As she lay there, panting, she realized the colors in her room had faded. *What time is it?*

She stumbled into the brightly lit kitchen. Suzette, dressed in a paisley housedress with her hair up in curlers, was quietly washing dishes. *Oh, no. It's later than I thought.*

"Did I miss everything?"

Suzette looked up from her chores. "Only the dinner. The other events are still going on."

"I'll be late for the contest. I've got to go."

"Eat first. You'll faint with nothing but a turkey leg from lunch in you."

"I'm probably too late anyway by the time I put on the costume." She wiped her forehead. "I was just so tired."

Suzette put a sandwich in front of her. "You'll have energy enough to join the festivities tonight, then."

"I hope Thyme's not disappointed. It was hard enough getting people to sign up. She had to bribe them with that new Nintendo thing."

"What's that?"

"Some game. The guys were all excited about it."

"Well, why don't you go watch. Cheer everyone on. I'm sure Thyme will understand. She was agreeable enough to let me skip the dinner tonight."

FAIRIES 2

Burke barged into the room where the heritage committee was meeting to go over the night's events. His clothes hung disheveled, his hair longer than it was at the puppet show.

Thyme put down her clipboard. "Did you just wake up? Shouldn't you be getting ready for tonight?"

"Who is she?" he practically yelled. "Tell me."

The three exchanged looks. "Who is who, dear?" asked Sage.

"The girl in my dreams. I can't see her face. The first time she ran from me. The second time as soon as she saw me, she faded away. I couldn't see her face."

"Did you talk to this girl?"

"Yes."

"And she answered?" Clove glanced at Thyme who had also shifted forward in her seat.

"Yes. She asked where we were."

"The girl from Paris. It must be." Clove stood. "I knew it." She directed this last bit at Thyme with a hint of triumph in her voice. She leaned over and whispered, "Her father grew up in Chapais, making her a more immediate descendant than any of the other girls visiting."

"How do you know it's the girl from Paris? She could just as easily be one of the local girls. Any of the visitors."

Sage stood between them, shutting down the conversation. "Have you had dreams before? Think carefully. This is important." Her face betrayed nothing, but she was squeezing her fingertips together.

Burke rubbed the back of his neck and began to pace. "Dreams, yes. But this was different. I *felt* the damp air on my skin. The smell of the yew trees was sharper than I've ever noticed before. Even my hearing was better." He pointed with force. "There was a hare not thirty meters away, and I heard it burrowing."

Sage reached for Clove and Thyme, squeezing their arms. "Then it's happening. You've not much time left. Your dreams are so vivid because you're turning into the beast."

He stopped pacing, his eyebrows coming together. "What does that mean, exactly? I already shave three times a day and have to cut my hair each morning. At the airport, the hair on my hands started growing, and I had to rush that American girl out before she noticed. How much worse is this going to get?"

Clove cleared her throat. "Much worse. It's time for you to break the curse if you don't want to be this way forever."

Burke narrowed his eyes at her. "You think I want to be this way?"

"Steady on," Clove said. "You *are* this way. Your outer self shows the beastly nature inside."

Sage shook her head. "Clove, you're too harsh. That's how we got here in the first place. No one else becomes a beast like this."

Clove crossed her arms. "Well, they should. Makes it clear for everyone."

"But what about the girl?" Burke asked, addressing Sage.

"She may be your only hope." Sage cocked her head. "For the first time, someone is seeing you in a new light. Tread carefully and find her before it's too late."

"Start with the girl from Paris," Clove said. "She leaves at the end of the weekend unless we can talk her family into staying longer."

"What about the girl from America?" Sage asked. "Thyme, you said you had a feeling about her?"

"She barely speaks French. How are they to get on?" Clove was adamant. "The girl from Paris. I'm sure of it."

Thyme stepped forward. "Whatever you do, don't scare the mystery girl away. You can't tell her you're turning into the beast. It'll muddy the waters. She needs to fall in love with you naturally."

"And I, her?" Burke said with a hint of hopelessness.

"Yes. You must woo the girl the old-fashioned way."

CHAPTER 8

*A*fter having such a dark dream, Margot found herself a little skittish walking down the dark lane. She was glad she was late, so she had an excuse to jog until she turned the corner where the stringed lights from the town square spilled onto the street. Shadows dispelled, she slowed down and casually took in the scene.

A cluster of girls dressed up as Belle stood at the side of the stage area in front of the head table. Two of them wore a variation of a medieval costume. Something that Belle would have worn before she met the beast. One of the girls was Tanvi.

The other five contestants wore ball gowns, including the pretty girl from Paris. These outfits were more like the princess-style prom dresses that were the current style. A throwback to the *Gone with the Wind* era with wide skirts.

Funny, when Margot's sister gave her the costume to wear, neither of them had thought of a ball gown. They both remembered Belle in her role before the fairy tale. Margot would have needed a whole suitcase to pack one of those prom dresses.

As she found an empty seat at a table at the back, Thyme caught her eye. Margot shrugged and mimed sleeping. Thyme nodded. Message received. Good. Because Margot couldn't shake her latest dream, even in the light and cheerfulness of this party. She just wanted to blend into the crowd and mull over what led her to such a dark dream. If she knew the trigger, she could prevent it from happening again.

Meanwhile, Sage began announcing each girl, who would then walk out by herself, turn, and then walk to the other side.

All the girls had a shot at winning. The judges might just have to draw names. Although, the ball gowns might give those Belles the edge over the peasant dresses. With the backdrop of the castle and the patio lights twinkling, the ball gowns in jewel tones of yellow, turquoise, royal blue, fuchsia, and white, made those Belle look-alikes shine like princesses.

Next were the boys. Margot watched the beast contest with interest. They had a tougher job than the girls. Who would be brave enough to act like a beast onstage? All the girls needed to do was walk and smile.

Five dressed like the beast with wigs and torn clothes. Tall, formerly blond Silvain stood out from the others, with the wildest long-haired black wig and fun fur shoved in his sleeves. He even had an impressive roar.

True to his word, Burke was not among the contestants. Margot scanned the tables, but he wasn't sitting down, either. Maybe he wasn't interested in finding out who was crowned most like Beauty and the Beast.

But the boy who she liked the best was the one dressed as the prince at the end of the fairy tale. With a Lionel Ritchie mullet and flashy Mr. T necklaces, he got the most applause when he walked across the stage. Margot laughed out loud. *I hope he wins.* Very clever. He didn't have to jump or roar. He simply walked across flashing the peace sign.

Once everyone had lined up on the stage, Clove came up with a card in her hand.

"And our winners…" She paused dramatically. "Monet is our

Belle. She is one of the town's descendants, but now lives in Paris. Her most recent ancestors ran one of the bakeries." Polite clapping ensued while Sage fixed a diamond tiara on Monet's head.

"Well, if I'd know they'd be giving out tiaras…" Margot said to the woman beside her.

A soft laugh came from behind, and Margot turned to see Burke with an amused expression. He must have slipped in after she did. He nodded at her and she smiled. *He's human after all, not always businesslike and uppity.*

"And now, let's welcome Jean Robert as our beast."

The teen guys in the audience all whooped the way the boys back home did at hockey games. Jean Robert was the one dressed as the prince.

Sage handed Jean Robert a single white rose. "Congratulations, you two." Thyme then hurried up on stage and handed each of them a large box. Margot assumed it was the promised game system.

"That's it for tonight," Clove said. "The joust continues tomorrow afternoon. We also have a sightseeing trip planned. For those who want to go on the tour bus, tonight is your last night to register. Sage has the sign-up sheets, and she'll be by the fountain for the next twenty minutes."

At least, that was what Margot understood Clove to have announced. She wasn't catching every word in French, but put it all together and she could make a good guess.

Now that it was over, Burke made his way to the front. He shook Jean Robert's hand and hovered around Paris girl. For a brief moment, Margot wondered if he would have shown such attention if *she* had won the contest. No matter. When a girl had an active imagination, she didn't need to win a costume contest to be Belle. After all, Margot was already dreaming of her own beast deep in the forest. Not that she would call dreaming of a beast a pleasant dream.

Usually, fairy tales played like animated movies in her head, but this dream was no cartoon. It was gritty. There had been movement on her skin, and she sensed other things moving around them.

"I thought you were going to enter the contest?" Tanvi sat beside her as the town square began to clear out.

Margot was grateful for the diversion. "I fell asleep. But you look great."

Tanvi flounced her peasant skirt. "Thank you. I didn't have a ball gown, so Thyme said our work costumes would be fine. I borrowed this one from my coworker."

"The prince looks proud of himself."

Jean Robert, dressed in his fancy prince costume, stood at the front of a receiving line of people who wanted to shake his hand.

"Come meet him. He's in our group."

"What about the girl?" Burke was still talking to her. Perhaps he'd found his equal in a girl crowned Beauty.

"The one Burke is falling all over? I've not met her. She's one of the tourists." She said it in a derogatory way, but quickly apologized. "I forget that you are also a visitor. You seem like you belong with us already, while she feels...foreign, even though she's from Paris."

Margot beamed, tearing her gaze away from Burke and Paris girl. What a nice thing for her to say. "You've all welcomed me like I belong." She hoped the warm feelings they felt for her would continue. And possibly rub off on Burke if he was going to keep working in the bookshop.

When Tanvi introduced Margot, Jean Robert bowed deeply before taking her hand and kissing it. "Bienvenue," he said.

Tanvi slapped him away. "Don't scare our guest."

"Silvain has already done that," Jean Robert said. "I saw him accost her after the puppet show."

Margot felt a blush creep into her face. "Where were you? I didn't see you."

"In the crowd, watching. Silvain is hard to miss. He likes to draw attention." Jean Robert waved at the tall boy

"Rawrr!" Silvain shouted in return.

"See what I mean?" They all laughed.

"Happy to meet you, Margot. You will stay out with us tonight? This town usually shuts down by nine, so we are all taking advantage while we can."

"Yes, but only if you stop speaking English. I need to learn to speak French."

"*Pas de problème.*"

CHAPTER 9

*M*argot quietly opened the door and started tiptoeing through the apartment. A snore from the rocking chair stopped her. Had Suzette waited up? Margot wasn't used to that. Dad was either better at pretending he didn't wait up, or he really did zonk out by nine.

Margot paused and debated whether she should wake Suzette up to tell her she was back. In the end, she decided to leave her high-tops in an obvious place by the door.

Jean Robert had been true to his word. They'd spoken French all night, and she'd learned more in two hours than in two years in class.

After brushing her teeth, she settled back onto the daybed. She pictured scenes from the night. The Belles, the Beasts. Burke. Now that it was all over, she regretted not dressing up. Tanvi had. It would have been fun to hang out with her in their peasant costumes.

And that Burke. He was an odd one, too. Sometimes he was friendly. Sometimes he was abrupt. And last night he hung out with Paris girl the entire time everyone was teaching Margot French. *Not that I'm jealous, or interested, or exhausted...*

The next thing Margot knew, she was back in the forest she had left a few hours ago. The air turned cold, and she pulled the blanket up to her chin.

There is something about this town. Suzette said history repeated itself here...

A twig snapped behind her, and she turned around. The forest was dark, and mist clung low to the ground. Anything could lurk beyond where she could see. *Where are you?* She searched for the dark shape of her beast.

"Hello?" she whispered.

"You're back."

His low voice sounded surprised, and that warmed Margot's heart. She turned toward the voice, but he remained hidden.

"Seems so. Where is this place?"

"I'm not sure myself."

"Are you bringing me here?"

"Not on purpose. Do you want to leave?"

She didn't know how to answer that. "Can I?"

"You have before."

"Oh. Sorry."

"You don't have to apologize. This is my world, not yours."

"Seems to be becoming mine. Who are you?"

"You haven't guessed?"

"Maybe." *Does he want me to say it? This is awkward.* "Can I see you?"

The mist shifted and Margot braced herself. She didn't want to run away this time. He didn't come forward.

"I don't want you to see me yet. First, get comfortable with my voice."

His voice did have an edge to it. An underlying sound like a growl. If Margot had walked past a dog making that kind of growl, she would back away slowly. Even now, she fought her instinct to flee.

"What next?" she asked.

"You must know the story. Help me."

"Yes, but you need Belle. Do you want me to find Belle for you?"

"It's not Belle I need. It's you. Help me."

Margot shook her head. "No, I'm observing. I'm not part of the story. You're getting mixed up."

"I'm not."

"What can I do?"

"To start, tell me your name."

Margot froze. She'd read enough fantasy to know that names were powerful in stories and that you didn't just reveal who you were without knowing who the other person was and what they wanted.

"I can't do that."

The beast exhaled, sounding like an angry snort.

"But is there something else I can do to help you?"

"I don't know. Start by finding me."

"Okay. Found you. You're right there." She smiled, hoping he would get her humor.

"No. When you're awake. I need you to find me awake."

Margot looked around the forest. Okay. She could find the forest.

"I'll try."

The forest grew quiet, and the mist went away. It took Margot several moments to realize she was staring at her curtains in the dark and not a stand of yew trees.

She closed her eyes and tried to get back to the beast, but was met with resistance. Her body was awake. As in, time-to-get-up-and-eat-breakfast awake.

A light clicked on, shining under her door. *Guess I'm not the only one.*

Margot made some noise as she left her room so she wouldn't startle her aunt, who may not be used to someone walking in on her in the middle of the night. Suzette had turned on the floor lamp with the gold fringe.

"Morning?" Margot said in French.

"You're a sight. Couldn't sleep?"

"I guess I'm just off schedule."

"You'll settle in soon. Me, I'm old. I sleep in bursts. Can I make you some tea?"

"If you're having some."

"I will. It's nice to share it with someone." She stood, holding on to the arm of the chair for a moment before going toward the kitchen. "You must have caught me sleeping when you came in last night. Did you see the costume contest?"

"I did. A girl visiting from Paris was dressed as Belle. She wore a turquoise ball gown and had done her hair in a French twist. Do you call them that here?" Margot mimed swooping her hair up.

"I haven't paid attention to hairstyles since the 60s, my dear. I don't know what anything is called these days. And the beast?"

"A local named Jean Robert. He was the only one who dressed as the prince."

Suzette nodded. "Sometimes it pays to be different."

"I've been different my whole life it seems."

"Oh? And that bothers you?" She handed Margot their same mugs from last night. Margot had paid little attention then, but noticed them now. Suzette's cup was dotted with pansies and said in fancy script: *I'd rather be reading.* While Margot's was pinstriped and said: *Books are better.*

"Usually it doesn't. I like what I like. My friends tease me sometimes."

"That's called peer pressure. Don't give in. Unless you're misbehaving. You're not, are you?"

"I'm too boring to misbehave." Margot added a spoonful of sugar to her cup before Suzette poured the tea.

"I doubt you're boring. Quiet maybe. Nothing wrong with quiet. The best writers are deep thinkers and look what they come up with." She waved a hand at the closest stack of books. "Adventure, romance, a glimpse into the human condition."

Margot sipped her tea. "Thanks for the reminder. I forget sometimes." She almost said, *I feel forgotten sometimes.* She was quiet Belle. Paris girl was ball gown Belle. Burke seemed to prefer glamor over quiet. Not that Margot cared. She was only making an observation.

Her dream was certainly not boring.

"Is there a forest nearby?" she asked, hoping she sounded casual enough. She didn't want to talk about her dream.

"Yes, on the north side."

"Easy to get to?"

"Yes. I'm told there's a jogging path, and several of the townsfolk go walking in the morning."

"Perfect." As soon as the sun was up, she'd take a walk and find the beast.

CHAPTER 10

How *ow long would the beast wait for her?*
That was just one of the questions she had. How was he pulling her into his nightmare? Why was he asking for *her* help? Not to mention the most fundamental of all questions… was there even a beast? The dream felt real enough for her to take action, but she wasn't going to broadcast it to anyone that she needed to go to the forest so she could find a beast and help him.

Suzette had gone back to bed after they finished their tea and Margot had settled in with her kid's book to practice her French. She found it hard to concentrate, constantly checking the window to see if it was light out yet.

As soon as the ferns were visible next door, Margot changed clothes. The morning was a little chilly, so she put on her sweatpants, Esprit T-shirt, and a light jacket, expecting the air to be cooler in the trees. With Walkman in hand, she quietly left the apartment and set out.

Taking Suzette's advice to get a sense of place before she went into the forest, she walked around the battlements and watched the sunrise. She didn't want to go into the forest when it was dark, anyway.

Since she hadn't been one for seeing any sunrise, let alone one over a castle in France, she was spellbound as the colors over the landscape came to life. *People in this town have been witnessing this event for hundreds and hundreds of years. It was a gift for her to see it today.*

Suzette said that walking around both the inner and the outer walls would give her about four kilometers of walking. *Whatever that was in miles.*

Her route on the walls gave her a good view overlooking the more modern city, colloquially called New Town. *Is* colloquial *a French word? I'm so bad at this.* And beyond that was the Mediterranean Sea. New Town didn't look that new but was built after the walled city outgrew its space.

Last night she'd learned that New Town was where most of the workers in the walled city lived, including Tanvi, Jean Robert, and Silvain. Margot didn't ask where Burke lived, and Tanvi didn't offer the information.

From looking over the wall, she found the path that led into the forest. The trees looked different from the ones in her dream and that worried her a little. *Did she have to find the exact tree they were standing near? She hoped all she had to do was find the forest and he would...what? Sense her? Smell her?*

As she entered the forest she briefly wondered if, despite the marked path, she should leave a trail of pebbles to find her way out. She slipped her headphones around her neck so she could listen for the beast.

When a woman with her dog overtook her on the trail, Margot wavered on her conviction about finding the beast. *This forest was smack in the middle of civilization. If there was a beast here, the townsfolk would know. There would be rumors. No one would go out walking on a carefully maintained path, and Suzette wouldn't have let her go alone.*

Still, she pressed on. She'd promised someone in her dream

she'd find him. In case there was another dream tonight, she wanted to be able to say that she tried, as odd as that sounded in the light of day. A jogger passed her, and then another one.

This isn't right.

She searched the trees trying to find an area that resembled her dream. But as she suspected, the trees were wrong. The feeling of the place was off. Too…modern. She looked up to the top of the trees where the light framed the topmost branches. These trees were old, but they were not yews. Some kind of pine.

"I'm sorry, Beast. You must give me more to go on." She waited, as if the creature in her dream would reply to her here, during the day.

In that moment, a group of joggers pounded toward her and she stepped to the side to let them pass. Silvain? In the middle of the pack, he looked exhausted, sweat soaking his surfer tank top.

He waved. "Find me later," he said. "At the fountain. Ten o'clock."

Margot paused midwave. *Find me.*

Silvain?

She thought she was looking for an actual beast. She chuckled at how wishful she was to have a fantastical adventure. Beasts were the thing of fairy tales.

There was no way Silvain was breaking into her dreams. It was probably her subconscious trying to tell her something. Look beneath Silvain's aggressive exterior and give him a chance? Or stay away from him, perhaps?

But the beast was so real.

Confused about what to do next, she turned around and retraced her steps out of the forest. The walk was refreshing and a good way to start the day, but it didn't turn out like she'd hoped. At the north entrance into town she looked back at the cluster of trees in disappointment.

"Margot!" called Thyme. She stood inside the wall, clipboard already in hand this morning. "Just who I was looking for." The heritage committee member joined up with her as they turned down a narrow alleyway.

Today, her dress was like a long gypsy gown, patch-worked in various shades of green. Her straw hat was ringed with fresh daisies and wildflowers. The scent was lovely. "Out for a jog?" Thyme asked.

"A walk is more my speed."

"Mine, too. Have you looked at today's schedule of events?"

"Not specifically."

"Excursions in the morning, a joust in the afternoon, and a tour of the Torture Museum for the teenagers at night."

"Torture Museum at night?" Margot said.

"Sage thought it would add something to the ambiance. What can I put you down for?"

"Well, I'm meeting Silvain later today. Maybe I'll see what he and the others are doing."

Thyme pressed her lips together like she disapproved. "What about Burke? Isn't he still helping your aunt with her computer?"

How can I put this tactfully? Silvain would *not* want Burke along. Besides, if Silvain was the one calling out for help, she needed to focus on him right now, and she found Burke to be infuriatingly distracting. "Burke seems to be busy with the computer. You'd have to ask him."

"Of course. And are you settling in, sleeping steady, having sweet dreams of days past in our medieval village?"

Margot nodded. "Yes. I think I've adjusted to the time difference."

Thyme's smile faded for a moment and then was back again. She was probably tired from putting on all these events.

"If you need my help with anything, let me know," Margot said. "I enjoyed working with the kids yesterday."

Thyme parted ways with her at the town center, leaving Margot with the feeling she'd disappointed the committee member somehow. Town events were great and all, but Margot had a mystery to solve. A beast to find.

She passed the fountain, an ancient stone monument, small by today's standards, but a pretty focal point in Chapais. Streams of water erupted from the center tower and cascaded down feather-like carvings turned gray with age. A thick edge surrounded the round basin at the base where people could sit and children could lean on their bellies and play in the water.

During the peak of day, there were too many tourists gathered around, and she'd not gotten a good look at it yet. There were still so many places to explore in this old town.

At the edge of the square, she stopped in front of the doll shop and pressed her nose against the windows. The display showcased small handmade people dressed in medieval garb. She especially liked the one who was a spinner, holding a distaff filled with wool in one hand, a spindle in the other. Amy might like that. But it was not tacky enough for her father. She still hadn't found something for him.

The door to the coffee shop beside her opened as the owner came out to raise the umbrellas over the three small tables he had outside. At the same time, the door to the toy store on the right opened, and a woman pulled out a bin filled with toy swords and shields.

She dodged them both and turned down the street to the bookshop. Margot had considered one of the plastic swords for her dad, but they were more fun than tacky. The T-shirt shop might have something. She'd have to go after the busy weekend was over.

The bookshop door nudged open and Suzette backed out, wrangling the narrow book table outside.

"Let me help." Margot took one end and, together, they placed the table under the window. Today, Suzette had put out European travel books to lure customers to stop and browse.

Margot stood back and admired the bookshop's square-paned

windows and earthy olive trim. It was the kind of bookshop you'd see photographed for magazines or you'd read about in novels. It wasn't modern and filled with bright lights and orderly metal shelves. It was more organic, growing up randomly from generations of readers perusing the shelves, and now also quirky with Suzette's arrangement into little nooks inside.

"Thank you, *ma chère*. How was your walk?" Suzette brushed some dust off her medieval skirt.

"Not what I expected."

"Oh?"

"The forest is more like a park. Lots of people were walking through."

Suzette nodded, then spoke in French to someone behind her. Margot turned to see Burke lift his hand in greeting before disappearing inside the store. His hair was wet, like he'd just come straight from the shower. It gave him that cute-puppy sort of look. Too bad that wasn't the look she was searching for.

CHAPTER 11

"*D*o you have a minute?" Suzette said. "I could use your help this morning."

Margot glanced down the cobblestone street. How long would it take for Silvain to finish his run, clean up at his home in New Town, and get to the fountain?

"Um... Sure. I've got time for you."

Margot stepped inside and watched Burke's retreating form until he went into the office.

"I got in a new shipment last night, and these book boxes can get heavy for me. If you and Burke can bring them up here, I can work my way through them at my own speed."

Margot thought of the tall freestanding towers of books collecting dust in the back. Suzette's speed was not lightning.

"Are you sure you just don't want one box? When you're finished with that one, I can bring up the next."

Suzette shook her head as she went around the sales counter. "They're crowding the back. I'd rather have them here. It'll be like a little bench behind the counter. They're the ten boxes near the door. Just stack them two high behind me here."

Margot breezed to the back and noticed that Burke was pretty focused on the computer. She let him keep working. How heavy could a box of books be?

She tested the weight of the first and found it heavy, but doable. After bringing three boxes up to the front, she was starting to sweat. Aunty Suzette's shop wasn't equipped with air conditioning, and the day was already starting to get hot.

Thyme came in as Margot dropped another box onto the floor.

"I thought Burke was here today. Why are you straining yourself?"

"She didn't want to bother him," Suzette said. She took a pair of scissors and cut the tape on one of the boxes.

"Nonsense." Thyme marched through and knocked on the office door to get Burke's attention.

Margot wasn't quite sure what she said, but something along the lines of letting a girl carry heavy things.

Firmly rebuked, Burke led the way to the final boxes. Margot tried to catch his attention to roll her eyes so he would know she didn't put Thyme up to disturbing his work, but he was too focused on getting to those boxes.

Margot squeezed her way past Thyme so she could get another box, but Thyme stepped back and bumped into one of Suzette's stacks.

"Watch it!" Margot called.

The stack wobbled and all three of them automatically dove for it, trying to steady it before it came crashing down. Too late, it all fell down in a heap, knocking the stack next to it. Thyme jumped toward the front of the bookstore, trapping Burke and Margot in the back. A small mound of books separated them from Thyme.

"Sorry, *les enfants.* I have to move on to heritage business. Can you clean this up yourselves?" She didn't wait for their response, but hightailed it to the front.

Burke narrowed his eyes like he couldn't believe Thyme left

them to clean up her mess. He said something under his breath, but Margot didn't catch what he said.

Margot glanced at the back door and considered leaving Burke here with the mess, too. But they were her aunt's books, and she couldn't do that. "There aren't many here," she said cheerily. "Besides, it'll give me a chance to shop before the books go out onto the shelves."

Burke gave her a look that didn't share her enthusiasm.

"I've got things to do, too," she said. "I'm meeting Silvain at the fountain." She didn't know why she added that last part, other than to let him know she wasn't thrilled about being stuck with him, either.

They started building four stacks, a more stable option than the original two towers. The books were old and dusty, and probably wouldn't ever see the front of the store.

"When my aunt gets through the new boxes of books, she can use the empties to pack away some of these books."

Margot couldn't tell whether they were heirlooms, and that was why Suzette was keeping them, or whether Suzette simply couldn't part with any book. Either way, these books were taking up space. If this were her store, she'd have some kind of system so things weren't so cluttered back here.

One book had fallen so far away from the others that it landed underneath the little side table Suzette kept for tea breaks. Margot retrieved the wayward book, a slim, leather-bound volume, the sort that you'd find in museums.

Handled often, the cover was worn in places where readers had gripped the spine. The edges of the pages may once have been gilded, but now were a dull copper color.

She flipped through it, noticing the old pen-and-ink drawings. A girl by a well. A fairy perched on a flower.

"They're fairy tales," she said. She sat on the floor and examined it more closely. The pocket-size book was written in

French, in a tiny font that was hard to read. But those illustrations!

Burke looked over her shoulder, and she showed him the cover.

"In the English it says *Once and True Fairy Tales.*"

"Thanks. For translating."

"Now, can you help me?" He pointed out all the books still lying haphazard over the floor. "Or am I to work while you read?"

Margot bit back her immediate response. *I don't even work here.* Instead of answering, she made a show of putting the book up on the table and out of the way. She picked up books from the opposite side of the pile from where Burke was working. In minutes, they'd cleared a path. Burke carried up the last box while Margot finished straightening the new stacks.

All organized, she grabbed the book of fairy tales and brought it up to show Suzette. "I found this in the back."

Thyme stood in the romance section and glanced up to see the book. *Huh. Some heritage business.*

"What can you tell me about it?" Margot asked as she handed it over.

Meanwhile, Burke quietly headed out the front door. *Well, good riddance.*

Suzette examined the faded cover. "I don't recall a book of fairy tales like that one." She flipped through it, pausing at the illustrations. "What a beautiful find. You may have it, if you'd like."

"Oh, it's much too valuable an antique. You could probably sell it for a lot. I'd be happy to look it over while I'm here and give it back to you."

"A forgotten antique. I didn't even know it was back there, and I pride myself on knowing where every book is in this store. I insist. I think the book chose you."

"Thank you," Margot said, running her hand over the cover. "Hopefully by the end of my trip I'll be able to read it."

"You've got plenty of time, yet," Suzette said. "Sometimes things like this happen all at once. You're surrounded by the words all day long; they make no sense, then *bam*, it all comes together. It's like your ears open up for the first time. You put all the pieces together, and you understand what's been in front of you all along."

"Like falling in love," piped up Thyme. She ignored Margot's shocked face and continued on. "Suzette is right. If you want to learn French, spend as much time as you can steeped in the language. Like a tea bag in water. Get that handsome stock boy back there to talk to you all day long. That'll motivate you."

Oh goodness. She didn't need all the old ladies of the town working on pairing her up. Especially not with Burke.

"He's here for the computer, but anyway," Margot attempted to change the subject, "some others my age are taking the time to help me learn French. I've improved a lot already."

After a glance at the fairy tale book, Thyme consulted her clipboard. "Well, there are things to do. Take my advice, young lady. You only get a summer like this once in a lifetime. Don't waste it." She took an envelope off her clipboard and handed it to Margot. "Here, I have a ticket to the jousting tournament this afternoon. You must watch."

Silvain! She'd almost forgotten. "What time is it?" She was supposed to meet him at the fountain.

"Almost ten."

"Oh, good. I was meeting someone at ten." She refused the ticket Thyme held out. "I'm not really into sports. I can't imagine watching by myself."

Thyme produced a second ticket. "Invite Tanvi. I saw you talking with her earlier. Make sure you sit in the red section."

Suzette was right about the heritage committee members being pushy. Margot knew when she was defeated. "Okay. Thank you." She took the tickets and put them, along with the fairy tale book, into her bag. "Thank you both. That's very generous."

"Our pleasure," Thyme said, seemingly taking credit for both the book and the tickets.

Before they could delay her any further, Margot scooted out the door and joined the flow of tourists. She speed-walked to the fountain. Silvain didn't strike her as the early type, but she was, and she hated to be late. Sure enough, a family of four and a young couple sat around the base of the fountain, but no Silvain. She had a feeling he would eventually disappoint her, but until he did, she would do her part.

It was well past ten when she gave up. The fountain was pretty, but even she could only stay there and stare into it for so long. She'd been stood up.

"Roar!" Silvain jumped in front of her. "Looking for me?" he asked in a growly voice.

Goose bumps erupted on her arm. He kind of sounded like the beast in her dream. She cocked her head. "I found you like I said I would." She waited expectantly for his response.

"Oui. Your beast is here." He draped his ever-present arm around her shoulder.

Hmm. He didn't give her a wink or a nod or acknowledge a secret message in any way.

"So, why did you want to meet?" she asked, pulling back.

"To make sure you came to my joust today. You can't go home without seeing the sport of kings." He put his foot up on the bench part of the fountain and leaned his arm against his knee.

"Well, you're in luck. I have two tickets."

"Fantastic. Sit in the yellow section and you can cheer me on."

Thyme had told her to sit in the red section. Margot deflected. "We'll see where I end up."

"Oh, ho. A girl playing hard to get. You want the chase, do you?"

Margot cocked her head. *Is he alluding to the dream or not?*

82   SHONNA SLAYTON

"The woman who gave me the tickets wants me to sit in the red section. Is that a better view?"

Silvain scowled. "They're all good views. But if you sit in the yellow, you will be backing me. If you sit in the red, you're backing my enemy."

"It's only a game, right?"

He stalked off without another word. Margot studied his lanky form. *He might be the beast and not know it.*

CHAPTER 12

*A*fter meeting with Silvain, Margot sought out Tanvi. Since they were friends, she might have some insight into Silvain.

Sometimes there were two employees working the stall, and Margot was hoping today would be one of those days. As Margot approached the flower stall, Tanvi was completing a sale. She wore a medieval costume, a long green skirt with a pale-yellow blouse embroidered with dainty flowers, and a ring of fresh flowers in her hair. They sold the flower hair wreaths, and before the summer was out, Margot planned to buy one.

It looked like the other girl wasn't there today. Margot turned to go, but Tanvi saw her and waved.

"Hello," Tanvi said. "Are you looking for me?"

Margot held up the tickets. "Mademoiselle Thyme gave me tickets to the joust. Can you take your break now and get away with me?"

Tanvi leaned back against her cart.

"I wish. I am working extra because my terrible coworker said she was sick. I think she is lying."

Three little boys ran between them, plastic swords drawn, followed by apologetic parents.

"And you've probably already seen the joust?" Margot asked.

Tanvi nodded. *"Beaucoup de temps.* The crowd enjoys it much. You can hear the cheers from here. You should go."

"Not by myself. I'm not really into sports."

"It is not like other sports. It's a play, too. The king and queen come and watch. There is a story with the knights."

"That sounds kind of interesting. Okay, I'll go."

Tanvi pushed herself off her cart and jutted out her chin. "Here my coworker walks now."

The girl, probably in her twenties, exchanged terse words with Tanvi. Their exchange ended with Tanvi taking off her apron and handing it to her coworker with an overly sweet smile.

"She needed to sleep it off and says she is fine now. I can go with you. If I stay here, we only fight. Jean Robert is working the crowd today. We can sit in his section."

They got in line for the entrance to the tournament arena behind an excitable little girl who kept darting in and out of line. Colorful flags snapped in the wind and the smell of roasted turkey legs added to the festival feel.

They handed their tickets to a jovial woman at the entrance. This time, the arena was packed with people eager to take in the joust. Teenage boys stationed at intervals around the fence called out jokes and heckled the tourists.

"There is Jean Robert," Tanvi pointed. "In the red area."

Awesome. The red section must be the best viewing place. Silvain couldn't fault her for sitting there, now.

Instead of royal attire, Jean Robert dressed in baggy brown pants with a loose white shirt. He stood atop a wooden crate and chatted easily with the tourists as they filed into his section.

"Jean Robert," called Tanvi to get his attention. "Remember Margot?"

He bowed, swooping his red-feathered hat to the side with a

flourish. "Nice to see you again," he said slowly in French. "How are you?"

Margot smiled. He remembered to help her with her French. "I am fine. Happy to see a joust." She mimed stabbing in case she said the word wrong. She was still tentative with her pronunciations.

"Very good. Sit here in my section. It is the best." He directed them to sit midway up the first set of bleachers. He pointed his hat at her. "Be ready. I have a special job for you today."

As they found their seats, Margot asked, "What kind of job is he talking about?" She had no intention of stepping into the jousting arena. Nor did she want to stand up and talk in front of a crowd.

Tanvi laughed. "Do not worry. It is all in fun. He will hand you a favor to give to the knight. That is all."

As Jean Robert waited for the other tourists to filter in, he juggled atop his crate and exchanged barbs with the tourists in English, French, and German. *Impressive.*

"We cheer for the red knight," Jean Robert called out to their section first in French and then in stilted English. For a few minutes, he had them practice cheering on his command. Then he launched into a monologue as if he was repeating something he'd memorized, ending with, "Who will give favors to our noble knight? A young lady who will wish him great fortune in his quest to impress the king."

Jean Robert dramatically searched the crowd before pointing at Margot. "You there, young lady." He waved her forward.

Tanvi nudged her, and, red-faced, Margot made her way along the bleachers. When she reached his perch, Jean Robert held out his hand to help her up, and then he handed her a fabric circlet wrapped in silky red with thin gold ribbons hanging down. "When red knight rides to you, put this on his lance and say, *bonne chance.* Good luck."

In his loud barker-voice, he yelled out for the crowd, "When our knight rides, his young lady will give him her favor."

With the instructions taken care of, Jean Robert scanned the arena. When the door into the viewing box opened, he turned and had the crowd in his section rise and cheer. The king and queen had arrived to preside over the tournament. The royal couple had changed into elaborate gold outfits, a neutral color, perhaps to not appear to favor any one knight over another.

They stepped to the front of their viewing box to wave to the peasants, and the rowdy crowd waved and cheered until the royal entourage took their seats. *Entourage. Another French word?*

Margot looked back and smiled at Tanvi who had joined in the farce, waving and cheering with the crowd. The knights entered the arena on horses bearing their colors. Red, yellow, green, and blue. They trotted around once, then paused in front of the king.

"Be ready," Jean Robert whispered. He called to the red section, "Here he comes, now!"

The crowd behind Margot erupted. She was nervous as she spied the red knight cantering on his horse toward her. He rode proud in the saddle, his helmet covering all but his eyes, which were fixed on hers.

Her breath caught. Is this what it felt like to have a knight in shining armor come for you? She easily slipped into the role of besotted medieval maiden and gave her knight an encouraging smile. *I was born in the wrong century.*

Silently, the knight lowered his lance so she could reach the tip.

Even though she was acting, her stomach fluttered with excitement. The red knight before her exuded strength and chivalry. It didn't feel like a play, his posture and the way his eyes bored into hers indicated he would fight for her honor.

Part of her wanted the red knight to remove his helmet, so she'd see what the object of her affection looked like. The other part of her wanted him to remain a mystery so she could imagine whatever she'd wanted to about him from here on out. Reality was rarely as good as the fantasy.

Holding his gaze, she slipped on the circlet, her heart skipping a beat as the crowd roared behind her. He wasn't the same red knight as the one who played with the children earlier. This one was younger; she could tell by the lack of wrinkles around the eyes. A friend of Silvain's perhaps? The way he looked at her was unnerving. She almost forgot what to say, but then remembered, "Bonne chance."

He nodded, lifted his lance with her favor attached, and then galloped off to preen in front of the crowd. She waved wildly at him until he was at the far side of the field.

Shaking, mostly from nerves, Margot made her way back to her seat. A tourist turned around and took her picture.

Tanvi laughed. "You are like a movie star now."

"No, but that was fun. I hope our knight wins."

"Do not fall in love with the knights. They are popular with lady tourists. A new damsel every weekend."

"It's all pretend," Margot said, watching her knight carefully. Feeling somewhat possessive about him, she understood the draw of a knight in shining armor. The other knights carried their helmets in their arms while they openly flirted with their fans, but hers rode stolidly around the arena, a dark and brooding warrior with his helmet on.

"Our knight seems moody."

"Moody?" Tanvi cocked her head.

"Set apart from the crowd. Not friendly."

"Yes. They each play a role. The yellow knight is funny. The green is strong, and the blue is handsome and ladies' man. The red is the proud knight with hot temper, but also best on the horse. The knights trade off. One day they ride, the next day they play armor bearer."

The joust began with their red knight squaring off against the blue knight. Jean Robert raised his arms, indicating that their section needed to cheer. Margot eagerly let herself get caught up in the excitement with the rest of the tourists.

The red and blue knights charged, lances pointed at each other's shields. There was a loud *crack* as the tip of the red knight's lance broke into pieces. The knights continued past each other, exchanging weapons with their armor bearers.

"They get points for touches," Tanvi explained. "More for broken lances."

With the roar of the crowd, the knights hurtled toward each other again. This time, her red knight hit the blue knight's shield square on and knocked him off-balance. Margot stood and cheered with the rest of the red section as the blue knight dramatically leaned over, almost falling off his horse.

The red section continued to roar their approval, and Jean Robert waved Margot down again. Without hesitation, she ran forward to give her knight a second favor.

"Congratulations brave knight," she said, as she held up the second favor.

Something about those eyes looked familiar. She cocked her head and looked at Jean Robert. "Who is he?"

Jean Robert shrugged. He wasn't giving anything away.

The knight continued to stare at her, almost daring her to guess his identity. He wasn't Silvain. She'd already seen him in his yellow surcoat.

Yes, she knew those rakish eyes.

Her heart did a little flip. "Burke?"

Her hands fumbled as she slipped the favor onto his lance. He removed his helmet and nodded at her. He had tied his hair back in a little ponytail at the nape of his neck. She didn't realize it was long enough for him to pull back like that.

"Why didn't you tell me you were one of the knights?"

He didn't answer, but put his helmet back on and rode proudly in front of the king, celebrating his victory. He held up his lance with Margot's red favors attached, gold ribbons streaming. And in that moment, Margot was glad she'd sat in the red section.

It might have been the role she was playing, or she might have felt a real spark between them. For now, it didn't matter. Margot reveled in the thrill of the tournament and the illusion of being picked out of the crowd to give Burke her favor.

After he finished preening in front of the king's box, he exited the arena. Margot quietly returned to her seat and the next two knights took their places. This next contest wasn't nearly as exciting for the red section, with their pride and joy gone. With Burke gone.

"Tell me about Burke," Margot blurted out to Tanvi.

While Tanvi studied her face, Margot tried to hide all romantic thoughts of Burke.

"That Burke always fools the tourists," Tanvi finally said. "They don't have to live with him the rest of the week."

"What do you mean?"

"Burke? He thinks he is the king and we are his little peasants. He's a beast."

Margot didn't know how to answer. She felt like she should stick up for Burke, but she knew nothing about him other than he picked her up from the airport, showed her around town, and knew something about computers. She'd also witnessed him picking up trash, helping with the kids, and jumping to help Thyme.

And how in each case he came off as prideful as Tanvi said.

"He never takes his helmet off," Tanvi mused. "I am surprised he did so today. He wanted you to see who he is." She said it like she thought Burke was showing off.

Margot thought back to her gaze locking with the red knight when she gave him her favor. *I see you, Burke.*

A knight? Who works in a bookstore? It's like he was tailor-made for her. Too bad he acted more like a haughty prince than a trapped beast in need of her help. She mustn't lose sight of the beast in her dream. He's the one she needed to find and befriend.

"Is there another forest?" Margot asked Tanvi. "I went for a walk this morning in the one outside the walls, but is there another? One with... different trees?" Margot spoke all this in French and hoped she said the words right.

Tanvi corrected her pronunciation, then said, "No. Those woods are the only ones that are close. You'd have to drive further inland for another."

How could she do that? Burke might drive her, but that would be awkward. Suzette was busy with the store.

"Look. There's Silvain!" Despite being in the red cheering section, Tanvi stood and yelled out to the yellow knight. He heard and came prancing over while Jean Robert led the group to *boo* at him.

He took it in good fun and preened all the more. Tanvi sat back down. "He loves the attention. All the knights do. If he doesn't watch it, his ego will be as big as Burke's."

Margot focused on the yellow knight on the field now. Silvain could be her beast.

CHAPTER 13

*M*argot parted ways with Tanvi at the flower stall. "Thanks for going to the joust with me. That was fun."

"Yes, but I'm afraid now the boys will be extra competitive in the field. Silvain saw us in the red section."

"They're not friends, are they?"

"No, their personalities do not mix." Tanvi put her hand on Margot's shoulder. "Now they will fight over a girl."

"Me?" Margot didn't believe it. She absently touched the ribbons on a hair wreath, then moved her hand back to her side when she realized they were the red and gold colors. "Burke likes Paris girl."

Tanvi shrugged. "But Silvain does not see it that way." She put her work apron back on. "Will we see you tonight?"

"The Torture Museum?" Margot made a face.

"Please come. You must see it. I'll be there."

"Yes?" she said it tentatively as she couldn't believe she was agreeing to such a thing.

"Excellent. See you then."

Margot returned to the apartment to rest up before the final reunion dinner. Her jet lag, combined with interrupted sleep, was confusing her body. However, she was hesitant to fall asleep for fear of what she would dream about this time. Would the beast be disappointed she didn't find him today? He didn't give her much to go on.

Instead, she went back downstairs to see if Suzette wanted help in the store.

"Do you need a break? I see you working so hard. Don't you have an assistant or anything?"

"Yes, I have a regular clerk, but she's taken vacation for the month. Terrible timing for your visit, but it was planned last year. I'm managing. Burke has been secretly helping me. He does things in subtle ways, so he thinks I don't know, but I do. For example, he's dawdling on the computer project, so he can cover for me when I need a break."

Burke? The same boy who has a reputation for being aloof and better than everyone else?

Suzette mustn't have noticed Margot's disbelieving expression as she continued on. "Besides, Clove wants me to hire a girl from Paris for the summer. She's one of the visitors for the reunion. Comes from the bakery folk, but I suppose she'll be all right with the books. Chapais has worked its magic, and she's not ready to go home yet."

"Oh." *Paris girl.*

"Have you met her?"

"She's the girl who won the Belle costume contest? No, I haven't actually met her."

"Nice girl. Clove brought her by while you were at the joust. How did that go?"

Margot thought of locking eyes with Burke and the spark that passed through them. Her. Passed through her. Maybe not him. Probably not him. "It was fun, actually. More of a play than a sporting event, so it wasn't too terrible."

Suzette laughed. "Well, at least now you've been, and you can stop everyone from telling you that you should go."

"So, what about this girl from Paris? Is she to start now?" Margot circled back to her concerns for Suzette and how hard she was working. Paris girl might not be the ideal—the last thing she wanted to do was hang out at the bookstore watching Burke and Paris girl make eyes at each other—but Suzette needed extra hired help until her assistant returned.

"Clove is trying to find the girl a place to stay before her parents will agree to it. But I suppose I could use her help. I don't seem to have the energy this summer." She looked wistfully around at her books. "I'll need to make some decisions about the place soon. The older you get, the younger you realize you are in mind than in body."

"I can help out while I'm here."

"That's kind of you, but I want you to enjoy your vacation. Isn't there anything else you'd like to do?"

"Tanvi was telling me about some woods farther out of town." *Suzette must wonder about my obsession with trees.*

"Yes, I think I know the place. But we have to drive there."

"Not a big deal."

The door opened, dinging the bell.

Burke marched into the store and stopped short when he saw Margot. His hair was wet, like he'd recently showered and his hair was no longer in a ponytail like at the joust. He wore a red linen tunic, the kind with the crisscross strings on his chest you see in movies set in medieval times.

Margot had no idea how he managed to put his hair into a ponytail during the joust. To her, it looked shorter again. She looked away, embarrassed to be so concerned with the hair at the base of his neck.

"Burke, would it be too much bother to ask you to take Margot sightseeing? The vineyard and out to the woods near the ruins? You should have time before the teenager event tonight.

I'm afraid I'm no fun as a host, and she should see more of the French countryside."

Margot didn't know how to respond. Yes, she wanted to go to the forest—especially near some ruins—but she couldn't go with Burke. How was she to find a beast when she had a moody knight trailing along with her?

"I'll go get my keys."

"No, you don't—" Margot found her voice, but too late. He was already out the door.

"Un moment." Margot ran upstairs to grab an extra negative disc for her camera. It was a gorgeous summer day for taking photos.

She also made sure her pocket English-French dictionary was in her purse. Burke didn't seem as fluent in English as some of the others were, or at least he wasn't as willing to speak it. That was better anyway, because she needed more practice.

She flew out the door, grabbing Amy's *Summer of Love* tape on the way. It would be awesome to hear those songs blasting out of the convertible.

Burke waited for her outside the bookshop door, along with Clove and Thyme. Suzette came out and waved. "Have a good time."

This felt like such a setup, as if all the elders in the town were playing Cupid.

Margot waved, and Burke shook his head at them. He turned and then silently led the way through the thinning crowd of tourists to the gate, and then out to his car in the dirt parking lot. This time the top was up on the car, and Margot was a little disappointed. She'd imagined herself riding Miami Vice–style through the vineyards of France playing Amy's summer-of-love tape.

They were silent during the walk to the car and Margot wondered if he'd rather be driving Paris girl somewhere. She couldn't come right out and ask. That would be tactless.

"You don't like our forest here?" he asked.

"It's fine. I'm used to something, I don't know…larger where I come from." *Larger?*

That comment seemed to offend him, too.

When they got inside the car, Margot waved her cassette tape at him. He raised his eyebrows before taking it and popping it into the tape deck.

Danger Zone blasted out of the speakers and Burke quickly reached over and turned the volume down. *Wow, he listens to his music loud.*

They zipped down the hill and through the streets of New Town. The buildings looked as dated as the castle grounds. Ancient stone structures with carved wooden signs fit the medieval theme, marred only by the people wearing shorts and T-shirts instead of jerkins and skirts.

Margot glimpsed the Mediterranean through a gap in the buildings. "I thought the forest was inland. Where are we going?"

"I'm hungry and want to make a stop. Besides, I prefer the sea to the forest. You'll like it better."

"Oh, you prefer. Do you always get your way?" Margot was miffed that he was taking her the opposite direction from what Suzette had asked. If he had no plans to take her to the woods, he should have said so before they left.

Burke found a parking spot near a restaurant and then turned off the engine. He rubbed his hands on his shorts. *Nervous?* And looked at Margot for the first time since they drove away from the walled city.

Margot thought they might go into the restaurant they parked near, but Burke headed toward the greenbelt behind them. This time he walked slower so she could walk beside him. He walked with purpose, and Margot wondered if he ever relaxed.

A group of teens was ahead of them on the street. Three boys and a girl. They started making gestures toward Margot and Burke. Talking and laughing.

Burke stiffened. He obviously knew them and was bracing for a confrontation.

The tallest boy called out to him.

Without answering, Burke took Margot by the elbow and quickly crossed the street in between moving cars. His actions made Margot nervous. Were those boys so dangerous they needed to risk crossing in the middle of the street?

Two of the boys followed, and Burke picked up the pace. The tall boy caught up to them and grabbed Burke by the shoulder, spinning him around.

Margot stepped back, wary of what might happen next. The group across the street stood watching, and the second boy who had crossed the street grinned in anticipation.

Immediately, Burke had the tall one up against the wall, his arm locked across his neck, muscles flexing. His fighting reflexes were quick to act.

Margot looked around for help, unsure of what to do. She kept her eye on the second boy in case he also went after Burke. At the moment, he hung back, but he'd balled his fists in readiness.

Burke spoke in short, terse sentences, glancing between the two boys. When neither made another move, he shoved the tall boy before letting him go. The boy straightened his shirt, sneering at Burke.

Silence crackled between them.

Burke stood his ground, placing himself protectively in front of Margot until the boys had crossed back to the other side of the street.

What was that? Adrenaline pumped through Margot's veins. If this was an example of what Burke had to go through...no wonder he kept to himself so much.

Once the group moved on, Burke turned to Margot. He raised his eyebrows at her questioningly.

"I'm okay. *Bien*," she answered. But somehow the trip through town had lost its appeal. "Could we go back?" she said. "Or for a drive?" She mimed a steering wheel.

Burke nodded in a resigned way. But before they turned around, he stopped by a small shop and purchased a bag of mixed olives—red, black, and green.

Okay. Odd choice. Margot kept watch on the street, not wanting to be surprised from behind. After Burke made the purchase, they started walking back to the car. He opened the bag and offered it to her.

She politely took one. *Who snacks on olives?*

He shoved a handful into his mouth.

She bit hard into hers and immediately spit it out thinking it was rotten and she'd bit the pit. Burke raised his eyebrows, looking shocked, then somewhat annoyed that she'd spit it out. Then the taste hit her. It was chocolate! She started to laugh, holding out her hand with the wayward chocolate-covered nut. "I thought they were really olives. Salty?"

Burke broke into a smile.

She laughed harder. It wasn't that funny, but apparently, she needed the emotional release. She'd been so nervous around Burke, and then he almost got into a fight and now she was busting it over chocolate.

Burke laughed with her. Not a lot, but it was the first time she'd ever heard him laugh. He was always so serious. Too serious.

She reached over and picked out several candies from the paper bag. Sure enough, it was a chocolate-covered almond with a candied shell to make it look like an olive. Nothing was as it seemed in the south of France.

Back in the car, Margot snagged a couple more candies. "I thought you were hungry. Is this all you're going to eat?"

He shook his head. "New plan. We're going to the beach. It's quieter there."

Margot wanted to ask about the bullies in town but didn't want to ruin the new lightheartedness she'd seen in him.

Ten minutes later, they pulled into a half-empty parking lot near a hot dog stand.

Burke ordered while she curiously watched the vendor cut off several chunks from a long baguette and then stab them onto heated metal spikes. Next, he took the sausages and dipped them in Dijon mustard before stuffing them into the holes left by the spikes and then wrapping the whole thing in brown tissue paper.

Margot tried to pay for her food, but Burke refused her money. He handed her one of the dogs.

"This way." He started walking through a gap in the trees.

The sound of surf grew louder as they cleared the path and ended up on the sandy beach. Cobalt blue water met pale blue sky.

"I want to touch the water," Margot said. The Mediterranean. It was beautiful. She balanced holding her food and taking off her shoes. *These feet are going in.*

She ran ahead of Burke and stood at the water's edge where the sand was packed firm. She eagerly waited for a wave to come to her. *Cold.* She jumped back when the water touched the sensitive arch of her foot.

Burke laughed. Again. She'd gotten him to laugh twice in one night.

"Are you going to eat that?" he asked, pointing to her hot dog. "Answer in French."

Demand much?

"You can't have it. I wanted to eat it in the sea." She spoke a mixture of French and English and then ate a big bite. *Mm.* The hot dog tasted as good as it smelled. Just the right mix of salt and sweet. She looked out over the water. *This is perfect. This moment right now.* "I could stay here forever," she said.

"Forever is a long time," Burke said. He wasn't looking out at the horizon but at his hands, balled into fists.

What is he thinking about? Dressed as he was in that huggable red tunic, she could picture him a warrior of old. He only needed his horse to ride on the beach to complete the picture.

"Do you like to joust? You're very good."

"I am."

Modesty is not his thing. "Is it hard to learn?"

"It takes practice. Some others don't take it seriously enough."

Margot wondered if he included Silvain in that list.

He glanced at his watch, then walked midway up the beach and sat on a log, waiting for her.

Margot took her time staring out at the waves. He wanted to come here; she wouldn't leave until she was ready. Every time she glanced back at him, he was checking the time. It was almost painful to watch. He obviously needed to be somewhere.

Fine. She carried her shoes to the log. "Ready?"

CHAPTER 14

The streets were sufficiently dark when it was time for Margot to leave for the Torture Museum. Despite the good time she thought they'd been having, Margot hadn't been able to convince Burke to join them. He said he had other plans, and they parted ways at the bookshop.

The Torture Museum frontage consisted of a door and a window. If it wasn't for the realistic-looking medieval mannequin trapped in the wooden stocks out front, a person would walk right by and not know what was there.

Two guys stood posing for Tanvi in front of the stocks.

"Quick, get in the picture, Margot," Tanvi said.

Margot jumped into the shot, making a peace sign along with the others. *Peace.* Another universal sign.

"These are Ed and Laurent." Tanvi introduced the guys. "They work with the jousting and around the stables."

Margot smiled at them and said bonjour to Jean Robert as he joined them. But then her smile dimmed as she recognized another boy as having been in town earlier.

"And this is Marc," Tanvi said, giving a name to the boy who stood by while Burke was harassed. Addressing Jean Robert, she asked, "Your sister didn't want to come?"

He shook his head, glancing at Margot. "She's seen it. Doesn't want to see it again."

Margot took the time to process their French. "Is it that bad?" Margot began to wonder if she should back out. Tanvi was the only other girl, and that Marc was not her favorite person in France. Also noticeably absent was the Paris girl.

"No," said Tanvi. "You'll love it. Or at least remember it. It's a good tourist stop."

Ed grabbed Laurent in a headlock and joked about putting him in the stocks instead of the mannequin. *Mannequin! Another French word she already knew. Why did she ever think learning French was so hard?*

"How did you like the joust today?" Jean Robert asked.

"I thought you did a great job. The crowd likes you."

Talk of the tournament reminded Margot of Silvain. She looked down the street for him. A torture museum seemed like his kind of thing.

Jean Robert smiled. "The people enjoy yelling at the knights. You should come back again tomorrow. It's different every time."

"Once more before I go home," she agreed.

After paying a man dressed in a reddish-brown robe, they entered a dark hallway. Spooky music floated in on speakers, and Margot felt herself getting jumpy already. She wasn't expecting ambiance like a haunted house. "How scary is it?" she whispered to Tanvi.

"You don't fall down when you see blood?"

Blood? "You mean faint? No." *But I usually close my eyes.* She was already regretting this museum visit. It was more immersive than the triple-horror experience at the drive-in back home. "Is there a snack bar?"

Tanvi looked curiously at her as if she didn't understand the word or why Margot was asking.

"Never mind. I'll stick with the group." Back home, her friends liked to talk her into going to three back-to-back horror movies at the drive-in theater. She spent most of the night hanging out with whichever clique floated into the snack bar instead of watching the movies. *Clique! Another French word.*

The first room they entered contained some kind of rack with another mannequin lying inside the contraption while another stood over her, apparently applying the torture. Placards in several languages explained the torture device and the crime that led the poor mannequin into her predicament.

Margot glanced at the scene, but focused on reading both the French and the English. She'd be able to go home and talk about medieval torture methods to her French teacher. It'd be great.

Another room held a mannequin about to be burned at the stake. Margot shuddered. She'd read about Christian martyrs during the time of Nero in Rome suffering such torture. How could people do things like this to one another?

Ed and Laurent continued ribbing each other.

"Ed says he would rather be burned than stretched to death," Tanvi translated. "And Marc says he'd pay them both to test one of big machines outside." She pointed out the open door they were coming up to.

Margot tried to catch a glimpse of what was coming but only saw the corner of some wood. "Oh, great. What's next?"

They went outside into a small courtyard where a gallows and a guillotine ominously filled the space. Music from the pub lent an anachronistic air to the scene.

"These contraptions would certainly be quicker," Margot said. She tamped down her imagination so she wouldn't picture actual people on them.

Seeing all these terrible death machines up close set her on edge. The way the boys were making light of it all made her wonder if they were desensitized because they'd seen it before, or if they were cracking jokes because they were disturbed by it, too.

Jean Robert led the way back inside where the lights were dim and spotlights shone on a chair of spikes on one side of the room. On display beside the chair was a coffin-looking contraption labeled *Iron Maiden*. The placard explained that when the lid closed, the spikes would...*well that's enough of that. So that's what that looks like.* She only knew it by the name of the rock band. She was glad the thing was closed, so she didn't have to see those terrible spikes. She turned away, but Tanvi pulled her to the placard and started to read it out loud.

Suddenly, the closed door on the iron maiden swung open and out popped a guy dressed in rags, with blood dripping down his head and on his arms.

Margot screamed.

Ed and Laurent slapped each other's shoulders in a congratulatory way. The others just laughed. They knew it was coming.

"Got you!" said Silvain, leaning out of the iron maiden and high-fiving the other boys.

"Haha. Very funny." Margot pressed her hand to her heart. It was beating so hard it felt like it would jump out and run away on its own.

"You know," she said, "I've heard that this isn't a real torture device. It became popular for medieval displays to show how barbaric they were in the middle ages, but the evidence for these is pretty slim. Not that I'm an expert..." Apparently she babbled out useless facts when she was scared.

They all paused in their laughter long enough to process her English, then all burst out again. This time Margot joined them. Now that she was breathing again, she could appreciate the joke. They got her bad.

The ghoulish Silvain jumped down from the platform.

"I'm glad you're not dead," Margot commented.

"I like this one," Silvain said, putting his arm around her. She let him keep it there this time. She was getting used to him and his hijinks.

"Where did you find her?" asked Ed.

"She is Burke's new friend," Tanvi said, her words laced with meaning.

The boy from town wrinkled his nose. "Burke has friends?"

Margot shot him an icy glare.

"Do you recognize Silvain?" the boy asked. "The yellow knight. Burke's sworn enemy at the tournament."

Silvain grinned like he'd done something amazing.

"Sorry he beats you so often," Margot said cheekily.

Scowling, Silvain removed his arm from her shoulder and said something derogatory about Burke.

Margot was taken aback. *He can give a joke but not take one.*

"Why didn't the spikes hurt you?" she asked, changing the subject.

Tanvi answered. "The trick is the spikes are made of rubber, so they are soft and they are short for the box. He can fit inside and not be hurt."

Margot nodded. It made sense that they wouldn't want a device that could actually kill someone. Especially when it was so accessible to the public.

Silvain continued with the group, and the good-natured tone changed. At every opportunity, he seemed to bring it back to Burke as the center of all his morose jokes.

"How does he not get in trouble for hiding in the iron maiden?" Margot asked Tanvi. "The owners can't be happy with him doing that?" She looked around for someone in charge, but they were the only ones in the room.

"Silvain's father runs the museum. They do that trick with all of us."

The jokes about Burke continued, and finally Margot couldn't take it anymore. Nothing she'd seen from him deserved this kind of treatment.

"He's not here to defend himself, and you shouldn't be talking about him behind his back. Never mind, you shouldn't be saying these things at all."

No one commented, though Silvain looked away, and the rest stared at their feet. If they didn't understand her words, they must have understood her tone.

They quietly went into the final room. It had fewer devices and more to read. No one seemed interested in reading, so they headed for the exit.

"We will go to New Town next," said Tanvi. The others walked ahead as if trying to distance themselves from Margot. "Will you come?"

Margot shook her head. She was done. The gore, the mood.

"They're only teasing." Tanvi spoke like it was no big deal. "They mean nothing by it."

"I still don't like it." From what Margot saw in town, there was more to it than Tanvi knew. For whatever reason, the tournament rivalry was spilling outside the arena.

"Besides," Tanvi said, "Burke's not any better than them. It's all bravado. These boys are like this all the time."

How could Margot explain about the Burke she saw? Yes, he was proud and arrogant, but there was also a caring side to him.

"He's nice to me," she said lamely. She couldn't keep both sets of friends happy. If they couldn't all get along, she'd choose Burke over them.

And if Silvain is the beast? He'll have to try harder.

"Why didn't he go out tonight?" Sage asked. She sat back in an armchair and put her feet up on the ottoman. Their rented apartment had a great view of the town square where they could keep an eye on things.

"He's tired of shaving. Wanted a night off." Clove looked annoyed. She added an extra scoop of cinnamon into the flour for her next creation. "If he dawdles too much, he'll seal his own fate and you two can't blame me for that."

"Give him a break." Thyme put her feet into a pair of fuzzy slippers. "All the boy does lately is shower and cut his hair."

"Yes, but if he gives up…" Clove chewed her lip and didn't finish the thought.

Sage eyed her warily. "The other one. He didn't give up, did he? You said it was taken care of."

"I said I took care of him, and I did. I'll do the same for Burke, now leave me be. You two never trust me."

"Fine." Sage put her reading glasses on and reached for her crossword puzzle. "What do you have planned for tomorrow, then?"

"I'm still trying to get Monet's family to stay longer. I thought offering her a job would help, but her father is determined she's going back with them to Paris."

Thyme smiled. "Good. It's only distracting him from falling in love with the right girl." She moved over the table where she'd spread out a jigsaw puzzle of kittens in a basket. "You know I'm right. The timing of the dreams. They started when she arrived."

"I suppose so," Clove said.

"Then why so reluctant?" Sage asked. "If we're agreed what needs to happen."

"I don't want him hurt." Clove put down her wooden spoon. "Girls these days are fickle. Not like in the old days."

Thyme burst out laughing. "Girls are the same as ever. Some are fickle and some are true. I know this girl. She is true. But that also means she'll be cautious. Her ideals are high and Burke might not be what she expects."

CHAPTER 15

$\mathcal{M}$argot didn't dream that night. At least, not of the beast. She woke disappointed that she hadn't seen him. Without dreaming, how was she to gather any more information on who he was or how she could find him? Had he given up on her already?

Suzette's door was still closed, so Margot quietly grabbed some breakfast before slipping on her Chuck Taylor high-tops. She'd left the *Summer of Love* tape in Burke's car, so she slid another mix tape into her Walkman. This tape was one she'd made off the radio. She'd spent hours waiting for her favorite songs to come on so she could hit the record button.

She silently opened the door and then almost stepped on a cassette left on the doormat. The label was handwritten in guy handwriting—bold capital letters. POUR MARGOT.

Pour. She was pretty sure that meant *for.* For Margot.

She looked down the alley and saw a man watering the hanging pots of geraniums on the street. No one else was about.

She popped open her Walkman and swapped out tapes. After pressing play, she started down the stone steps. A deep, rich voice filled her head and her heart about stopped. She'd been expecting music, but what she got was some guy speaking in French.

What is this?

Given the cadence in his voice, the guy sounded like he was reading something to her. The voice was so immediate in her head that he must be nearby. She looked again, but no; it was just her and the gardener, whom she'd never seen before.

Who could have left the tape? It wasn't a professional recording, as there was too much background noise for that. No, this was a home job.

She briefly considered that Burke left the tape, but that didn't seem like something he would do or have time for. The other guys were always goofing off, but Burke seemed to disappear a lot, working or running errands for the heritage committee.

Silvain was the obvious one to leave her a gift; an attempt to make up for being such a jerk in the museum?

The voice was hard to place. French and male were all she knew for sure. But she couldn't tell if it was Silvain. It could also be Jean Robert. He knew she was trying to learn French. When either of them spoke to her, it was in a mixed-up version of English and exaggerated French. She would have to pay attention to their voices today to determine the identity of the mystery speaker.

Here she was in France, walking down a medieval street while watching the sun rise and listening to a husky voice speaking directly into her thoughts. Nothing this romantic happened in real life. At least, not in her life.

Whoever sent her this was very sweet, and the gesture put her in a great mood, even though he spoke too fast for her to understand anything he said. By the time she reached the walkway leading to the battlements she'd decided the tape was probably Silvain trying to make up for yesterday. Even if Tanvi put him up to the recording, the thought warmed her heart. She would have to forgive Silvain after this.

At the town center, she ran into Sage near the castle. "Bonjour." Margot stopped the tape and took off her headphones.

"Where is Suzette, is she coming?" Sage removed her reading glasses and let them dangle from the silver chain around her neck. She tucked the clipboard under her arm.

"Coming for what?"

"The families are meeting in the chapel. We have a vicar from New Town here for Sunday Services. She was to hand out programs."

Margot shook her head. "I came home too late last night for her to tell me about it, but when I woke up this morning, her door was still closed."

Sage looked up at the sky as if determining the time from the sun. "Please check on her. I can find someone else to help, but I know she wanted to be there."

"She's mentioned that she's been unusually tired lately, but I'll wake her so she doesn't miss out. Where is the chapel?"

"In the castle."

Margot looked over to see the chain-link barrier removed and the door standing open. She'd been wanting to get inside that castle. It seemed a likely place for the beast to be. *If he is still waiting for me.* She'd gotten too preoccupied with the activities from the reunion weekend to focus all her efforts on solving the mystery of the beast.

"I can help pass out the programs, too. What time should we be there?"

Again, Sage consulted the sky. "Fifteen minutes. That should give us plenty of time before the guests arrive. The vicar is already here."

Margot scooted home with mild concern. She hoped nothing was wrong with Suzette that a good night's sleep couldn't fix.

"Suzette?" Margot called as soon as she stepped into the apartment. "Are you up? Miss Sage is looking for you."

The door to the bathroom opened, and Suzette exited

wearing a light cotton dress and prim green hat. "It must be later than I thought. I needed the sleep, though. Are you going to chapel?" Suzette politely eyed Margot's shorts and T-shirt.

"Yes, I'll change quick."

She hadn't brought anything fancy, but had packed a jean skirt and blouse. She pulled her hair back in a ponytail and wrapped a scrunchy around it. "All set." She traded her high-tops for her jellies and followed Suzette back to the town square.

There was no payment line today in front of the castle. They allowed visitors to walk right under the portcullis into the vestibule, though ropes funneled them straight to the chapel.

Finally. The castle.

Margot lingered in the entrance, studying the cut of the stones, the worn paths where she walked over the footsteps of knights and ladies and servants. She also peered into the dark corners searching for the beast. There wasn't much in the way of hiding places. Walking into the castle was like walking into a house that someone had moved out of, taking everything but the light fixtures.

"I can't believe I'm inside a real castle."

Suzette chuckled. "Your enthusiasm is refreshing. I'm afraid those of us who grew up here are rather lackadaisical. We're used to these old stones, and they're used to us."

Sage met them just inside the entrance and gave Suzette a stack of bulletins to hand out. "Good morning!" She touched Margot's arm. "Be sure to stay for the tour afterward since you missed the one on Thursday night."

"I wouldn't miss it."

A harp began to play, and Margot continued into the chapel to see what it looked like. The large mahogany harp that Thyme played sat to the right of the altar, which was a simple platform compared to the detailed architecture surrounding it. Margot's gaze immediately lifted to the large stained-glass windows which filtered light through slivers of blue, red, and yellow.

The chapel had been built to direct one's eyes heavenward. Huge marble columns spanned the space leading up to layered arched ceilings and those stained-glass windows. Carved statues filled the alcoves that cut into the walls. The way the light from the stained glass and other windows played with color and illumination on the carvings was a masterful work.

Five rows of wooden pews fanned out from the altar, with folding chairs taking up the rest of the space to make more room for the extra guests that morning. When people started to come in behind her, Margot returned to Suzette's side to hand out the programs.

"Well?" Suzette asked.

"It's gorgeous in there. Better than the photographs."

"Keep in mind the entire castle used to be more ornate, but most of the items have been relocated to museums or private collections."

"I wish I could have seen the castle at the height of its use. Even so, it's still special to be inside."

Suzette hugged Margot's shoulder. "I'm glad you love the place. Some find our town dull after they've seen everything."

Paris girl arrived with her family. Margot smiled and handed her a program.

"Merci," Paris girl said and smiled back.

Margot attempted to ask if she'd be staying long.

After Suzette corrected Margot's pronunciation, Paris girl shook her head. They were planning a few more tours outside town before going home. Knowing Paris girl was leaving soon made Margot relieved. After the girl walked on, Margot whispered, "What will you do?"

Suzette shrugged. "Carry on as usual."

After a few more minutes of handing out programs, Suzette nudged Margot. "It's filling in. Go find us seats that are easy for me to slip into when I'm done here."

"There are two right there." With one last look outside, she retreated into the chapel. She'd wanted to linger and see if any of her new friends were coming. And if they were still friends after the Torture Museum. Especially Silvain so she could mention the cassette.

"Are those seats taken?" she asked an elderly man. She first spoke in English, then attempted French. One day she'd remember to lead with French.

"By you," he said.

They fumbled through a short conversation about the reunion weekend before they ran out of things to say.

Margot turned around and looked to see if any of her friends had slipped by her. Yes, she found Silvain, sitting with a man and a woman who looked like they might be his parents. She waved and mouthed *merci* trying to hint that she was thanking him for the cassette to see if he would take the bait and confess. He waved back, not giving anything away, but as friendly as ever.

Margot's gaze lifted to Burke slipping into the back as the last chords of the harp faded. His eyes briefly met hers, bounced to Silvain, and then he found a seat near Paris girl and her family. Again, he looked like he just got out of the shower, clean-cut and freshly shaved.

Suzette slipped in beside her as Thyme walked off the platform. "We have a nice crowd today," Suzette said.

As the vicar began his sermon, Margot's mind began to wander. She tried to listen, but she only caught half of what he was saying. Her understanding was better than the day she arrived, but she still had a ways to go. It didn't escape her notice that she was sitting in a chapel where people had come to worship for hundreds of years. She could picture the people dressed in their linen tunics and skirts quietly shuffling in, pausing in their work for the week to commune with their Creator.

After the service, a line began to form as people shook hands with the vicar on the way out. Thyme stood by with her clipboard to organize folks into tours.

When Margot and Suzette reached the vicar, instead of shaking hands, Suzette put one hand to her forehead and stretched the other one out like she was preparing to catch herself in a fall. The vicar, anticipating, reached for her and helped steady her on her feet.

"Suzette? Are you okay?" Margot asked.

"I better sit," she said.

The whole entourage moved with her to the nearest pew. Suzette, the vicar, Margot, and Thyme. Sage joined them within minutes and took the place of Thyme, who resumed organizing the tours.

"Can I get you some water?" The vicar quickly left to track down a drink. Sage, meanwhile, felt Suzette's forehead. "You're a little warm, but nothing alarming."

Suzette answered in quick French, and Margot lost her hold on the conversation.

"She says she felt faint of a sudden," Sage explained. "She may have gotten up too fast. We'll wait for her to settle then walk her home. One of us on each side of her."

"Should I get someone to take her to the doctor?" Margot asked.

"Across the street, with the ferns," Suzette spoke in gasps. "But he is gone till tonight."

While Sage and Suzette held a brief conversation, the vicar returned with a paper cup filled with water. Suzette sipped it until it was all gone, and they had made plans for her.

They would return to the apartment together, then Sage would monitor her during the afternoon. If she got worse before the doctor came, they would take Suzette to the emergency room. "Margot, can you drive Suzette's car?"

"Technically? Yes, but I don't know where anything is."

Thyme chimed in. "Burke will drive." The tour she arranged left the room through the archway behind them.

Where was Burke? Margot expected him to be hovering in the background like usual, but he wasn't there. In fact, everyone had left by this point. So, while the heritage committee members talked particulars, Margot took the time to wander the room. *Would she be able to see the beast if he was trapped in here?*

When she got to the other side of the room, she whispered, "I'm here," in French.

"Margot?"

It was Thyme, signaling across the room that they were ready.

"Coming."

Chapais was still fairly empty, so maneuvering three across was not difficult, even down the narrow cobbled street that led to the bookshop.

"You are all making too much of a fuss," Suzette kept saying, but their progress was slow, and Sage wasn't backing down an inch.

"Are you a nurse?" Margot asked.

"No, why do you ask?" Sage maneuvered them around a café table.

"Seems like you would make a good one."

"I like to do what needs to be done."

Margot wanted to add *just like a nurse*, but let it pass.

They got Suzette situated back in bed, elevated with an extra pillow. Sage moved a kitchen chair near her bedside. "I'll stay with her until I'm certain she doesn't need emergency care. Would you please go make some tea?"

Margot appreciated having something to do besides stand there and worry. Not only did she get the tea ready, but she fixed some sandwiches and chopped up a fruit salad.

While they waited for any change in Suzette, Margot finished the letters home that she'd started. One for Dad and one for Amy.

Dad's was filled with descriptions of Chapais. Amy's was filled with descriptions of Burke, Silvain, Tanvi, and the others.

Sage came out of the bedroom as Margot was licking the envelope addressed to Amy.

"She's agreed that I can call the doctor later if she's not recovered, but regardless, we don't want her working so hard this week."

"What about the store? Her assistant is still away on vacation."

"Yes, we ought to do something about that. We'll leave it closed for today and see what happens on Monday."

"I could help, but I don't know that I could run it on my own." Margot yawned. These dreams she was having were messing up her sleep.

Sage noticed the yawn. "Why don't you get some rest this afternoon. I suspect you were out late with the other young people. I imagine the half of you who didn't sleep in this morning will nap this afternoon."

Margot nodded. "It's been a busy weekend. Thank you for your work in putting the town reunion on. I'm glad I came."

"We are, too. I can't tell you how much."

CHAPTER 16

*A*fter putting the letters on the table by the door, Margot settled onto the couch with the fairy tale book she'd found in the bookshop and tried her hand at reading it again. The words weren't as elusive as when she first arrived, but she was by no means fluent.

Maybe her idea of going to France for school wasn't the best plan. While it would be fun to take lessons in a castle, living in the walled city had taken that edge off her dream. She was falling in love with Chapais itself. Whether it was the romance of the old stone structures or the kindness of the people, she couldn't tell. Probably both. No wonder her mother wanted to live here. And no wonder Dad didn't. Not a ball field in sight.

Sage joined her. "Your aunt is sleeping now. I suspect on top of everything else, she was dehydrated." She sat in Suzette's rocking chair and picked up a book of crossword puzzles.

Instead of reading, Margot flipped through the artwork again. Pen-and-ink was her favorite style of illustration. It was deceptively simple, only lines and dots and spaces.

She'd not recognized many of the tales by the illustrations and wondered if the stories predated Charles Perrault. Just because she didn't know of any collections that predated the Perrault collection didn't mean they didn't exist.

As she flipped through, one drawing of a group of three fairies caught her eye. They were hanging out in a tree overlooking a wall. On their side of the wall, a girl sat reading a book, and on the other side was an orchard with a classic French *château* behind it.

"Sage, these fairies look like your heritage committee." Margot held the book up. "In the story *La Belle et la Bête.*"

The illustration caught her attention because of the puppet show recently given of Beauty and the Beast. She'd never read the original story herself, so maybe she'd be able to work her way through it now. Even if it took all summer.

Sage lowered her reading glasses down her nose and leaned forward to study the picture. "I don't see it." She slid her glasses up and continued working on a crossword puzzle.

Margot examined the drawing closely. Same upturned nose; hair was curlier in the image, but the cleft in the chin and the demeanor were spot-on. The model for the illustration could have been her twin.

"You say Thyme gave you that book?" Sage crossed off a clue on her puzzle.

"No, I found it mixed in a stack of old books. Well, Thyme helped me find it, because she knocked the books over to start with."

"*Hmph.*" Sage sounded like she disapproved.

Margot adjusted position on the couch so she was lying down as she read. A dangerous position if she wanted to stay awake, but she was getting tired. As long as Suzette was resting, Margot probably should, too. If they were to end up at the hospital, who knew when she'd get to sleep later.

Reading French was faster for her to process than conversational French, but this book had a lot of words she didn't know. As she worked her way through the first paragraph of a story, her mind began to wander and she found herself in a stretch of meadow surrounded by woods. Finally, there were the trees she was looking for. She walked closer to them until she heard a guttural sound come from her right. She stopped and listened.

"Did you look for me?" The beast spoke out of the shadows in his growly voice.

Relieved he was still there, she answered. "I did. I went to the forest, but you weren't there. I can't do this on my own. You want me to find you when I'm awake, but you hide from me during the day."

"I don't mean to." His voice came out softer, if that were possible in a growl. "This is all new to me, too. If you would only tell me your name, it would make this easier. I could find you."

Margot wasn't prepared to do that. "Or, you could tell me yours."

"It's Beast."

"So not helpful. Who names their child Beast?"

"No, not Beast. It's Beast." He growled.

Margot listened to his tone. He wasn't meaning to be funny. "You said Beast every time. Are you trying to say another name, and it's coming out Beast?"

He lowered his head. "Yes. They told me it would get worse. What if that's all I am now? A Beast. Forever." He sounded despondent.

"No, not forever." Margot tried to offer hope. "I'm still here. That means you still have a chance. We only need to figure things out faster."

"I need to see you more clearly. Don't be scared. I'm coming out." He stepped out of the shadows, and when he did, she found herself now in darkness.

"I won't hurt you," he said. "Let me see you."

Margot tried to come closer, but with each step he was just as far away. "I'm trying, but something is keeping us apart."

"Run to me," he said. At the same time, he sprinted toward her. The scene changed. Now they were running parallel to each other. Margot switched course and tried running straight to him, but he adjusted his gait. No matter what they tried, they couldn't get close.

She stood still, and he began running in a circle around her. On all fours. Margot tried not to shiver or let her face show how shocked she was by this beast. She didn't want him to feel worse than he already did.

"What kind of curse is this?" she whispered.

He stopped running, and the scene changed again. This time she felt like they were indoors, but it was still dark. "A terrible one. One that will never end for me."

"Where are we now? The trees are gone." She couldn't see the beast anymore, but knew he was near. They might be in a castle. Where else would a Beast hang out? The air was humid like the forest, but there were no trees. There was vegetation, though. Overgrown plants set up on tables. "Is this a greenhouse, do you think?"

"Yes. I come here often."

"During the day?"

"No. I forget where I go during the day. My life in the light is different from here, but when I'm here, I can't remember who I am there."

She couldn't see the walls. "Is it always night here?" *How terrible.*

"I prefer it to be dark so you can't see me."

The book Margot had been reading slipped off the couch and landed with a *thump*. She blinked open her eyes, but continued to lay there collecting her thoughts. She'd had another dream. The poor beast.

She'd tried to make things happen in the dream, but she couldn't control it. No matter what she did, she couldn't find out where the beast was. Or even get a good look at him. He'd wanted to see her clearly, too, but something wouldn't let them get close.

In fairy tales, the enchanted always escape their altered forms. The frog becomes a prince. The wild man becomes a king. The prince is released from the iron stove.

Resolve shored up, Margot was determined to find the beast today.

Sage was no longer in the chair, but Margot found her in the bedroom.

Suzette lay sleeping while Sage continued to work on a crossword puzzle beside her.

"How is she?"

Sage put down the puzzle and looked over the top of her glasses. "About the same. Doctor's been and gone. He'll be back in the morning with new medication for her. I'm afraid we exhausted her with all our planning. I forget sometimes how the human body needs recovery time."

"That's good news, then." Margot noted Suzette's color was back. "Is it all right if I go out for a bit?"

"*Oui.* I'll send someone for you if there is a significant change."

"Thanks."

Margot grabbed her bag and left.

First, she went to the castle to see when the next tour was. The castle seemed the most likely place for the beast, but they wouldn't let her in until four. That gave her time to explore the forest again, just in case she missed something.

Taking the exit closest to the castle, she followed the dirt path around the back of the tournament grounds to the other side of the walled city, in case there was something of a forest on that side.

As she walked, she listened to the tape Silvain had left on her doorstep. She wished she could have had time to thank him properly. His voice worked its way into her conscience. Some words sounded familiar, but he spoke too quickly for her to understand or follow an idea all the way to completion. So frustrating. How long was it going to take her to master the basics?

Around the back wall, a stable butted up against the stone wall and a smaller paddock extended into a field. *Of course.* This must be the warm-up field for the tournament horses.

A horse and rider galloped away from her along the length of the distant fence. The horse on the field was a proud, muscled charger, exactly the kind she'd expect to see a medieval knight riding. She glanced around, wondering if she was allowed back here. Seemed it would give away some magic of the tournament if she saw the knights jousting in jeans and cowboy hats.

Several ranch hands worked with the horses in the stable, but aside from the lone rider, the field was empty. The rider wasn't tall and lanky enough to be Silvain. Broad shouldered and confident on a horse, he might be Burke. Now at the far end of the field, the rider turned around. *I think it is Burke.*

She took a step back from the fence and was about to run away in embarrassment when he turned his horse and started toward her. She couldn't leave, now. Her face warmed as he got closer.

When he got close enough, he said, "What are you doing here? This area is for the knights only."

"Sorry, I didn't know." Before he could ask her to leave, she continued on the trail past the field as it rounded the other side of the walled city. How did she keep getting herself into awkward situations with this guy?

On the other side of the city, she passed a small vineyard where the grapevines stretched up to the sun. Back in Washington, Margot walked near the apple orchards. The view changed with the season, from buds in the spring to the fragrant white blossoms to the fruit-laden limbs in the fall. Here, she didn't know the first thing about grapes and their seasons.

Currently, the grape clusters were all small and green and the rows of vines stretched into the distance like she imagined feudal fields would have looked back in the day.

A faint and narrow path cut through a gap in a copse of trees and she eagerly ducked through, wondering if these were the trees she was looking for. The path ended at a short wall, and what looked like an even less-worn path continued along the length of it, so she went that way. Soon, she came to a wrought iron garden gate, beyond which she could see an overgrown garden. Curiosity pulled her in farther. She'd been fascinated with *The Secret Garden* in elementary school and always wanted to find her own secret place.

The garden would have been surrounded by walls if the walls were all intact. But the entire area had fallen into disarray and the walls were mostly missing, with a few crumbling sections to show where they used to be. Dead thorn bushes suggested that this used to be a rose garden.

"Beast? Are you here?"

She didn't remember seeing any rosebushes in her dream, but there had been a greenhouse, she was sure of it.

Margot picked her way through the overgrowth, imagining herself a young maiden from the village sneaking into the prince's secret garden. The garden suffered from neglect with the prince away protecting the kingdom and by extension, protecting the young maiden from invaders intent on pillaging.

"No one else is here, if you'd like to come out," she said.

A song bird trilled, and the wind whistled around the corners of the garden. No guttural sound. No growl. No beast.

While she waited, she pulled out the weeds around one of the rosebushes. *That looks better. Maybe now it'll grow some roses.*

She'd fix up the garden for the missing prince so that when he returned, it would be alive again, and he could go there to relax and recover. Because, of course, he'd return with a war wound and need to spend hours in the sun as part of his healing regimen. The prince would search high and low for the loyal subject who had taken the time to keep the garden, and finally, he'd be directed to a tiny cottage on the far side of the village where the poor girl lived alone with her dying mother. The prince, seeing her genuine goodness, would fall instantly in love and invite them both back to the castle where, under the prince's doctor's care, the mother would recover and go on to maintain the castle's herb garden.

While she daydreamed, Margot continued to tidy up the small rose garden. Several dead plants were easy to remove, and she placed those near the wall. She didn't plan to go all out in this abandoned garden, because there was a fine line between being kind and doing something that no one wanted you to do. However, if this was one of the community gardens Suzette had told her about, she'd be allowed to putter as much as she wanted.

She was thrilled to uncover a stone bench that would make a great place to sit and read, or eat lunch. Thinking of food, she realized it was probably close to dinner, and she'd missed the castle tour again. It was time to go back, anyway.

"Okay, Beast. I'm going home now. You know how to contact me." *Apparently.*

She reluctantly left the prince's secret garden, walking past the moody knight still practicing in the field outside the city walls, and entered the city near the castle gate. Ah, magical France.

When she arrived back at the apartment, the entire heritage committee was in the living room. Sage held court in Suzette's rocking chair while Thyme and Clove sat on the edge of the couch. They all had intense looks of concern on their faces.

"Suzette?" Margot asked, fearing the worst. *I shouldn't have stayed out so long.*

"She will be fine," Sage said. "I don't want you to worry, but we are making her rest this next week. We're discussing how to handle her affairs until she is ready to walk about."

Margot sat on the floor across from them all. "What do you need me to do?"

"Enjoy your vacation. We three feel responsible for overworking her. We'll take care of her and her little bookshop."

Thyme grinned. "I've always wanted to work in a shop."

"And I'd like to try that machine. The computer," Clove added.

Sage narrowed her gaze. "We are only to maintain things for her. Not disrupt anything."

"I'll help, too," Margot said. "I can't just have a vacation while everyone else is pitching in."

Sage nodded. "I expected no less from you. Good. All hands on deck tomorrow morning."

CHAPTER 17

*M*onday morning Margot woke without a memory of a dream. She missed the beast and wondered what had happened. If he was in control of visiting her in her dreams, why hadn't he tried to see her last night? And, obviously, the secret garden wasn't his hiding place either. Margot's leg muscles ached after all the bending she'd done as she pulled weeds.

"Rise and shine!" Clove swooped into her room and drew back the curtains. "We're having a staff meeting in twenty minutes. Hop in the shower. Don't worry about breakfast. I've baked some of your American muffins. You like blueberry?"

So that's what the delicious smell is.

Margot quickly got moving as Clove took the pillow out from under her head and began to fluff it.

By now, Margot was used to hanging her clothes on the back of the bathroom door so they didn't get wet from the whole-bathroom-is-the-shower concept.

When she got out, the three members of the heritage committee were seated around Suzette's table.

Thyme beamed at her. "Margot, we have big plans for you."

"Oh?" She joined them and put a muffin and some fruit on her plate. Just when it felt like the busyness of the reunion weekend was over.

"Don't worry. You'll have plenty of time for fun with the other young people. Burke in particular," Thyme said.

"Oh?" she repeated. Suddenly, this was feeling like a setup again.

Clove explained. "His parents left today for vacation, but he is staying behind to help run things while they're gone. They want us to keep him busy and out of trouble."

Sage dabbed her mouth with a napkin and dropped it onto her empty plate. "I'll check on her."

After Sage left, Thyme looked around the corner, then whispered. "Do you know who Burke's parents are?"

"No. Should I?" Margot whispered back, wondering what all the secrecy was about.

Clove leaned forward with an eye on the hallway. "You've seen them. At the dinner and again at the joust?"

Margot felt like they were leading her down a path, but she didn't know why. Who did she see at the dinner and the joust besides everyone in town?

Thyme mimed putting something on her head. *A crown?*

"The king and queen?" *Cool.* "I thought they were actors brought in. Their costumes were awesome. They looked real."

Clove spoke first. "For our reunion weekend, we tried to have as many people playing their historic roles as we could. Some people were easier than others as they've kept their family ties in town, like Suzette and her bookshop. Same with Burke's family."

The two looked at Margot expectantly.

Burke's family. His parents dressed up as the king and queen, and he played the role of a knight.

Understanding finally dawned, but Margot couldn't quite believe it. "I'm sorry, are you saying he's a prince?" Burke. A prince. Or at least descended from one.

Clove shrugged. "The days of princes in this land are long passed. But, yes, had you and he been born in a different generation, you'd likely be curtsying to him when he walked by."

Margot thought of the way the others talked about Burke. How high and mighty he was. "The others think he wants us to bow to him now."

"You like him," Thyme said. "Don't you? In spite of yourself or the way everyone talks about him…or how he acts sometimes."

"He's okay," she said. How could she explain to these ladies her feelings about him when she didn't know herself? She had a wall up between them for sure because she couldn't trust his actions and didn't want to get hurt.

Sage returned, and Clove and Thyme stood up at once. A look of confusion passed over Sage's face, then she held out her hand. "Clove, here is the key. You can open the bookshop."

"I really should tend to these dishes," Thyme said. "Help me, Margot?"

They worked silently until Margot whispered, "Why is this all a secret from Sage?"

"It's not. She knows. But she didn't think you needed to know."

"Why not?"

"Sage has her reasons. I wouldn't worry about it."

But Margot was starting to worry. New ideas rolled around in her mind and the implications shocked her.

She'd thought the Beast could be an actual beast trapped somewhere in Chapais. She'd believed it to the degree that she'd gone out searching for him, just in case.

She'd also toyed with the idea that Silvain was the enchanted prince who came to her as a beast in her dreams, but had human form during the day. Silvain had said so many of the things that had matched up in her dream. It would be like the opposite of the lion in *The Singing, Springing Lark*. In that story, the prince took his human form during the night, but was a lion during the day.

Such a situation was an easy fix for his bride, as they slept during the day when he was a lion and lived their lives at night when he was a man.

But if Burke was a descendant of a prince in real life…

Margot needed time to process what she thought of that.

After the dishes were put away, Thyme sent Margot down to the bookshop.

Margot helped Clove put the small display table outside and then turned the sign to *open*.

Burke arrived not long after, wet hair and freshly shaved. Today, he wore his red linen tunic which was quickly becoming Margot's favorite shirt.

"Food in the back," Clove called out from the office.

Burke. Descended from a prince. She had to talk to him.

"I'm sorry for going to the stables," Margot blurted out in half English and half French as she followed him to the snack table. She wanted a way into a conversation, and that's all she could think of. "You didn't get into any trouble, did you?"

Burke glanced at Clove and then pulled out a chair for Margot to sit.

"Oh, thank you," Margot said. She considered also telling them about the garden, but held back. It wouldn't be a secret garden if she told everyone where it was, nor would it seem special anymore if they all knew and told her the real history behind it and it turned out to be less exciting than her imagination.

"They don't like tourists to go back with the horses," Burke said.

"But his uncle breeds the horses," Clove added, "So I'm sure they wouldn't mind if you went back as Burke's guest. He's been riding since he could walk."

Burke raised his eyebrows at Clove, and she gave him a look Margot couldn't quite interpret. He put two of Clove's pastries on a plate and she added a third.

"I didn't mean to go where I shouldn't," Margot said. "I don't even know how to ride a horse."

Clove elbowed him.

He looked up, locking eyes with Margot. He cleared his throat. "I can teach you to ride."

"Really? I'd love that." *Learning to ride from a prince.*

He nodded. "Meet me there in the morning. We'll go instead of your walk."

He knows I walk? Aside from noticing she didn't speak French very well, she wasn't sure Burke noticed anything about her. He'd been too preoccupied with Paris girl.

The back door opened, and Thyme sashayed in. "What did I miss?"

"We're talking about the stables," Margot said. "Where the knights practice for the tournaments."

"Oh, I love the tournaments. Two men on horses trying to kill each other for sport."

Could Burke get badly hurt in a joust? Margot wondered if the lances were replicas of what knights really used in history, or if they were more like Hollywood props.

"How real is it?" She directed the question to Burke, thinking of how his lance had shattered.

He answered in French, but before Clove could translate, Thyme leaned in with a smile. "He says, 'How real do you want it to be?'"

Margot's gaze met Burke's, and there was another spark. His eyes were so expressive; stormy and wounded all at the same time. Her breath caught, and she suddenly felt nervous. Sometimes Burke could be a little too much knight for her. "I-I should get up front. The customers will be here soon."

CHAPTER 18

For once, Margot was glad for early morning summer sunrises. As soon as the light hit her window, she was out of bed and looking for riding clothes. Learning to ride a horse in the shadow of a castle was a life goal she didn't realize she had until yesterday.

By the time she got out of the city and behind the wall, Burke was already on his horse, taking it through the paces. He could hold his own at any rodeo she'd seen. Not that she was an expert, but he looked mighty fine up on that horse.

When he noticed her at the fence, he stopped and stared across the field at her. What she wouldn't give to hear what was going through his mind right now. He'd either not expected her to show up, going on with his day presumably the same way he'd done so every day before she arrived. Or, he had been trying to get his practice in before she got there, and she'd interrupted him too soon.

She hoped he welcomed the interruption. She wasn't in the mood for him to show off what a great rider he was compared to her.

Margot had only ridden a horse once. A pony ride at the

county fair when she was little and scared at how big the horses stood when they were up close. It was one thing to see a horse in a book, another in real life. But that was the way with most things. A rose was pretty in a book, but when you saw it in real life, smelled the fragrance, touched the silky petals, and pricked your finger on a thorn, you *knew* what a rose was. You couldn't learn that in a book. Not what a bookworm like her wanted to admit, but some things were best experienced outside the pages of a story.

Burke met her at the fence, dressed in jeans, T-shirt, and a cowboy hat and looking more like a western cowboy than a medieval knight. He stood close to the animal, stroking its muscular brown neck and whispering in its ear.

Her heart raced ahead of her thoughts. If he was an enchanted prince, did he know it? Could she tell him her suspicions without sounding crazy or without spoiling her ability to break him out of the enchantment?

"I hope you're telling that horse to be nice to me, and not buck me off," she called out to announce her presence. She'd worn her stirrup pants and an oversize T-shirt. It was the closest thing she had to riding gear.

Burke looked up and jerked his chin in greeting.

"You have no idea what I'm saying, do you?" she asked.

He raised his eyebrows questioningly. "A little."

She felt her face turn red. *You Take My Breath Away. Summer of Love song #3.* Her reaction didn't need a translation, and she hoped he wouldn't guess her thoughts. She couldn't help noticing that he looked extra handsome today.

To take the attention off her burning face, she looked around for the way into the stables. Burke pointed and then met her at the gate to let her in.

"So, what do I do?" She clasped her hands together.

He demonstrated how to put a foot into the stirrup and mount the horse. He made it look so easy; just swing that leg up and over. From atop the horse he said something she didn't understand.

He hopped off and indicated it was her turn.

"You mean, now?" She thought there'd be more buildup to getting on the horse. Talk to it first or something. She petted the horse, not knowing if that was the thing to do. "Nice fella. You'll go slow, right? No sudden movements?"

"Her name is Estelle," Burke said.

Margot repeated the name. "You be nice to me today, yes?"

Burke helped her get her foot in, holding her steady, because that stirrup was higher off the ground than she'd like. She jumped, one, two, and Burke put his hands around her waist to boost her up. She swung her leg, and she was up! On a horse. Tall on a horse.

"Yee-haw!" she said.

Burke laughed.

"I guess that's a universal word, huh?" She smiled back at him.

He handed her the reins to hold, but then led the horse himself by holding the bridle and slowly walking around the pen. When Margot started to relax, he directed her to move the reins herself.

"Okay. I can do this." She nudged the horse to the right, and it turned. She nudged it to the left, and it turned. Pleased, she looked over her shoulder to say something to Burke, but he was gone. Before she panicked too much, he opened the gate and brought in another horse. He mounted and then led the way out onto the practice field.

"I don't know if that's a good idea," she called. "Non?!?"

He glanced back. "Oui."

Margot sized up how far off the ground she was. She would survive a fall. If the horse was standing still. And not running. *Bump. Bump. Bump.*

"What are we doing?" Her horse wasn't running, but it wasn't walking anymore. "Burke. I'm not so sure about this."

He turned and must have seen the scared look on her face because he slowed his horse right down until they were barely moving.

"Merci. This is totally more my pace." She could walk this pace.

Because they were going so slowly, they didn't go very far before they had to turn around in time to help open up the bookshop.

"I'm going to feel this later, I can already tell," she said wiggling in the saddle.

Burke got off his horse and secured it to the fence.

Without waiting for help, Margot swung down and then patted the horse. "Thanks, that was fun." The horse turned its head slightly and adjusted its foot on top of hers.

"Ow. Get off. You did that on purpose." She tried pushing the horse over, but he wouldn't move.

"Burke?" She didn't want to spook the horse, but she was afraid for her toes.

He hurried over and pulled the bridle. The horse slowly moved.

"Ah. Ow." Margot's foot throbbed. She took a tentative step, but instantly lifted it at the first twinge of pain.

Burke looked questioningly at her, and she shook her head. No, she couldn't walk on it. She started hopping to the fence, but he reached over and scooped her up.

"Oh, well, aren't you the strong one," she said.

Her face burned, but she looped her arms around Burke's neck. Her heartbeat raced as she held on, her cheek resting against his chest. Was that *his* heartbeat she felt?

Then he dumped her onto a hay bale and went back to secure her horse.

Hmm. That was probably more romantic in my head than in reality.

She carefully removed her shoe, not remembering from first

aid class if she should keep it on to stop the swelling, or if she needed to remove the shoe to keep the swelling from getting worse.

Too late now, and she wanted to see it. She peeled off her sock to reveal a red foot and—gross—a big toe that was turning colors.

Burke jogged over, the horses being taken care of by a stable hand. He kneeled in front of her and examined her foot.

How embarrassing.

Burke shook his head and pointed at her foot. "Can you walk?"

"I could try walking on my heel." She pushed herself up. *Ow.* She winced. To get back to the bookstore, she'd have to walk down the path along the wall, up the slope to the gate, and then through the streets before the tourists arrived. She took another step before Burke swooped in again, and next thing she knew, she was in his arms. "Non, non, non. It's a long way," she said.

He shook his head and kept walking.

Oh, goodness. He'd have to carry her all the way back to the bookstore. She'd never been self-conscious about her weight, but she'd also never been carried so far before.

She lay with her arms crossed for a few minutes, but that was awkward, so she wrapped her hands around his neck. He paused and then bounced her up a little, so she would get a better grip without strangling him.

After they walked a few minutes, she became increasingly aware of their closeness. It was terribly intimate to be hanging onto the neck of some guy she hadn't known for very long. It was like a really long slow dance, minus the music and multiply the awkwardness.

"I'm not too heavy, am I? Because if you need a break, you can take one."

He glanced at her, his face so, so close to hers, then focused back on the uneven path.

"Okay, you're in it for the long haul." Margot tentatively

rested her head against his chest and listened to him breathe. He smelled like sweat and horse, with a little bit of fabric softener thrown in. If her foot wasn't throbbing in pain, and if she wasn't so mortified, this would be a whole lot more fun.

He started talking about how she needed to stay off her foot and his voice rumbled into her head. As he talked, she began to feel familiar with the cadence. Then it dawned on her. The cassette left on the welcome mat.

"*C'est toi,*" she said looking up at him. "You left me the tape."

"You wanted to learn, but everyone kept practicing their English with you. I thought the tape would help."

"What are you saying on it? You speak so fast I can't make out the words."

"You'll get it. Tell me when you figure it out."

Margot nestled back into his arms. He made her think about him. In her waking hours, and maybe even in her dreams...

She'd noticed the stubble growing on his face; she was that close. And she'd noticed that when she'd arrived at the stables, he'd freshly shaved like he had every morning. Not only that, she was positive his hair was already longer than it was this morning. She didn't want to talk herself into believing he was the beast, but all of her observations couldn't be in her imagination alone. Burke could literally be the guy of her dreams.

CLOVE AND THYME rushed out of the store like they'd been waiting.

"What happened?" They looked accusingly at Burke. He started to explain, and Margot interrupted to let them know it was not his fault.

From his arms, she explained. "My horse stepped on me. I'm pretty sure she did it on purpose because she looked right at me before she did it."

"Margot didn't wait for me to show her what to do," Burke said as he carried her through the door and dumped her on the stool behind the cash register.

Margot opened her eyes wide in mock accusation. "Okay, so maybe it is his fault." Burke was one for ruining a sweet moment.

"Let's get you some ice," Sage said, ignoring the sudden shift in Margot's tone. "Then we can assess what to do with you."

Margot insisted she keep helping them even though they all wanted her to rest with her foot up in the air until it healed. She needed to be near Burke in order to study him. Gallant and chivalrous one moment; arrogant and annoying the next.

Besides, her foot looked worse than it hurt.

Thyme set her up behind the counter with another chair and a pillow to rest her foot on. "Let me know if you need anything."

By midmorning some of the swelling had gone down and a deep purple bruise began to take over her foot. Perhaps feeling somewhat responsible, Burke gave her his stash of chocolate olives on his way out the door for the tournament.

Then, during the afternoon lull, Tanvi came into the store. "*Salut.* I didn't see you walking this morning. I was going to join you."

Margot waved her to look behind the counter.

"What happened?"

"A horse stepped on my foot. Burke was teaching me how to ride, and when I got off the horse it stepped on me. I didn't let it run fast enough. I don't know."

"Does it hurt?"

"Only when I walk on it. It's not broken or anything; I think it's just bruised."

"I do not know how you can spend time with Burke." She whispered it, with an eye toward the back.

"He's fine." Margot held up the chocolates. "And he's taking care of me."

Tanvi huffed.

In reply, Margot offered Tanvi the chocolates, but she refused them.

"Some friends are going to Jean Robert's house tonight to play his NES game. Do you want to go?"

Margot didn't want to go without Burke. There was too much she needed to uncover first. "Tonight might not be the best. Another night?"

Tanvi shrugged. "Silvain will be disappointed. You might not get invited again."

CHAPTER 19

hen Sage found out what happened at the
stables, she confined Margot to her room,
insisting on bringing her dinner in bed. "The less you move, the
better."

Margot thought it was overkill, though, and around eight,
when it seemed like they'd forgotten her, she got out of bed. She
tentatively took a step by putting her weight on her heel and it
wasn't excruciating. She took another. And another.

She hobbled into the kitchen to tell the others her foot was
getting better.

"Guess what—" The words died on her lips as they turned
around with surprised faces, and Thyme sent Margot's book of
fairy tales flying up above their heads.

Where it stayed.

Margot cocked her head. Her book hovered in the air above
the three women.

Sage lowered the teapot in exasperation. "Thyme, really?"

"I panicked. I didn't want her to see what we were looking at,
so I just threw it up there."

"Because that's not suspicious at all," Clove said. "You did it on purpose." She directed her attention to Margot. "What are you doing up? I thought you couldn't walk."

At that moment, Margot's vintage book of fairy tales fell from the ceiling...and back into Thyme's hands.

Margot gaped.

"Oops. I'm sorry ma chère," said Thyme. "We have a confession." She held her hands out in an apologetic shrug.

"How did you get that book to float up there like that?"

They exchanged looks.

"What book?" said Sage, giving a commanding look to the others.

In the same moment, Thyme said, "You caught us. We're fairies. We are the fairies mentioned in the book of tales." She tapped the fairy tale book as if it explained everything.

Clove huffed. "You didn't try very hard to keep it a secret. What if you've ruined everything?"

Sage stepped forward. "Clove, don't get snippy. She's here to help you clean up your curse."

"It's not a curse, and I was doing fine on my own."

Thyme put her hands on her hips. "No, you needed our help. And look." She raised a hand at Margot. "Things are taking a turn for the better."

Sage waggled her finger at Thyme. "The situation was improving until a minute ago when you crossed the line."

Margot pinched herself. Nope, this wasn't another dream.

"This is the modern era," Thyme insisted. "Girls aren't used to discovering princes trapped inside the bodies of frogs and the like. She will need some education and a certain amount of time to come to terms with the news." Thyme turned to Margot. "You know why we're all here, don't you? Goodness knows we've dropped enough hints from the beginning. *La Belle et la Bête?*"

The blood drained from Margot's face. Though not a complete surprise, the announcement left her weak-kneed, anyway.

"We'd best sit down." Sage put down the teapot and grabbed hold of Margot's elbow to guide her toward the living room. "Can I get you some water?"

Margot shook her head.

"How much should we say, now that Thyme has decided to share secrets?" Clove plunked down on the couch beside Margot.

"I didn't decide exactly." Thyme held her empty cup steady for Sage to pour the tea. "It was on the spur of the moment. I saw Silvain send that flower girl to talk to Margot today, and I'm worried his involvement will delay progression with Burke. We don't have time for that, do we, Sage?" She looked at Sage as if challenging her to disagree.

"But the love interest can't know without feeling obligated. You might have ruined everything." Clove was usually slightly on edge, but now she was angry and refused Sage's offer of tea.

Her wits catching up with her, Margot tentatively entered the conversation. "Sometimes the love interests do and sometimes they don't. In the story of *The Twelve Huntsmen*, the prince forgot his first love and had to be reminded. The princess always knew, and it was up to her to rescue him."

Thyme nodded. "Well done, Margot. You believe us? Without us having to show you anything?"

"I'm falling for an enchanted descendant of a prince. You think believing in fairies is a stretch?" It kind of was, but she was in too deep already to question much.

Thyme put down her tea and gave a tiny clap. "I knew it. I knew you were the one from the moment you walked in on our welcome dinner." She reached out and took the fairy tale book, opened it, and showed it to Margot. "Read."

"O-kay…" Margot started reading, and she could understand all the words. Some were written in French and some were now in English.

"Since you didn't ask, I gave you a sign. As you learn more

French, the English words will all become French again. Think of it as a teaching tool. My gift to you."

Clove rolled her eyes. "Can we get back to the task at hand?"

"Margot, let's start with you. What do you think you know?" Sage sat in the rocking chair and gently started rocking back and forth.

Margot had been analyzing this all day and had several ideas. "I think Burke is somehow a beast. Maybe physically at night, so he has to shave and cut his hair in the morning." She paused. "This is so strange to say out loud."

"Go on," Sage said, not put off in the least.

"And I might be able to help him, though I haven't figured out how yet, and I'm not certain if he knows what's happening to him."

"Helping is easy," Thyme said. "You are like Beauty. Burke is like the beast. You fall in love and the curse breaks."

Clove made a squeaking noise. "You weren't supposed to come right out and tell her. She was meant to discover it on her own."

Sage ignored the outburst and leaned toward Margot. "He's under a curse, so the more beastly part of his nature is manifested physically. It's partly, well, mostly our fault, so we want to help him break free."

"How is Burke cursed?"

Clove jutted out her chin. "Can we agree to call it a lesson and not a curse? Curse indicates ill intent."

Sage and Thyme exchanged a look before Clove spoke again.

"We don't know exactly what has happened, but the symptoms Burke exhibits seem to be a holdover from the original Beast, who turned out lovely, if I say so myself."

Thyme *tsked*. "Clove went overboard, and the curse continues to flow through the family. Burke is the first boy in generations and is showing strong indicators he's being *tested*." She looked pointedly at Clove.

"Does he transform into a beast at night then?" Margot asked. Finally, she was getting answers.

Sage shook her head. "No, he is slowly taking on a beastly form. Several times a day he needs to cut his hair, shave, shower. This summer it started accelerating."

"I thought something was odd about his hair." It was never the same length.

Clove shrugged. "I told him to let it grow long and be done with it. That mullet style, like Jean Robert. But he says it grows too fast for that, and it would be a ponytail to his knees."

"So, he knows about the curse? And you all? That's good, I guess. But why me? Why do you think I'd be like Beauty?"

"You're perfect." Thyme's exuberance continued. "You've got heart and imagination, and it will take someone with a lot of both to carry this through. But most of all, Burke sees you in his dreams. At least, we assume it's you. He says he cannot see who the girl is."

"I've...also...been having dreams." Saying it out loud made it all seem more real. She was glad it was real and not her mind playing tricks on her. *But it is real.*

She stared at the book she held. *Once and True Fairy Tales.* The book that fell out when Thyme knocked over a stack of books in the back of Suzette's bookshop. She looked up at Thyme, who was grinning from ear to ear.

"So tonight, if I dream again, I can tell him I know who he is."

Clove jumped up in front of Margot, blocking her view of the other two. "You can't tell him anything."

"Why not? You want us to fall in love?" She thought of being in Burke's arms and that didn't seem like such a bad proposition. She was halfway there already. However, she'd had unrequited crushes before.

"We must move forward with caution. Don't scare him away," said Clove.

"I'm not exactly an expert in these things," Margot said. "I've never been in *love*, love. I wouldn't even know what that feels like. I've liked guys before, but that's probably not what you're aiming for. You'll need something strong enough to break a curse."

"We're willing to give it a try," said Thyme, leaning around Clove.

Margot sank back into the couch. "I'm so glad I've got someone to talk to about this. My dreams were getting strange. I can't imagine what they are from Burke's perspective. Does his family—the king and queen—know about the curse?"

"Yes, and no. They joke about the family curse, a legend passed down along with other family heirlooms. But they don't know the extent it has affected Burke."

"I still don't understand why he can't know that I know the secret now. Wouldn't that make him feel better? Not alone?"

Clove shook her head vehemently. "He'll think it's something we've done. That you don't actually like him, but that we've talked you into it somehow."

"But I do like him." *Bring on the blushing. Why were these things so embarrassing? Fear he doesn't feel the same way?*

The three women—fairies—quietly watched Margot, studying her reactions after all she'd just learned. She wilted under their scrutiny.

Having confirmation about Burke was a good thing. But at the same time, she suddenly felt a huge weight land on her shoulders. They all expected her to break Burke out of his beastly form. Like she could make that happen of her own will.

Finally, Thyme said, "If you need any help, we're right here."

"But I'm sure you won't." Sage glared at Thyme. "Because we need to let things run their course with no more interference."

———

THAT NIGHT, Margot sat at the window overlooking the cobbled street below. All she wanted to do was fall asleep and dream so she could talk to the beast, but her head was spinning. She'd expected her summer in France to be unique, but this... *This.*

What would she tell the beast if she saw him in her dreams tonight? He wanted her to find him when she was awake, and she had. But the fairies wanted her to keep it a secret, even from him. What was the right thing to do? She knew about him before she learned of the fairies, and her loyalty was with him. If the circumstances were reversed, she'd want to know.

"Sipping chocolate?" Sage passed her a hot mug filled with a thick, dark chocolate drink with a dash of cinnamon floating on top.

Margot took a tentative sip and the sweet drink went down smooth. "*Mmm.* This might be the best thing I've ever tasted."

"Good. Drink up. It'll help you sleep."

Clove and Thyme had left after Margot had spent all her questions. Almost all. "What about Aunty Suzette? She's not one of you, is she?"

"No, Suzette is not one of us," said Sage. "She is your great-aunt and a descendant of a bookselling family. She does not know who we really are." Sage looked over the top of her glasses. Her eyes were piercing.

"I won't tell her. It's Thyme you have to warn."

Sage sat in the armchair watching Margot sip her chocolate drink. "I want to let things sink in for you, but tomorrow, we should have a serious talk."

Margot nodded. There was only so much she could absorb at once, but she wasn't looking forward to what kind of serious talk she would have with Sage.

A group of people walked past the bookshop below. "Pub's closed," she said absently. The last of the day-trippers walked by on their way out of town, completely unaware that something very odd was occurring in their midst.

"I'm a bit woozy. I should go to bed." Margot dropped her

mug, and it landed on the area carpet with a dull *thump*. A bit of the sipping chocolate spilled onto the beige fibers. "I should clean that up." The words sounded mumbled coming out of her mouth.

Sage came over and helped her up. "That's it. This way. Ease back into bed. Watch your head. Sleep well."

CHAPTER 20

*T*he early morning light filtered through the curtains, but Margot resisted waking up. *Why didn't the beast come to me last night?* Now that she knew who he was, had they lost their secret connection? She'd been so eager to see the beast and hint that she recognized who he was in real life.

Yesterday had been an unusual day. She half expected to wake up this morning and find out it had all been a dream. Fairies! Curses! A beast!

But even her far-out imagination couldn't have created all that on its own. She languidly flipped open her fairy tale book on the bedside table to confirm she could still read it. Yes, it was a mix of French and English, the way Thyme changed it for her.

Margot couldn't lay in bed forever, but she felt sluggish. And her teeth had a thick coating on them like she'd neglected to brush. She must have been so tired she'd forgotten.

Sage was already up and puttering in the kitchen, and the doctor would come first thing to look in on Suzette. Margot ought to dress and be ready in case the doctor had time to look at her foot. The only real concern she had from yesterday was her big toe, which had an ugly red and purple bruise under the nail.

The rest of her foot looked bad, but didn't hurt like it had yesterday. In fact, her foot held no pain at all.

She tentatively stood, wondering if she'd be able to take her walk today. Or at least, a shortened walk, going as far as the stables to see Burke?

Margot tested her foot all the way into the living room where Sage had already set up in Suzette's chair.

"Sleep well?" Sage asked with a quick glance up from today's crossword puzzle.

Memories surfaced of Sage half carrying her to bed last night. The mug falling to the floor and the sipping chocolate spilling. No wonder her teeth were so grimy.

"Aren't you going to ask me how my dreams were?"

Sage took her reading glasses off and let them dangle from her silver chain. "How were they, dear?"

"I didn't have any. Did you put something in my sipping chocolate last night?"

"Only cinnamon." Sage put her glasses back on. "And a little fairy dust."

Margot snapped her fingers. "I knew it. Why?"

"You needed to settle first before you talk to him. I didn't want you rushing off and blurting out everything you learned. It'll be tempting for you, so I intervened." She picked up her pen and filled in a word on her puzzle. "I don't approve of what Thyme has done, despite her reasonings. No one—not even Burke—can know. Don't cross us on this."

"He's got to find out sometime."

"He will. On his own." Sage looked seriously at Margot. "Thyme rushed into things with you. She must have had her reasons. But from this point onward, we must let things develop at Burke's pace." Sage leaned forward and grew even more serious. "Try to continue as you have been. Be friendly, but not obvious. Don't change yourself to accommodate him or this new situation. Be yourself. *Cliché*, but it's true. There's no use helping Burke only to lose yourself."

Margot nodded. How was she to act normal knowing what she knew? She was never particularly good about keeping a secret. "What about my foot?" She changed the topic to something more neutral. She rotated her ankle for good measure.

"Feels better? A happy side effect." Sage drew a line through a clue on her puzzle.

Margot took her actions as a dismissal. "I'm going for a walk." She returned to her room and quickly put on her shorts and T-shirt. When she stepped outside, she noticed another cassette tape lay on the welcome mat. *POUR MARGOT #2* written on the white label in Burke's thick hand.

She smiled and imagined Burke sneaking quietly up the stairs and leaving this for her. Sage might have tried to keep her away from the beast last night, but Burke had been thinking about her. Did that mean he was hoping she was the girl in his dreams?

I know who you are, but they don't want me to tell you. She popped the new tape into her Walkman, and Burke's rich voice filled her head.

Now, what would Burke record on a tape instead of telling her in person? In a conversation with someone, there were context clues and facial expressions to help guide her understanding. But here, it was only Burke's voice in her head.

However, on this new cassette, he spoke slower and with careful pronunciation. The cadence, the words, they finally started to feel familiar. She turned up the volume and really listened. There were the words. She got it! Most of the words. He was reading to her from a book of fairy tales. This particular tale involved a girl and a dragon.

He could have talked jousting or computers, or any other interest that he had, but he figured out what she liked. She realized that the timing of the first tape was the day after the two of them got trapped behind the pile of books Thyme spilled.

When Burke came over to tell her to keep working, she'd gotten annoyed with him, but he'd noticed her interest in the fairy tale book.

Margot climbed up to the battlements with the other morning walkers, the old man with the dog, the two middle-aged women speed walking with headbands and hand weights. But she didn't want to be out here on top of the walls. The draw to the stables was too strong to resist. She had to tell him she'd figured out what he was reading on the tape. And to thank him for helping her learn to speak French. The fairies wouldn't fuss about that, would they?

She descended the nearest stairs back into the town where she could cut through the town center.

"Margot!" Tanvi caught her before she could exit near the stables.

"Good morning," Margot said in French.

"You missed a great party last night," Tanvi said. "Even Paris girl came."

"Oh?" Margot smiled at the good news. If Paris girl was at Jean Robert's then she wasn't getting to know Burke better.

"What are you listening to?" Tanvi reached for Margot's headphones. "I'd like to hear the American songs."

Margot pulled back. "I'll get you one of my tapes. You wouldn't like this one."

"Why not? Let me listen."

"It's French lessons, not music."

"Oh." She lowered her hand. "Are you going home already? I was hoping to walk with you this morning. I need to get into exercise."

Margot glanced at the way out to the stables. Burke would have to wait.

"Sure. We have time for a couple laps of the battlements before opening."

"WHY CAN'T I STAY?" Thyme asked Sage. She'd met them at the front door of the bookstore with a basket of treats.

"Buttering me up with *choux* buns won't make me change my mind. You and Clove are supposed to be working on that other thing."

Sage said the words with great weight, which made Margot curious about what that other thing was. But before she could ask, Sage turned to her and said, "Lift."

They moved the book table outside. Today, they were showcasing books about Chapais alongside children's picture books of castles. The doctor had agreed with the plan for Suzette to rest while the heritage committee ran the bookshop for her. He said she'd be up and around next week, but she would need to have help until her assistant returned.

"Clove made the choux last night. Besides, we're getting nowhere with that other thing." Thyme pushed her way inside and sat at the till. But Sage was on her heels and shoved her right back off the stool.

"Because you two are distracted with the daily soap opera." She glanced at Margot.

My life is a soap opera now? I don't remember seeing anything like this on All My Children. She dusted her peasant skirt.

For helping in the bookshop, she'd worn her sister's costume with her mom's scarf wrapped around her curls. Margot was transforming herself from a tourist into something more like a proper town descendant.

"Any more updates?" Thyme looked hopefully at Margot.

"Get." Sage shooed her out.

"Tell me tonight," called Thyme over her shoulder as she left.

Burke walked in moments later. Freshly showered and shaved, like normal. His eyes lit up at the basket of treats.

"Seems that Thyme can butter up one of us." Margot

laughed nervously and handed him the basket. *Why was she extra nervous now? Maybe because their interactions were being watched. Analyzed.*

"How is your foot?" Burke asked. He looked like he hadn't slept at all last night. Dark circles under his eyes, he yawned twice before he got to the counter.

"Bien," Margot said.

He nodded and then took the basket with him to the back room. As soon as he left, Margot whispered to Sage, "Wouldn't it be easier if we tell him? I mean, you tell him? He ought to know if we all do."

"Or, it could lock the curse in tighter. These things can be tricky. It's not worth playing with Burke's life. Thyme already took a big risk in revealing who we are."

"Speaking of lives," Margot stopped whispering, "is the doctor sure my aunt will be okay?"

Sage sighed. "Her condition is manageable. He'd already given her medicine for it, but she hadn't been taking it because she didn't like how it made her heartbeat irregular. They're working on adjusting the dosage now, and he wants her to rest all this week."

The bookshop door opened with the first customer of the day.

When Sage went to help, Margot slipped away to the office. Burke had already turned the computer on and spread out Suzette's inventory papers on the desk.

Margot leaned on his work, forcing Burke to look at her. "Conte de fées," she said. "Fairy tales. I figured it out." She was proud of her strides in learning French.

"I know what girls like," he said with a smirk, and went back to his work.

Margot stood up straight. She'd expected a touching, possibly romantic moment similar to what they shared yesterday.

Burke's arrogance hit her anew. "You only think you know,"

she said and stalked out of the room. *The nerve!* No wonder his curse hadn't been broken yet. He was too irritating.

Margot fled to the front of the store and began processing the boxes of books behind the counter. Burke was so confusing. One minute he acted like he liked her, and in the next he pushed her away. Now she couldn't tell him who she was for fear he'd be disappointed to learn he'd been dreaming about her.

Sage completed a sale and waited for the customer to leave before she turned around. "Something the matter?" she asked.

"No. Everything is fine. I thought I'd get these put away for Suzette so she doesn't have to worry about them."

"And Burke is...?

"At the computer, as usual."

Sage let out a sigh. "I told you this would not be easy. Every friendship has its trials, never mind one that is tarnished with a curse."

"Don't you mean a test?" Margot bit her lip. "I'm sorry. I didn't mean to be sarcastic. Or take anything out on you." She sat back on the floor. "Now that I know what's going on, I thought it would make it easier to get to know him, but it's not. I still react to the way he is. He doesn't seem to like anyone."

"Maybe that's why Thyme thought you should be brought into our secret. So you would persevere."

"Don't say anything to him about who I am, please. You were right. He can't be told. He's got to figure it out himself."

Sage nodded. "Yes. I'm glad you see it our way."

Margot pointed upstairs. "I'm going to check on Suzette."

"HOW ARE YOU FEELING?" Margot brought Suzette a fresh cup of tea.

"Ridiculous. What I've put all of you through when I should have been taking my pills." She took a sip. "Thank you."

"You'll be happy to hear we'll be through your boxes of books by the end of the day. When the doctor tells you to take it easy, he means it."

"You've been a great help. It's good to have family here. Tell me what you think of your visit so far."

Margot started with her arrival, spending lots of time talking about the town and very little talking about anything fairy tale related. "And I've enjoyed spending time in your bookshop. It's got a nice atmosphere to the place."

"Would you bring me that green book right there?" Suzette pointed to the thick book on top of her dresser. "There's a family keepsake in there that I want you to have."

Margot retrieved the book, then sat on the edge of the bed while Suzette flipped through a small stack of old photographs she'd stuck inside the cover. She pulled out a small black and white.

"Ah, yes. There was a resemblance even then." She handed a photo to Margot. "Your mother. All this sitting around has given me the time to think where I've put things. You can keep that."

A little girl with a mop of brown curls stood outside the bookshop. She held a small reader in both hands as if it were a precious gift.

"We don't have any pictures from when she was a child. Thank you so much, Aunty Suzette."

"My pleasure. It's time to pass these things on to the next generation." She sighed and looked around the room as if she were talking more philosophically.

"Is there anything I can do for you before I go back down? The tournament is letting out soon. I should go back to help during the after rush. I don't know how you did it all by yourself."

"When you do a job for a long time, the work sneaks up on you. I should have listened to the warning signs. It's time for me to slow down."

CHAPTER 21

*A*fter the tournament, Burke returned to the store wearing his red tunic and carrying a box filled with red pennants and other paraphernalia. He had a small cut on his cheek from where a broken lance might have hit him.

"What's all this?" Clove asked. She'd taken the afternoon shift while Sage sat with Suzette.

He told her and then proceeded to bring the box to the back. Clove stopped him. "Oh, no you don't. Take these around town like you're supposed to. Margot can help."

"Can help what?" Margot only caught parts of what Burke had said so quickly.

"Team spirit." Clove grabbed the box and put it on the counter. "The knights are to rally support from the local businesses to help make the tournaments look more exciting. The shops are supposed to hang their favorite knight's colors in the store." She pulled out a red ribbon to tie around Margot's arm. "You show your loyalty by wearing his colors."

Why did that comment feel so charged? Did Clove sense the drop in temperature when she and Burke were in the same room? Margot still wasn't over the brush-off this morning.

"Sure, I can help," Margot said. "What do I ask?"

Clove gave her a suggestion, and Margot practiced saying the words. "Great. It'll be fun." Her enthusiasm would counter Burke's scowl. Or, Burke could stay outside while she went in alone to make the request. Besides, there were a lot of shops she hadn't been in yet, and this was the perfect excuse to see what she'd missed and even find her dad a tacky souvenir.

Burke reluctantly picked up the box, glancing at the red ribbon around Margot's arm. She caught him smiling before going out the door.

They skipped the stores that already had chosen their knights. The yellow, blue, and the green knights had all been busy while Burke had likely gone off to shower and shave again. Their color pennants flapped on most of the outdoor signs and hung strategically in windows. Only one or two stores held red pennants. Margot pointed them out. "Your partner?"

Burke shrugged.

"This is kind of a big deal," Margot said as the more they walked the more colors they saw. The town was really getting into it. Silvain and his friends were high-fiving as they left the town square having emptied their box. She noticed that Burke didn't particularly like seeing the yellow pennants and wondered if things were continuing to heat up between him and Silvain.

When they passed Tanvi at the flower stall, she and Margot eyed each other's arm ribbons. Tanvi wore yellow. Margot couldn't help but see it as a deliberate slight. Tanvi was just as friendly with the blue and the green knights as the yellow. It was like the whole group of teenagers had decided to take a stand against Burke. In such a small town, the slight was glaring.

"There he is." Burke pointed to a man in a red tunic who was carrying a similar box to theirs.

"He's your partner?" she asked. He looked their way, and she waved. He waved back. "There's someone who doesn't hate you," she said. The man joined them and introduced himself.

"*Je suis* Arturo."

"I'm Margot. Visiting here from America." Thought she'd slip that in so he wouldn't think she understood everything he said.

"Ah. I'm a visitor here, too. Burke's squire for the summer." He spoke with a Spanish accent. "This is a nice little town. And he is a good fighter." He slugged Burke in the arm. "I haven't found many shops to wear our color. The other colors are jealous because we are so strong." He winked. "Thank you, Margot, for helping us find support."

"You're welcome. I've only been to one joust, but it was great."

He pointed at Burke. "Because of this guy. He shows up ready to work. Some of these guys go out partying the night before and are a mess the next day. I trust him. I don't have to worry about a sword in the back."

Burke soaked up the praise.

Margot got the impression that for these red knights, what they did was part of a long and proud tradition. Especially Burke, with his lineage. He took it more seriously than just a show for tourists.

"Nice meeting you," Arturo said, holding up his box. "Let me get rid of these, so I go home and relax."

"Bye. Thank you for being kind." Her eyes fluttered quickly to Burke and back again. She didn't want to embarrass him, but surely Arturo knew Burke didn't get along with many in town.

Arturo nodded once before leaving.

She and Burke continued down the street, popping in and out of businesses. Some refused any colors, complaining they had small enough windows as it was and didn't need any more clutter, but most were happy to hang a pennant or two.

Margot popped into a pastry shop she'd passed many times during her morning walks but hadn't gone into yet. The smell coming out the open door was overwhelmingly yummy, and she felt her pockets for change.

When she stepped through the door, though, she stopped short. Behind the counter was one familiar head of pinkish hair. Thyme's eyes opened wide, and she gave a little wave. "Bonjour, Margot."

Margot slunk up to the display case and placed her hands on the glass. She glanced around. "What are you doing here?"

Thyme leaned in conspiratorially. "Don't tell Sage. She gets annoyed at my side jobs. But I say, you only live once. May as well enjoy the days you're given and try new things. Speaking of which, have you tried our *éclairs*? They're heavenly. I need to get Clove to make these for me." She smiled wide and pointed to the tray of pastries decorated with chocolate icing.

"Sure. I'll buy two." Margot exchanged her money for the treats.

Thyme was about to say something else when a kerfuffle outside caught her attention. "Oh, dear," she said.

Silvain and Burke stood toe-to-toe exchanging words. A crowd quickly formed around them. *Why is no one breaking them up?* A woman elbowed her friend and took a picture of her in front of the feuding knights.

They think this is for show.

Margot ran outside, with no plan for what to do next. Silvain pointed his finger into Burke's chest and Burke retaliated by shoving Silvain's shoulders back. Silvain fell into the crowd and was quickly shoved back into the circle that had formed around them.

The two women with the camera decided they'd seen enough and moved on.

"Burke," Margot called. He glanced her way, and she waved him to follow her. While his attention was diverted, Silvain got in a punch to his jaw.

Margot gasped and stepped forward, but Jean Robert beat her to the fight before Burke could retaliate. Muscling his way between the two, Jean Robert separated the angry knights. The crowd clapped and began to disperse, thinking the show was over.

Margot pulled on Burke's arm. "Allons-y." He stood his ground, watching Silvain until Jean Robert had him walking down the street. Then he relented and picked up the half-empty box of red ribbons.

As they walked away, Margot smiled. She'd said the words in French! Automatically. Without thinking about it. This was a personal victory. She glanced at Burke, but he hadn't noticed. She could tell he was still bothered by what had just happened. Before going back to work, he needed to cool off. Margot could suggest a drive, but in his current state, that probably wasn't a good idea. Same with horseback riding. Besides, the horses were probably resting from the tournament.

"How about we go for a walk, and I'll show you the garden I found, *le jardin?* We can eat these éclairs there." He needed to get away from the walled city. Somewhere quiet and relaxing.

Burke shook his head and stopped. He looked at his watch before holding out his free hand to her.

Unsure of herself, Margot put her hand in his and let him lead her back to the busy town square.

We're holding hands.

She fought back a smile. Maybe he didn't want her getting lost in the crowd. Or he wanted to communicate without talking and making her mad at him. But even when the crowd thinned, he didn't let go. He adjusted his grip so that their fingers were interlaced. Like boyfriend/girlfriend interlaced. And he held on tight.

He led her all the way to the front of the line waiting to go into the castle. He whispered something to the woman organizing the tours, who then opened a little gate to let them in the employee's entrance. She looked curiously at Margot, paying particular attention to their joined hands before going back to the tourists in line.

Burke hurried her along until they met up with a small gathering of tourists standing before an English-speaking guide. The guide, a middle-aged woman in a beautifully crafted peasant blouse and skirt, met his gaze and visibly adjusted her demeanor. She was about to speak when Burke shook his head slightly. He dropped Margot's hand and left her while he took the box and disappeared down a roped-off hallway.

Margot wondered if the guide would point him out as the red knight, given he still wore his tunic. Instead, she welcomed everyone to the tour and began to give a brief explanation of what they were going to see.

When Burke returned, he'd taken his red knight's tunic off and was only wearing the thin peasant shirt he wore underneath, the laces open at the neck. If he thought changing would help him blend in with the tourists, he was wrong. He looked even more like a gallant knight on his day off. He stood next to her, but didn't take her hand.

When their guide noticed he'd returned, she announced to the group, "We have a special guest joining us today. As I mentioned before, this castle was bequeathed to the heritage society by the original family who owned it. They had one stipulation, and that was that we maintained an apartment for the family to use. This summer, we are privileged to have the youngest heir staying here in residence with us."

CHAPTER 22

*M*argot silently gasped with all the other tourists. Even though she already knew his lineage, it was shocking to hear he also lived inside the castle. *How cool is that?*

Everyone turned to get a good look at Burke.

Margot was dying to say something, but not when everyone was watching. Besides, Burke wouldn't look at her. He was too busy playing the role of a reigning monarch, standing aloof and politely nodding now and then. One audacious tourist even took a photo. Burke raised his eyebrows at the guide, and she continued with the tour.

"What you see here is the conclusion to many years of building. The original structure of the castle was a simpler manor house which builders added onto over time, even more so as the threat of war came."

When most of the attention was off him again, Burke finally looked at her.

"You live here?" she mouthed.

He shrugged and then nudged her along as the group started to move to the next room. *Shrug?* Like it was no big deal. What she would give to live inside a castle. She was learning French so she could experience what it was like to live in a castle, for the school months at least.

The guide brought them through several rooms, many of which were empty. She described what the rooms would have looked like with their tapestries hanging over the stone and with rich furnishings and carpets.

"It may not look like much now, but in its heyday, this castle was famous for its hospitality, the center of which was a grand banquet table that stretched the length of this room. The nobility would come here for hunting parties and retire here at the end of the day for feasting. Let me show you the kitchens where twenty cooks and kitchen maids worked from before dawn to feed everyone."

Like little ducks, they followed the tour guide into a surprisingly small space at the back of the castle. "There are almost twenty of us on this tour, imagine all of us busy chopping vegetables at the table or stirring the soup over the coals in the hearth." A few token pots and pans were on display, and several clumps of spices hung from the rafters. The old hearth stove was blackened with use. Margot imagined a kitchen maid at her left chopping carrots and a cook farther down the table adding spices to a hunk of raw meat.

"In good weather, much of the preparation would have happened outside near the garden. People lived out-of-doors back then more than we do today."

The group shuffled forward to peer out the oversize door that was propped open to show a small herb garden beyond.

Next, the tour guide led them back through the passageways and out near the beginning of the tour. "We'll view one more space that was added to this side of the castle, and then you are free to spend as much time as you want looking around. I'll be here for the next thirty minutes to answer questions. Thank you for being such a fun group, and thank you, Burke, for joining us. Your family has given the world a wonderful gift in this castle."

Everyone turned and gave Burke a little clap. "This way, folks." She walked into the chapel where the sun was shining through the stained-glass windows.

Burke grabbed Margot's elbow, keeping her from following.

"I'd like to see the chapel again," Margot said, pointing after the crowd. Now, she could view it in context to the rest of the castle and with the history she'd learned behind it.

He whispered a response in French, and the part she understood was what she thought meant a personal tour later. He inclined his head toward a spiral staircase cut into the back wall. She eagerly followed, wondering where he was taking her.

The stone steps were barely big enough for the length of her foot. These stairs were definitely made for protecting against invasion and not for carrying a load of laundry down to the washing machine. The ancient builders didn't have much of an eye to the future other than building a sturdy structure and protecting the royal family. She imagined a siege with knights trying to stream upstairs to capture the king and having to take tiny steps in their armor.

The echoes of their shoes on stone was the only sound. At the top of the stairs they turned left down a short corridor which led past several doors. Burke opened the last door and stood outside, allowing Margot to go in first.

The apartment was a modern open plan, with a living area, dining, and kitchen—with a microwave—all in one space. A hallway beyond led to more rooms. Regular drywall covered the castle stones, sponge painted, wallpapered, and everything.

"This is not what I expected," Margot said.

"What? You thought we still lived like in medieval times?" He scoffed. "Everyone does."

"Well, it is a castle." *Watch it, Burke. You're more lovable in your beast form.* "Don't you want to uncover the stones behind these walls so you can see you're in a castle?"

"Speak French," he said. "You'll never learn if you don't."

He was right, but she didn't like the tone he used; like he was commanding it.

She stepped in farther to examine the place. *A coffee maker in a castle.* She had a hard time grasping the concept.

Meanwhile, Burke collapsed onto the leather couch, which was covered in discarded T-shirts. A book splayed open on the coffee table, marking the spot where its reader had last left it.

Burke lay face up, with his arm draped over his eyes like he was blocking out his life.

She hadn't realized the toll the afternoon had taken on him. From getting in a fight with Silvain to having to put on his royal face for the tourists, it must have taken all his self-control.

"Is it okay if I look around?"

Burke responded with a raised hand, and Margot took that as permission.

She ventured down the hallway and noted Burke's bedroom door was open, a double bed, unmade with tousled sheets filled most of the room. She didn't snoop farther in that direction, but returned to the main living area. The kitchen was like any ordinary kitchen. Dirty dishes filled the stainless-steel sink and various food boxes cluttered the counters. "I guess you don't have a maid," Margot whispered.

Next, she checked out the view from the tower. On one side, she saw clear out over New Town and beyond to the Mediterranean Sea. *Impressive.* The other set of windows overlooked the tournament grounds. Two groundskeepers were out raking the dirt, smoothing over where the afternoon scuffles had taken place. What a strange existence Burke lived. To wake up in a castle every day and watch tournaments from your living room window (or compete in them). And everyone who lived in your house wore period costumes, yet you wore track pants and a beach shirt most days.

Back to the apartment. The living room contained a mix of modern decorations and medieval objects. Photographs of a smiling family hung alongside a battered shield. A digital clock on an antique side table. And a telephone hung on the wall in the kitchen. In a medieval castle. So much scope for the imagination, Margot could hardly stand it.

"Your family?" she asked, standing in front of the photographs. Burke looked a lot like his dad. They were both tall and stared down the camera like they were staring down another knight in a duel.

Margot spotted an antique gold-framed hand mirror on a display table. A family crest was on the handle where it attached to the mirror. *Is this what I think it is?* They wouldn't just leave out the magic mirror from the Beauty and the Beast story for anyone to find? It was heavier than she suspected and wondered if it was made of more than gold leaf.

After confirming that Burke was still crashed on the couch, she peered into the surface and made a silent wish to see Clove at the bookstore.

Nothing happened, and her eyes focused back on herself. Her cheeks were a touch sunburned from sitting in the sun during the jousting, and her hair had gone a little flat.

She put the mirror back and surreptitiously scrunched her curls. "I guess not. That would have been cool."

Burke let out a little snore and Margot giggled. He must have been tired. All that dreaming he did. Would he go to the forest and try to find the mystery girl?

"I'm right here," she whispered.

She pulled a chair over to the window to watch over the tournament arena. After a while, she felt someone watching her. She turned back and saw Burke leaning up on a pillow.

"Good evening," she said in French. She tried to come up with a clever way to ask about his dreams and hint that she knew all about them, but when she looked at Burke, her mouth went dry. She liked him; that's all there was to it. And she couldn't tell him until she knew how he felt.

Margot tore her gaze away from his, but she'd looked long enough to notice that his hair had grown and was looking rather shaggy after his nap. She pretended to be distracted by something outside before he realized that he'd pulled his shirtsleeves up to the elbows and that the hair on his arms had also grown an unusual amount. She didn't want to put him on the spot and think he couldn't spend unguarded time with her anymore.

"You have a beautiful view," she said, acting like she'd seen nothing unusual.

"Yes, I do," he answered.

She glanced back briefly, and he was looking right at her.

She quickly turned around. Hair covered his chest at the opening where his shirt ties were.

"Don't be a tease. That's more Silvain's style."

Saying Silvain's name broke the moment, and the leather creaked as Burke shifted and got up. "I'll be right back." The door to the bathroom shut, and moments later the shower turned on.

Margot would have preferred to stare into each other's eyes all night, but Burke had to notice soon that he needed to take care of some beast business. She didn't know how he would react to her learning his secret like this and wanted to continue keeping their friendship intact.

He trusted her enough to fall asleep in her presence and that was a big deal.

She moved over to the leather couch, taking his place. It was still hard to believe that they plunked this modern apartment down in the middle of a medieval castle.

When Burke returned, his hair was short again and his arms were bare. It must be tiring to keep shaving like that.

"Ready to go back to the bookshop?" he asked.

"Oui." She wasn't, but how to tell him that? She'd rather continue to wander through the apartment and daydream of living like a princess. The wish she'd made as a child burned brighter now than ever. Her skin almost tingled along with her imagination.

"You're so used to what's around you, this castle, do you even see it anymore?" Or did he simply take it in stride that he was heir to all this?

He waved his hand to the door, indicating she should go first. "Sometimes it's all too real to me."

They descended the spiral staircase and walked back through the public parts of the castle. Margot could hardly believe her eyes.

Red pennants hung in the windows of the castle and all the workers were wearing red ribbons. Her heart soared. Did they know how important their support was to Burke? Did Burke realize? He hadn't asked them to do it. He could have, and they would have hung his color because of his family connection. They also could have ignored the box he'd brought in and stayed neutral, hanging pennants of each color.

She glanced his way, not wanting to embarrass him, but trying to gauge his reaction. He took it all in, but remained his stoic self.

Margot bit her lip. *Let them in, Burke. These people want to be a part of your life.*

CHAPTER 23

*W*ith encouragement from the fairies, Margot attended the joust the next day, along with half the town. She was still floating after a lovely dream chatting to the beast that night.

She had kept her promise to the fairies and didn't tell him who she was or what she knew. She and Burke simply talked. Burke in beast form was a really nice guy. Burke in human form was often beastly. It would be nice, when this whole thing was over, for the best parts of Burke to be put back together.

Margot bumped into Tanvi while going through the entrance gate to the tournament area. "Why is everyone at the joust today?" Margot asked. She'd noticed that most of the town's workers usually didn't go, leaving the excitement to the tourists.

Tanvi shrugged. "The advertising is working. They've put up the colored banners around New Town, too. And our gang has come out to support Silvain. He told us it would be an especially exciting match today."

Margot looked into the yellow section and spotted the usual gang joining the boy from town who had picked a fight with Burke. He stood and yelled to Silvain. The yellow knight raised his arm, hand in a fist, to the yellow section, with his other hand in a fist over his heart. Margot got a sinking pit in her stomach. Today felt different. Silvain had too many of his friends watching.

"Will you sit with us?" Tanvi glanced at Margot's red ribbon.

"I better not. Someone has to cheer for Burke." The undercurrent of trouble that followed Burke around was building into something unavoidable. Did he know?

Tanvi smiled patronizingly. "And it'll be you cheering for him, then?"

"Yes, it will." They parted ways as Tanvi turned toward the yellow section, and Margot headed straight for Jean Robert in the red section.

He waved when he saw her.

"Can I give the tokens to Burke again?" She spoke in French, determined to get around using the words she knew.

"I'm sorry. I need to ask a tourist," he said.

"I am a tourist!"

Jean Robert took in her medieval costume she'd worn for working in the bookshop and raised his eyebrows. She'd already gotten so used to dressing up with everyone else that she'd forgotten.

"The first one? I need to talk to him. Silvain is planning something." Margot hoped he understood. She didn't know how to say *warn* in French. Or, *those guys are being jerks, and someone needs to tell Burke, so he doesn't get hurt out there.*

She pointed into the yellow section. "They all came to watch."

Jean Robert scanned the yellow section. His jovial expression dimmed in concern. He nodded. "Stay here with me." He held out a hand to help her up onto the hay bale.

The knights were still warming up the horses, and Jean Robert tried to wave Burke over, but Burke never noticed. Too late; they had to exit the field for the show to begin. The acting king and queen entered with their servants to open the games.

Margot's stomach churned. The arena was filled with adults, surely someone would step in if things got out of hand?

Finally, it was time to give favors, and Jean Robert handed her the first one. Burke came trotting over to receive the gift.

"Watch Silvain," Margot said. "He wants to kill you." Probably an exaggeration, but it was the only French word she knew that came close to what was going on. The helmet masked Burke's expression, and Margot couldn't tell from his eyes what he was thinking.

Burke nodded, and she hoped that meant he understood and would be careful. There was no more time for conversation. She placed the red circlet on his lance, and he raised it up, turning the horse around to line up in front of the actors playing the king and queen today.

"Merci," Margot said to Jean Robert. She gathered her skirts and hopped down.

Jean Robert gave her an encouraging nod, and then she ascended the stands to find a seat. Someone in a white sun visor waved to her. "Clove?"

"Saved you a seat." The words came straight to Margot's ears like she was sitting next to Clove, not halfway down the bleachers. Margot continued the climb to the top and then squeezed past several tourists to make her way to Clove.

"What are you doing here?" Margot said as she sat down.

"I come to most of the games," Clove said. "Thyme usually joins me, but she's in the bookshop with Sage."

"This tournament might be more intense today." Margot pointed at the yellow section. "Silvain's friends came to watch. I think they've planned something."

"Oh, dear." Clove leaned over to get a good look. "That tall boy who just stole his friend's hat?"

Margot watched the group toss the boy's hat around while he tried to intercept it. "Yes, that's them. Can you help Burke from here if he needs it?"

Clove set her lips in a line. "We'll see how bad it gets. But don't worry. Burke is a tough opponent. They might have plans, but he's got skills."

"You're right. I've seen him practice." All those hours of drills in the morning made Burke a great competitor.

Margot felt better for the reminder, but that didn't mean Silvain would play fair. He's the one who liked to pull pranks by scaring people in the Torture Museum. Margot wouldn't be surprised if he did something underhanded to Burke on the field. Or off the field. Hopefully, Arturo was paying attention as Burke's squire today.

The knights all left the field, and moments later, Burke and Silvain returned to the arena for the first duel. Burke, riding tall and proud, stopped and stared down the yellow section. It was as if he was challenging them all.

Margot's heart skipped a beat. *What is he doing? I warned him so he would be careful, not make things worse.*

The yellow section erupted in *booing,* and Burke pointed his lance at them before taking his place at the center near the tilt barrier. The two knights positioned their horses on opposite ends of the jousting arena, waiting for the signal. Burke's horse did a nervous side step, and Burke had to rein him in. *Did he sense something was amiss?*

The signal flag lowered, and the knights charged. Silvain aimed his lance for Burke's head, and Burke immediately raised his shield to protect himself.

"Is he supposed to be that aggressive?" Margot leaned forward. Silvain's lance hit Burke's shield. Burke's lance didn't make contact; he was too busy keeping balance after the off-script attack. The king stood. *Good, he'd seen.*

So had Arturo. He stood with his arms crossed, shaking his head. When he helped Burke prepare for the second pass, they kept the lance in play. He and Arturo both checked out the integrity of the shield and it appeared to have passed muster.

During the next contact, Burke's lance exploded with a loud *crack*. Splintered wood flew off in chunks, and Silvain lost his balance.

Next, Silvain jumped off his horse and his squire handed him a sword. He ran at Burke, who likewise jumped off his horse and obtained a sword. The squires quickly collected the horses and led them off the field, leaving the knights to fight in close contact alone, much to the delight of the crowd. Adrenaline pushed through Margot's body and she rose to her feet, along with the rest of the red section. The fighting took place at the end of the field, closer to the yellow section.

But the crowd didn't know this wasn't staged, and that it was serious. Both helmets were off now and the yellow section went wild.

"Clove?" Margot didn't like that Burke was off his horse, his position of strength. Her stomach clenched like she was going to be sick.

"Hold steady." Clove put a hand on Margot's arm.

Silvain swung, but Burke ducked out of the way. After that first swing, arms and legs moved swiftly, and it was hard to tell who had the upper hand.

Now the queen and the rest of the royal entourage were on their feet. The tourists in the red section were picking up that this fight was personal between the two knights. The good-natured cheering gave way to silence while all attention was focused on the fight. The knights were too far away to see how many blows were landing.

Silvain was taller, with longer arms to reach Burke, but Burke was agile and able to duck many of Silvain's charges. Based on the crowd's reaction at that end of the arena, someone was getting hurt.

When the two squires returned to the field, they looked at each other and then rushed forward. The yellow squire stood back while Arturo got in between the knights, eventually separating them. The crowd cheered, whether in relief or appreciation for a good fight, Margot couldn't tell. She was pretty sure though, that both Burke and Silvain had blood on their faces.

She remained standing after the red section sat down. Clove tugged on her skirt and Margot sat, too.

"He'll be okay," Clove said. "It's not the first fight he's been in, although he's usually good about avoiding them. They've got a medic back there to help with any injuries."

"That doesn't make me feel better," Margot said. She wrung her hands to keep them from shaking. "Silvain planned that."

"And Burke handled it well. He's stronger than Silvain. He could have done a lot of damage, but he held back." She leaned in and whispered. "As the beast, he is incredibly strong. He's learning to keep it under control."

"Are you saying I should have warned Silvain, not Burke?"

CHAPTER 24

*M*argot waited in the town square, hoping to see Burke after the tournament. All the tourists had already exited the arena, and she'd spotted several of the guys involved in the jousting leaving. Still no Burke. She'd not seen Silvain either.

Tanvi came over from her flower stand with a headdress made with red and gold ribbons. "Truce?" she asked, holding it out. "Silvain was too hard on Burke. He didn't deserve that."

"Yes, Silvain has been terrible. Thank you for noticing and thanks for the flowers. I've been eying these." Margot accepted the gift. "How bad was it? You were closer to the action."

Tanvi shook her head. "They both walked off the field, so that's a good sign. I'm sure wearing the armor helps." She laughed. "What is up with these guys? Their hands probably hurt more than anything."

Margot agreed.

Tanvi secured the flowers over Margot's curls. "Wear it the rest of the day. You can keep it in the fridge to make it last longer and wear it again tomorrow, and then you can leave it out to dry, so you can take it home to America with you. Still friends?"

"Friends."

"If you want to do something later, let me know. We can take a canal boat down the river. I haven't done that in ages."

"Sounds fun. I'll let you know."

After Tanvi returned to her flower stall, Margot ventured outside the walls and risked going to the stables. Now that she looked like a worker from the town, she hoped no one would mind if she wandered behind stage.

Several of the stable hands were working with the horses, taking off their colorful caparisons, wiping down their coats, and checking their feet. A door opened in the barn, and Silvain walked out with a scowl. His right eye was puffy and turning red. That would look nasty tomorrow. Worse than her foot. Well, served him right. He was the one who attacked Burke. She tried to step out of his line of sight, but he saw her.

"You okay?" she said.

"I'll live." His gaze flickered to her flower wreath in Burke's colors. He said no more, but brushed past her.

She waited a little longer, but still didn't see Burke. A young stable hand walked to the barn. He stopped with his hand on the handle. "You here for Burke? He's in the field." The boy pointed to the field beyond the stable.

"Merci."

Margot walked over to the fence and saw that Burke had stationed himself at the end of the field, as far away from everyone as possible. He wasn't riding the horse; rather, he stood with it, feeding it something from his pockets. She slipped through the fence and crossed the field.

He noticed her coming about halfway across. He had a cut on his nose and another under his cheek, but at least his eye wasn't swollen and probably wouldn't turn purple like Silvain's would in the morning. When she stood in front of him, he reached out and fingered one of the red ribbons on her wreath.

"This is Bisou," he said, feeding it a carrot. He held one out to Margot.

She took the carrot and tentatively offered it to the horse the way Burke had. When Bisou gobbled it up, she grinned. This horse might like her better than Estelle did.

"Do you want to ride?" he asked. "With me?"

"Now?" She considered her skirt and decided it was full enough to arrange modestly. She slipped her foot into the stirrup.

Burke tried to help her up, but when she stumbled back, his hand automatically went to his ribs. Silvain must have done more damage than Burke let on.

"*Ça va?*" she asked.

He nodded, quickly lowering his hand. He led the horse to the fence for Margot to get a boost up.

She scooched up to the front of the saddle. Even though this horse was bigger than the one she rode, she wasn't afraid. She trusted Burke to control Bisou and keep her safe. Although, she wished she had her camera so she could get a picture of herself on a horse while wearing her medieval maiden costume.

She looked at Burke and smiled, letting him know she was ready.

He swung up behind her, and she settled back into him while he put his arms around her to help her manage the reins.

"Your ribs?" she asked in English, putting her hand on her chest to show him what she meant. "I don't want to hurt you."

He shook his head and indicated she should resume her position. She did, but didn't dare lean back too much.

She was nervous about leading the horse, but Burke kept his hands wrapped around hers. His grip was firm, and he expertly set out in a walk around the field.

He kept the pace slow and meandering, and Margot focused on the moment. A breath between the craziness of the tournament and thinking about the curse. Although, she noticed that the hair on his arms and hands was thicker than normal. She was determined to distract him, so he wouldn't cut their ride short.

"When did you start riding horses?"

"I have no memories of not riding. Everyone in my family rides, and we all have our own horses. You road Estelle, my first horse and the one we use for the pony rides. I'm the only one to joust, now, though. My father did when he was younger, and my mother still does accuracy demonstrations for the crowd when she is here."

"That's right, they were the king and queen at the welcome banquet." *Banquet. Another French word!* "Will they be home soon? I heard they were on vacation."

"They're not far, so they'll come home on several weekends to play their roles in the joust."

"When was your first joust?"

"Against a competitor and not my parents? A real joust? They made me wait until I was fifteen."

"Did you win?"

"What do you think?"

Even though she couldn't see him, she imagined the smirk on his face. Classic Burke. "How about I ask it another way? Have you ever lost?"

"Not to anyone who mattered."

High achiever. That didn't help to keep his modesty in check. But she'd seen the dedication that went into what he did and knew his skill was earned. Those around him, however, would prefer a little humility be attached to his skill.

A man approached the fence and called out to Burke.

Burke waved acknowledgment. "It's Arturo. He wants me to practice hand-to-hand with him."

Alarmed, Margot asked, "Why? Are you planning on another round with Silvain?"

Burke snorted. "No. I think he's done. But Silvain isn't the only one who wants to bring me down."

Oh, dear. Burke didn't help himself by staring down the entire yellow section at the tournament. Any one of those guys might try their hand at knocking Burke down a peg. When they reached the fence, Arturo waited for Burke to help Margot off the horse.

"Nice to meet you again," Arturo said. He opened the gate.

"You, too."

Burke walked the horse through the gate and over to the paddock. He indicated goodbye to Margot with a jerk of his chin.

"Bye," Margot said, wanting to linger but realizing Burke had already moved on to the next thing.

She returned to the walled city. An afternoon of horseback riding was more in line with what Margot expected out of her summer vacation than dreams of a fairy tale beast. Actually, snuggling up to Burke was *better* than what she expected in her summer vacation. It was too bad Arturo interrupted them when he did.

If she could capture this moment, she would die happy. Well, that might have been an exaggeration. There was so much more she wanted to do with her life, but this moment was pretty near perfect. Despite the odds, she and Burke had grown closer, at least comfortable with each other. They hadn't fallen in love... yet. But there were definite *feelings* happening. At least, she hoped Burke didn't go horseback riding like that with any of the other summer visitors.

CHAPTER 25

*C*love was in the kitchen baking when Margot returned to the apartment. She pulled off her oven mitts and came around to the living area. Her gaze rose to Margot's flower wreath.

"How is Burke?" She looked as conflicted as ever about Margot's role in her plans. Her fingers worried the bottom edge of her apron. The hope and pain in Clove's expression were hard to deny. Margot was new to the problem, but to Clove it was personal.

"He's sore. But still proud."

"And Silvain?"

"Has a nasty black eye."

The corners of Clove's mouth rose slightly. "I'm sorry to hear it."

Sage came down the hallway and marched into the kitchen, her brows furrowed. "Clove, can't you smell your shortbread burning?" She pulled out the tray and fanned the oven mitt over the biscuits. "Open the window before Suzette kicks us out of the apartment for setting the place on fire."

Clove hustled back to the kitchen and then began to slide the shortbread to a plate.

Sage brought out a glass of water for Margot. "Here. It's hot out there. So, you spoke to him after the fight?"

"You heard?"

"The whole town is talking about it. Fortunately for them, the tourists loved it. But they'll not joust each other for the rest of the season, I can tell you that."

"After seeing both of them, I'd say they won't mind." She pictured their banged-up faces. Neither of them was strutting around afterward. Their boss probably had sharp words with them as well.

"For Burke, it's not as easy to walk away," Sage said. "As he grows more beastly, he's putting out hormones that affect those around him. We're seeing it happen already. Soon, he'll have the whole town against him." She stared pensively at the cookies Clove put out as if remembering a similar event.

"Half the town is already against him. At least those his own age are. They all showed up today and sat in Silvain's section. You should have heard the way they talked about Burke that night we all went to the Torture Museum. It was awful. They complain about Burke, but none of them saw how badly they themselves were acting."

Sage pulled out a chair and then sat down at the kitchen table. "We rarely see the plank in our own eyes while we are pointing out the speck in someone else's." She crossed her arms and leaned on the table. "Does this experience give you more compassion for our dear Burke?"

"Some."

"You've spent time with Burke. Does their behavior help him or encourage him at all? Does it make him want to change?"

"No. It probably eggs him on. He knows there's no point in trying to fit in."

Sage held up a finger. "Ah, but there's where you're wrong

about his intentions. Why do you think he tries so hard in the tournaments? The jousts aren't real; they're a spectacle for the tourists."

Margot thought about Burke getting up early every morning to practice. None of the other knights were as dedicated.

"It's something he's good at." Margot said. "A way to show he's part of the town."

Sage nodded. "There you go. So, he does care."

"Then shouldn't we tell him about my dreams so he knows he's not alone?"

"He's not alone. I've not left him," Clove said, getting defensive like a mother bear.

Sage ignored Clove's comment. "When you saw him after the joust, what was he like? How was his demeanor?"

"Is a mix of sadness and anger an emotion?" Perhaps the emotion she was searching for was *resigned*. Resigned to his fate and a little bit mad about it.

"And how did he react to you?"

She sucked in her lips and looked at the tabletop. "He invited me to go horseback riding with him."

Sage raised an eyebrow. "You caught him in a vulnerable moment, and he didn't push you away?" She and Clove exchanged a winning look, and Margot was glad Thyme wasn't there to supercharge the meaning behind their smiles. There was still a long way to go in freeing Burke.

Margot said, "Tell me how the original curse was broken. Maybe that will help."

Clove joined them sitting at the table. "The *lesson* was learned after the prince was given a second chance."

"A second chance?"

"There's always a second chance," Sage said. "The prince had many lessons to learn, actually. He lived a self-centered life, not knowing how to put anyone ahead of himself. He did what he wanted, when he wanted to. Beauty demonstrated sacrificial love to him. Inspired him to treat her well. She didn't scold him into it; she was an example, and he was ready to learn."

"But they fell in love," Margot said.

"Yes."

"What if we don't? What if all we can get to is friendship?" She thought of the easy way they rode the horse together. Wrapped in his arms, she'd felt nothing like that before. They'd not known each other long enough to be in love, but she hoped it was the beginnings.

Sage glanced at Clove and smiled. Margot realized she must have a faraway look on her face. She blinked and tried to come back to the present.

"That's where it starts, dear," Thyme said as she entered the apartment. "*Mm*, something smells good. We're all for forward progress, no matter how slow." Thyme squeezed Margot's shoulder on her way to the kitchen. "Clove bakes when she's worried."

"I'm not worried. I like baking."

Thyme laughed. "I closed the shop early, is that allowed? No one was coming in, and I was bored. What's happening up here?" Thyme sat and reached for one of Clove's shortbreads. "Is Suzette sleeping?"

Sage nodded. "We can talk openly."

Thyme leaned toward Margot. "Well? Sounds like I missed an exciting joust this afternoon."

Margot looked at her in disbelief. Why was Thyme always so happy about the situation? Didn't she see how hurt everyone was? "It was horrible. I don't want to see Burke get into another fight again."

"The curse is still accelerating," Sage said to Thyme. "Like before."

Margot could imagine what the original beast had gone through. "He's not helping himself any," Margot said. "Most of the time Burke is arrogant and proud." She pictured him staring down the yellow section at the joust. What he did was more than simply play to the crowd. He was making a point to Silvain. "It gives the impression that he thinks himself better than everyone else."

Thyme cocked her head. "And? This is too much for you?"

"That's not what I said." He was also helping her to learn French and to ride a horse. "He has moments of kindness and gentleness that come out of nowhere."

"There you go," Clove said. "The curse should break any time now."

Sage's face pinched. "We all know it's not so simple."

Thyme spoke more colorfully. "Have you gone soft? The original beast had to suffer, so did Belle and her father. Not to mention..."

Sage cleared her throat and, with a glance at Margot, Thyme stopped talking.

"Just be his friend without any expectations," Sage said. "We all know he needs one."

Thyme took a sip of tea and selected another of Clove's shortbreads. "I should join Margot in her morning walks." She patted her hips. "Either that or we've got to fix this quick so Clove stops baking."

Clove slid the plate toward Margot. "Here. Take these to your aunt before Thyme eats them all. I made them at her request, and she's just woken up."

Gladly. The conversation had somehow turned weighty in ways she didn't understand. She tapped quietly on Suzette's door.

"Come in."

"Hi, how are you feeling?" Margot asked quietly.

Suzette pushed herself up, arranging her pillows.

"Much better, but even though I just woke up from a nap, I'm still so tired. Have you tried Sage's sipping chocolate? It's heavenly and puts me right under. I'll have to get the recipe from her."

Margot smiled and handed over the cookie plate.

"How do you enjoy working in the bookshop?" Suzette asked.

"I'm not doing much, since, the, *um*, heritage ladies are doing most of the work."

"Probably for the best. I'm not sure what the tax laws are with you working, anyway." She put the plate on her bedside table. "Would you have an interest in taking business courses at school? To learn accounting so you can do bookkeeping and that sort of thing."

"That's an idea. Why do you suggest it?"

"There's no point in me being subtle, I suppose. I'm wondering if you have an interest in continuing the family business. I've enjoyed the time off, and if I knew the shop would go to you in my old age, then we could start to plan."

"You mean, move here? Permanently?"

Suzette smiled understandingly. "Don't give me an answer now. It's a suggestion. An option for you to consider when you get back home and can talk properly to your father."

"Okay. I'll think about it."

There were lots of things Margot needed to think about. Not the least of which was that there was still one thing bothering her about the Beauty and the Beast story, and she couldn't admit it to the fairies.

In the original "test" the beast watched Beauty sacrifice her life for her father's. That was a powerful example of sacrificial love and a turning point for the beast. But this was the '80s and her family wasn't even on the continent. How could she demonstrate anything as powerful as that?

CHAPTER 26

*W*hen Margot didn't dream of the beast that night, she grew concerned.

She had hoped to talk to the beast and make sure Burke was all right after the joust. The beast's mood would give her a clearer picture of how Burke was really feeling, without the bravado.

When she'd left Burke at the stables, he and Arturo had planned to practice hand-to-hand combat maneuvers, and that was the last she'd seen him.

Knowing that others wanted to hurt Burke worried her. One-on-one fighting in the arena was one thing, but what if Silvain and his friends attacked Burke as a group? Clove said he could hold his own, but would that trigger something that gave away his secret? What if a burst of adrenaline caused a flight-or-fight response that made him burst out in hair all over?

She didn't wait for the sun to rise before she was up and tossing on a pair of shorts, along with a polo shirt and light sweatshirt over top. None of the fairies had arrived yet for the day, so she left a note telling them she'd gone out. She slung her bag over her shoulder, with plans to bring back a breakfast treat for everyone.

The stables were quiet when she got there, but before she continued on to the field, the barn door opened, and Burke stepped out with his horse, Bisou. Somewhat hidden under the cowboy hat, Burke's hair was already long and pulled back in a ponytail. He looked scruffy, like he'd only done a minimal tidy-up to hide his curse. When he noticed her, he startled like she'd scared him.

"You shouldn't be back here," he said. His voice was gravelly like he'd just woken up. "Knights and stable hands only. I've not been strict about it before, but I mean it this time. You can't stay."

Margot looked around for Burke's boss. There was no one in the field, no one in the paddock. They were all alone before anyone else was up. Burke didn't need *that* much training. *Okay then.* We're back to this.

"May I feed carrots to the horses today? I'd like to stay in their good graces." It sounded like an excuse to check up on him, which it was.

"My boss is pretty ticked about yesterday, and I need to work, which I can't do with you around."

"Right." One romantic step forward, two back. Maybe because she was hoping to relive the ultraromantic day yesterday, the brush-off felt worse. She shook her head and backed away.

He sighed and then tied off his horse, but she turned and speed-walked away, acting like she'd been out for her morning walk, anyway. She didn't want him to see how hurt she was. If she was caught up in the whirlwind of a fairy tale, it seemed she was the only one riding the wind.

When she heard him follow behind her, she quickened to a jog around the far corner of the walled city, through the trees, then slipped into the wild garden, hoping he'd think she'd gone over the ridge and down the valley already.

She was too sensitive for this, too easily offended. Even though Burke didn't mean how half of what he said sounded, she couldn't stop her reaction to it, nor was she sure she should.

But moments later, he followed her inside the garden.

Margot couldn't look at him. If she did, he would know everything she was thinking. Just be a friend, huh? Pretend her heart wasn't on the line. That her stomach didn't already flip-flop when he looked at her, or that her heart didn't race when she heard his voice. No problem.

"Margot."

She groaned. The way he said her name. It should always be said like that. Back home, her name fell flat when other people pronounced it, but Burke gave her name life.

He stopped short and looked all around the garden space like he'd never been in it before, or it had been a long time since he'd seen it.

"*Le jardin*," he whispered.

"Yes, this is the place I suggested we go to the other day..." Margot left the rest unsaid, not wanting to remind him of his fights with Silvain. "You've never seen it?" she asked.

He shook his head.

"I planned to clean it up a little in my spare time, but haven't gotten around to it." Margot took in the weeds and wild nature of the thorn bushes. The places where she'd pulled weeds out had already grown back.

Burke bent down by one of the dry bushes. "One of the town's legends is about a garden that is cursed with growing thorns, but no roses. I thought it had been built on top of by one of the buildings in town."

He snapped a dead branch off the bush and then quickly sucked his thumb. "A thorn." He held out his thumb and the blood oozed out.

"I have a bandage," Margot said, digging through her bag. *Always be prepared.* She held it out to him.

Instead of taking the bandage, he kept holding out his thumb to her.

"Fine." She ripped open the package as she took a step closer to him. She'd bandage him up and then leave. That French accent wasn't going to overcome her hurt feelings of how he spoke to her.

She stuck down one side of the bandage on his calloused thumb, then adjusted his hand so she could properly stick down the other side. Her stomach fluttered when they touched. She looked into his eyes and swallowed. "You're done." She held his hand a little too long, and a flush crept up her neck.

His gaze locked on to hers as she dropped his hand and took a step back. She looked away, her gaze lowering to the thorn bush he'd pricked his finger on. She gasped.

A small, green bud had appeared near the base of the branch he'd snapped. The bud was the only sign of life in the garden other than the weeds.

"Look."

Burke glanced down briefly, but his attention was focused on something behind her. His eyes narrowed, and he shook his head slightly like he was trying to adjust his vision.

"Qu'est-ce que c'est?" he whispered in awe.

Concerned, Margot turned around. An early morning mist had formed, obscuring their view of the trees and the city walls behind them. But, no, that wasn't quite it. The trees, the walls, all were faint, giving way to a clear view of the castle. Only it wasn't the castle anymore.

"What is that?" she echoed Burke's question.

The building was more like a manor house, the way the tour guide explained the original royal hunting retreat. It was as if they were seeing back in time.

Built of white stone with spires and chimneys rising out of the blue-gray roof and dotting the skyline, it stood in commanding contrast to a dark green forest behind. Lush green lawns surrounded by low hedges and sculpted trees created a symmetrical pattern leading the eye right back to the mansion.

Margot couldn't look away, but she felt Burke at her side. He touched her shoulder as he passed her, walking toward the vision. He moved slowly, head cocked as if trying to decipher what he was seeing. *"Le château."*

She caught up with him, and they approached the apparition together, wondering if it was real. There was no movement on the grounds. Nothing in the windows to give any indication of life, but the house felt almost watchful. Like the entire scene was focused on them.

They walked on a gravel pathway, the hedgerows bordering their way fading in and out as if being blown in the wind. When Burke reached the edge of the garden, the mansion faded into the mist and disappeared like it had never been there. With Margot's next blink, the city walls were back, and the birds began to chirp. She'd not noticed their silence until they started up again.

"Did you make that happen?" Burke said.

She shook her head. No. She had nothing to do with this. Could the mansion be a glimpse of the past? Or something from the curse that tied the ancient to the present?

Burke continued, speaking such rapid-fire French that she couldn't make out what he was saying. He was more earnest than she'd ever seen him.

Reluctantly, she shrugged. She wished she had insight for him, but she had no clue what any of this meant. She pointed where the mansion had appeared and nodded. "I saw it. I saw it, too." Still stunned, she couldn't recall any French to converse with him.

Burke ran from one side of the overgrown garden to the other, frustration etched on his face. He examined the ground; he scratched his head. He spoke into the air.

He's never seen the mansion before.

The realization hit Margot hard. A new thing was happening in the garden that couldn't be denied, but what was it? Some kind of fairy-tale magic had been stirred, woken up.

Margot found the thorn bush Burke had pricked his finger on

and examined the little bud which had already grown since she last looked at it. Now it showed a narrow strip of white where the petals were beginning to put pressure on the green part of the bud. She reached out and touched it.

"What are you doing little thing?" she asked it. "This is a garden of thorns; are you trying to take it back?"

Burke shot past Margot and out of the garden. She followed right behind. He only paused at the stables long enough to put his horse back in the barn and that's where Margot caught up with him.

"I'm sorry, I need to go." He tried to leave her at the stables, but she followed.

"I must find Mademoiselle Clove. The heritage committee."

"I'm coming with you." She wouldn't tell him that she already knew why he wanted to talk to Clove.

He tried to argue more, but quickly gave up. "Where are they now? The bookshop?"

Margot noted the empty streets. "No, it's too early, still. At my aunt's apartment. They've been meeting there for breakfast. I was going to bring them something today."

"You go to the bakery. I'll go see Clove."

Not getting rid of me that easily. "No, I'm coming with you."

Sage met them at the door, blocking entrance to the apartment. Suzette must be out of the bedroom.

"Yes?" Sage said. "May I help you?"

"We have to talk to Clove." Burke examined his thumb where the bandage was. "She saw, too, and wants to know what it was." He looked up with an expression like a wounded puppy. "We both do."

"Go downstairs. We'll be there soon." Sage shut the door.

Burke paced in front of the bookshop. It was taking the fairies forever to come down. Margot kept quiet, letting Burke work through what they'd seen and what part, if any, Margot had in it all. Finally, the fairies arrived, Sage in the lead.

"Let's open early today," Sage said, shuffling everyone toward the door.

They all scrambled in, and Thyme locked the door behind them.

"What is it?" Sage asked. "What's happened?"

Burke spoke first. "We saw le château."

Clove and Thyme looked shocked, but Sage's expression never changed. Either Sage knew something, or she was better at hiding her feelings than the other two.

"Where?" Clove asked. "Inside the castle?"

"No," Margot said. "We were outside the city walls, in an overgrown garden." She glanced at Burke, wondering when he would realize that she knew the heritage committee was more than a group of enthusiastic promoters. "The walls faded away, and we could see clear to the château and the hedged gardens all around it."

"Show us." Clove started for the door.

"It's gone now," Burke said. "Do you know how to bring le château back?"

Clove stopped with her hand on the door. "No. I don't. Thyme and I have been looking for the garden all summer. How did you find it?"

Burke looked at Margot and everyone followed his gaze.

"Margot?" Clove said, stepping away from the door. "Is there something you haven't told us?"

She held her hands up. "It was just there. I found it during one of my walks. How was I to know it was something important?"

Burke's eyes narrowed slightly as he studied her, glancing back and forth between her and the fairies. Margot held her breath. Now that the excitement was dying down, Burke was beginning to process.

He bit his lip and looked away.

Margot waited for an outburst, but there wasn't any. His silence was worse than him getting mad at them.

Sage noticed Burke's reaction, too. "Let's go out there now and see what happens."

Meanwhile, a stodgy man came up to the windowpane and cupped the sun from his eyes as he peered into the bookshop. Seeing them in there, he tapped at the glass and then looked at his watch.

"You go on without me," Thyme said. "I can run the store."

CHAPTER 27

The sleepy old town had begun to wake up with shopkeepers opening for the day. Soon the tourists would descend and not long after that, Burke would have to attend Arturo at the joust.

"Mademoiselle!"

A coffee shop owner tried to flag down Sage as their group marched through town, but she simply waved as they bustled by.

No one spoke even after they'd gone out the gate. Margot hung back, letting Burke lead the way and deal with the news that she knew more about him than she'd let on. She waited uneasily for him to ask about just how much she knew, but so far, he'd said nothing.

Once in the garden, they gathered around the budding rosebush. No flowers had burst forth yet, but more buds had formed and the leaves had turned a dark green. The live rosebush stood out like when color had been added to a black-and-white photograph.

Margot faced Burke square-on as she watched him connect all the dots while he stared at the bush come to life. He worked his jaw as if going over what to say, but holding back.

Finally, he said, "If this was a dream, I'd know the perfect thing to say." Only then did he look at Margot.

She gave him a tentative smile. He wasn't mad. He wasn't disappointed, only surprised. Her heart opened up a little more for him. "I've had some really good dreams since I arrived in Chapais."

He flashed an unguarded grin before turning stoic again. "Clove, what does all this mean?"

"Good news, I think." She deferred to Sage, who nodded in confirmation.

"We have no advice for how to proceed, other than do so together."

Burke and Margot exchanged glances. *So not helpful.*

"Then leave us alone," he said, extending an arm toward the garden entrance.

Clove looked hurt. "Oh. But we can stay and help come up with ideas."

Burke shook his head. "Margot will help me."

They waited for the fairies to leave, then Burke turned to Margot and put his hands on his hips. He didn't look too angry, but determined that by the end of the conversation, all would be said.

She tried to smile disarmingly. "There's a bench here somewhere."

Burke found it first and cleaned it off for them. They sat, and he reached for her hand. He held it sandwiched between his hands like he was making doubly sure of her.

"Tell me everything," he said. "When did you learn about me?"

Margot had a hard time concentrating the way he held her hand and fixed his stormy gray eyes on her. "I had the first dream, well, you remember. The first night I was here. I ran from you because I didn't know who you were, or what was happening."

He nodded. "I'd had nightmares before, but none of them

came close to that dream. You appeared in a glow." He twisted his lips. "Like a large firefly I chased through the forest."

"Interesting. That's very fairy tale–like."

"My world. One big happy fairy tale."

His sarcastic tone was tired. For Margot, the idea that one could have a fairy tale was still exciting and new, but for him, it was akin to living a nightmare. She supposed that if she was the beast, she'd have a completely different perspective about a modern-day fairy tale.

They talked until Margot had filled him in on every encounter from her point of view. "Does it help?" she asked.

Burke let go of her hand and stood staring at the place where the magic happened earlier. "Not really. Seems I'm no better off now than I was yesterday."

Margot tried not to be overly sensitive, but he should feel better off now. Not only had he confirmed who he'd been dreaming about, but something had changed significantly that morning.

She hesitated before reaching out. He wore that huggable shirt that she loved on him, but he wasn't acting huggable. Instead, she grabbed his arms and turned him around to face the rosebush.

"Count your blessings. I don't know how or why things have changed, but the fairies are excited. This rosebush is growing when it used to be dead. Be patient. Fairy tales are about a series of obstacles for the hero to overcome."

"Every day is an obstacle. How many do I need to overcome?" He stared at the rosebush.

"And, according to Clove, they're about learning a lesson." She gave a teasing smile, thinking of Clove's insistence it wasn't a curse. Besides, Margot wasn't going to come out and say that he had to fall in love and be loved in return. Clove should have already told him that part.

WITHOUT RESOLVING ANYTHING, Burke went to the arena, and Margot returned to the apartment. She was drained emotionally and needed time alone to reset.

Burke would have to muster all his energy for the tournament. Good thing he wasn't jousting today, so he didn't need to be as sharp as usual.

After a quick peek in on the sleeping Suzette, Margot sprawled out on the couch, hoping for a quick nap. Since Burke was busy at the arena, she should have a restful, dream-free sleep. After putting a fresh set of batteries into her Walkman, she listened to Burke's voice reading fairy tales to her. She wished there was a way she could help him, but no one had any ideas. They were all waiting for the next change.

As Margot drifted off to sleep, she felt the now-familiar pull inside the fairy-tale dream and she eagerly walked into it. *Shouldn't Burke be at the tournament? Why was she dreaming now...?*

Soon, Margot was walking through the woods. Beast? Margot searched the trees, listening closely. The air had a different smell today. Muskier. Darker, if she could describe an odor as dark. How unexpected, yet exciting to talk to Beast today in her dream. For the first time she didn't have to be careful about what she said for fear of giving herself and the fairies away.

A growl sounded behind her, and she whirled around, heart pounding. *What was that?* The spine-chilling sound was from an actual wild animal. A large wild animal. She searched the dark spaces for it while simultaneously backing away. She wanted to call out for Burke's help, but she didn't want to alert the animal on the slim chance it hadn't noticed her yet.

"Welcome woman-child." The deep voice dripped with derision. "It's nice of you to join me."

The hairs on the backs of Margot's arms rose. The voice was different.

"Who are you?" she asked, still searching for the creature but not seeing him. She took a step backward. She'd never touched fear like this, even during that first dream when she was running from the beast, before she knew he was Burke.

Her mind screamed at her to wake up, but she couldn't.

"Let me go," she said. "I shouldn't be here now."

The beast laughed. "You aren't here, but you are coming to me."

"No. No, I'm not. Go crash someone else's dream."

He laughed, a deep, guttural sound. "I don't have you yet, but I will soon."

Margot woke to Suzette holding her in her arms and rocking. *"Shh. Shh.* It was a dream. You're all right."

Margot wiped her eyes.

"I thought you were being chased by wolves in here. That was quite a dream you were having."

"Yeah. I don't remember much of it." She was confused. The dream was so similar to those she shared with Burke, yet it couldn't have been more different.

"Okay now?" Suzette asked. "Go have a shower and wake yourself up. I'll put the kettle on for tea."

"Sure. Thanks." Margot pushed her sweaty hair out of her face.

What was that? Was it real, too?

She had to warn Burke. They weren't alone in their dreams.

CHAPTER 28

argot spent way too long in the shower, and her shorts fell off the back of the door and onto the floor, getting soaked. Minor irritations, but she was already out of sorts after the dream.

"Tea?" Suzette called out while Margot dressed in stirrup pants and a fairy tale T-shirt.

"Chamomile would be great," she said. Something calming while she waited for the jousting to end.

Suzette, seemingly happy for the company, told Margot more about the history of the bookshop and the day-to-day operations. "I've got my regulars who like the new books, and the tourists who prefer books they won't find elsewhere."

When the clock neared the time Burke would be finished with the joust, Margot excused herself. "Speaking of the bookshop, I should see if the ladies need anything."

"I'll come," Suzette said. She eagerly tossed aside the light shawl she wore around her shoulders.

"No, no, no." Margot held up her hands. "Doctor's orders, you're to stay away until next week. He knows it's hard for you to resist going back to work. Why don't you read? It's the next best thing."

Suzette exaggerated a frown. "Fine. But tonight, we'll go for a stroll after hours. I'm getting cabin fever. Surely the doctor won't object to exercise."

"Yes, a great idea." Except now, Margot would observe the town with different eyes, knowing that the mansion and gardens were all there behind today's buildings and streets.

When Margot walked into the bookshop, the first thing she noticed was that it was empty of both customers and fairies.

"Hello? Is anyone here?"

"Is that you, Margot? Come through; we're back here."

The fairies sat around the table, discussing the appearance of the mansion and what it might mean. Rather than the scent of old books, the air smelled like vanilla, which was a good sign that Clove had been in the kitchen recently.

Margot looked for the telltale plate of treats but didn't find it. But there was a gray cat curled up on Thyme's lap.

"New friend?"

"Poor thing was mewing at the back door. I wonder if Suzette feeds it from time to time?"

Margot eyed it with uncertainty. She would accept nothing at face value anymore in this town. "Is it friendly?"

Clove huffed. "It's a cat. As a rule, they're not friendly."

Thyme made a face. "This one is. Isn't she sweet?" She lifted the bundle of fur who didn't look particularly happy about the treatment.

"It can't stay here," Sage said. "It's not a domestic cat. The town has always used the alley cats as mousers for the village." *Sage, the voice of reason.*

Margot was about to pet it, then flinched away. "You mean, that cat is a descendant from the time of the original beast?"

Thyme looked up, a quizzical look on her face. "Don't go looking for trouble." She stroked the cat. "You're surrounded by descendants and artifacts here. It doesn't mean they're out to get you."

"Get rid of it," Clove said. "It'll have hair all over the shop before you know it."

"Not if I'm holding it," Thyme shot back.

While they bantered back and forth, Margot contemplated her most recent dream. Whoever or whatever she saw and heard from was definitely beastly, but also, not Burke. Not even close. So, was he someone who lived in town? And what could he possibly mean by saying she was coming to him? Because, obviously, that's something she would not be doing voluntarily.

Thyme touched her arm, and Margot jumped. Thyme frowned. "Come with me."

She took Margot and the cat to the front of the bookstore.

"What's wrong, dear? Here, have a ladyfinger while you tell me. It'll fortify you. I like the ones dipped in chocolate. Sage put them up here because I was eating too many." Thyme held a plate out to her and after Margot had taken one, took two for herself. "Clove is getting really good with her bakes. The more stress she feels, the more she feels the need. I'm loving it. Now, what's on your mind?"

Margot glanced at the bookshop door. "Shouldn't we lock it or something?"

"No need. Sage has already closed up for the day. No one will come in."

"But the sign…it still says open."

"To you. And to Burke. He'll be able to come in as well. Now, what's got you so upset?" Thyme scratched the cat's jaw, and it leaned into her.

"You said that's a female cat?"

"Yes, we're all girls here, now out with it. What's bothering you?"

Margot hesitated. She still thought it best to tell Burke first. Finally, she said, "I'm worried that what you're asking of me is impossible. Falling in love requires communication and trust, and I don't know. Lots of other things I'm guessing. I don't see how it can happen in the short time I've got left here. Burke and I have already kept secrets from each other."

"But you like him, right?"

"Attraction and love are not the same. This isn't a fairy-tale story that's wrapped up in a few pages; it's real life. I'm not a curse breaker."

Clove's voice shouted out from the back. "Not a curse." Her voice was tense. "A lesson to be learned."

Thyme scowled. "So much for privacy," she called back. She put the cat down and let it explore at her feet.

"And Burke doesn't seem to be learning anything. He hasn't changed from when I got here." As she said it, she realized it was true. He was still proud and arrogant, with small bursts of kindness. She'd only planned to give Thyme a reason for her mood, but now she'd come up with more worries for herself. The situation was worse than she thought.

"You only say that because you didn't know what he was like before you got here. He's taken great strides since the reunion weekend. Just because things haven't gone in a straight line doesn't mean they're not going forward. If you had been here in the spring when we planned the reunion, you would have seen a very different Burke. His, *erm*, hairy situation has humbled him."

"I'll have to take your word on it."

"That's what I'm here for, dear. You can't give up now. When you look back, you'll have a greater perspective and see for yourself. Right now, you're the frog in the pot and don't realize how hot the water is."

"Wrong analogy, Thyme." Clove called out from the back. "What Thyme means is that you can't see the forest for the trees."

Thyme pressed her lips together. "Might as well join the others if they won't allow us a private word."

Margot followed Thyme to the back.

"Where's the cat?" Thyme asked.

Margot thought she'd been keeping a good eye on it and was sure that when Thyme put it down, it walked to the back room.

"Out," answered Sage.

Thyme made a small noise of protest. Meanwhile, Clove had lost her characteristically morose expression. "Things are changing," she explained to Margot. "So, this is good news. You are making a difference, let me assure you."

But Sage clucked. "Let's not be hasty and lose our guard. It could be that Burke is getting close to the time when the curse becomes permanent. Perhaps he'll disappear into that mansion."

Clove fumbled her tea cup with a clatter.

Margot leaned forward with her elbows on the table. "Permanent? Can that happen?"

Thyme opened the door and called "Kitty, kitty?" At no response, she closed the door and joined them. "What's in your heart, Margot? What does Burke mean to you?"

"Shush," said Sage. "Don't put her on the spot like that."

Margot sent Sage a thankful smile. She didn't want to have to answer that just yet.

"I say we go back to the garden and check it out again," Clove said.

"Without Burke?" Margot shook her head. She wouldn't leave him out of anything again.

Sage's mouth formed a line. She cocked her head. "Consider the time. Burke should have been finished with the tournament long ago."

"He went there without us?" Margot looked at Thyme. *See? He's not changed. He still thinks he's better off on his own.*

Sage stood. "Let's you and I take a walk."

Neither Thyme nor Clove protested. *This must be serious.*

Margot grabbed her bag and followed Sage out the back door.

"We'll go up on the wall," Sage said, pointing to a staircase Margot had never seen before. When they climbed up to the wall, she said, "Burke has lived with this curse for a long time, mostly on his own. He's not trying to shut you out on purpose."

"No, I get it. He doesn't want to be a bother."

Sage smiled. "*You* wouldn't want to be a bother. He only wants a way out. He's not thinking of your feelings yet, which is part of his problem."

"If he won't let me in, how do I help him?"

A group of tourists walked by with their camera bags, and they all had to walk single file on the stairs going from one section of the wall to the next. When they were alone again, Margot said, "There are other ways to break a curse." Meaning, ways that don't rely on the couple falling in love.

"Oh?" Sage stopped and leaned against the wall, her eye watching the next group of tourists walk closer.

"I was reminded of some from the fairy tales I've been reading." *Or listening to.* "We could throw him against the wall, like the princess in *The Frog King*." Margot shrugged, knowing it was a long shot. "He turned back into a prince after that."

Sage struggled to suppress a grin. "Do you think you could lift him?"

"Could you turn him into a frog first?"

Sage shook her head.

"I could remain silent for six or seven years. The shorter time period is if I also make him a shirt of nettles. And it might help if I'm his sister. Does he have a sister?

"No sister, and we don't have that kind of time."

"Could we find a wisewoman to break the enchantment like the one in *The Lambkin and the Little Fish*? That seems the easiest."

Sage raised her eyebrows. "I am a wise woman."

"Oh."

"Well, my last idea might not be popular."

"Oh?"

"In *Brother and Sister*, once the sorceress was dead, the brother who was transformed into a fawn returned to his human form."

Margot stared out over New Town, not wanting to see Sage's face when she realized the implication.

Surprisingly, Sage laughed. "Don't let Clove hear you talk like this. She might think we're serious. Besides, she's not a sorceress."

Margot sighed. "That's all I got."

"You have more than you think. What you're lacking is patience."

They waited for the next group of tourists to pass by.

When they were alone again, Margot said, "Seems like a lot of these curses are actually character tests of some sort."

"Yes. Clove was testing the original prince, to see if he had the right strength of character to be with Beauty. When he immediately failed, she was angry. She was overly protective of Beauty and that led to a harsh test. She was even reluctant to give him the second chance, but she did."

"Tell me more about this second chance. I've not heard it explained that way before you three talked about it."

Sage started walking again. "It's not always described as such by the fairy tale historians. Clove gave the prince a white rose when he transformed into the beast and told him it would guide him to value true beauty." Sage's mouth turned down disapprovingly. "Hardly instructive, but he worked it out."

"How?"

"By caring for the rose, keeping it alive, the prince learned to pay attention and nurture something other than himself. As long as he kept the rose alive, he had hope. He nurtured it into a beautiful bush, and in its enchanted state, it bloomed year-round. Understandably, the young prince was overly protective about that rosebush. Belle's father found out how much. Then when Belle came along, she awakened him to loving someone else. Truly loving her."

"And that was supposed to be the end of it?"

"Yes. The last few generations of descendants have all been girls. They all lived normal lives."

"Until Burke."

Sage paused before she answered. "And that leads us to Burke. What a shock he was to the family."

"What is his second chance?"

"The second chance has already been used up. Clove didn't give Burke a test, so she can't give him a second chance."

"That sounds ominous."

Sage nodded. "It's more serious than we've been letting on."

Oh, I know that. She was *this close* to telling Sage about her dream. Although, walking with Sage made the fear disappear, like she shouldn't be afraid of whatever was taunting her.

"Seems like Burke might get a second chance in the rose garden. That bush is growing now."

"Yes, the rose garden. Do you know the significance of that?"

Margot shook her head.

"It's quite romantic, really. The prince planted the garden himself for Beauty. It was the first thing he'd ever built with his own two hands. He found out all her favorite roses, favorite colors, and then imported as many as he could find from other lands. On their first anniversary, he blindfolded her and led her down into the garden. The first inkling she got was the fruity scent of roses rising up over the hedgerows.

"The prince had demonstrated love to Beauty before that, but to watch the two of them—Beauty exploring the garden, and Beast sharing in her pleasure, was a happy conclusion for us all. Well. We thought it was a happy conclusion. Little did we know what was to come."

Sage pursed her lips and thought. "I don't know of any second chance for Burke, but it seems like there should be one."

"A little more fairy-tale magic couldn't hurt, could it?" Margot herself would love to see what else the fairies could do, so she was pushing to see if Sage would agree. "To create a second chance for him?"

"Mixing fairy magic with human actions or intentions doesn't always produce the desired results. No, we use our gifts sparingly. We're not to interfere if we can help it."

"But Thyme—"

Sage held up her hand to cut her off. "If we can help it. And what Thyme did for you was merely extend an invitation. You took it from there. Just like you need to do now."

CHAPTER 29

Margot left Sage standing on the city wall and walked by herself to the garden. She suspected the fairies would not stay away for long, but that Sage was giving her a chance to see Burke alone.

At the opening to the garden, she paused and took a deep breath. She'd decided to wait and see what Burke said to her before rushing headlong into any of her theories or telling him about the dream she'd had. He'd lived with the curse and was more motivated than she was to end it.

He looked up when she entered. Wearing his red jousting tunic, he sat on the bench, elbows on knees and his head resting on his hands. He stood.

"Bonjour." She walked to him and he wrapped her in his arms. *The huggable shirt.* Margot squeezed back and buried her face in his shoulder. He was solid and real and not a dream. He released her way too soon.

"*Ici.*" Burke held her hand and brought her over to the rosebush. Several buds had burst now, and the fragrance was intoxicating.

"Try something with me. I can make le château appear and it stays for five minutes each time. Do you want to go inside?"

"You waited for me?"

He nodded. "You need to be here, too." He looked at her with a hopeful expression, then immediately jabbed his finger hard onto a thorn. He wasn't messing around, nor was he giving her time to think about going inside the original hunting mansion.

They waited, and after a moment, the trees and walls began to fade, replaced by the carefully manicured gardens of the past. When the château slowly appeared, on impulse, Margot jabbed her finger on another thorn. *Ouch*. She didn't want to leave anything to chance. If Burke was getting in that house, so was she.

He squeezed her hand, and they ran, not taking their eyes off the mansion. With each step, the gravel path formed solid beneath their feet, and the hedgerows beside them grew a brighter, deeper green.

"But the fairies," Margot said at the garden boundary.

"They'll guess where we've gone."

Gone. She hesitated, pulling back on his hand. "Will we come back?"

"You don't have to do this."

He started to let go of her hand, but she grabbed onto him with both hands. After all, she was the one who'd wanted to live a fairy-tale life since she was a child. Of course, that was before she realized what that might feel like.

"You're not leaving me behind," she said.

He leaned over and kissed her forehead. "Thank you." He let out a breath that betrayed how nervous he was. Again, her heart opened more for him.

The vision never wavered, as they passed the place where the garden ended, nor after they'd crossed the area where the city walls were today. Soon they were standing before the flight of stairs going up to the front door. The mansion was large, and Margot could see where they later added on the chapel and other rooms that would turn it into a full-fledged castle. The building in front of them now was a striking country home with large windows, ivy climbing the walls, and an inviting front door with a lion knocker.

"I can't believe we've gotten this far," Burke said.

They looked at each other and then at the same time placed a foot on the first step. It held, and then they raced up the remaining distance, laughing.

Margot waited for Burke to open the door. This was his heritage, and he should be the one to see where it went first. Plus, she didn't want to be the one to do anything to make the vision disappear again.

The doorway was dark, but Burke entered and Margot followed right at his heels. They were greeted by the smell of old furniture polish and cold air.

The door shut ominously behind them, and Margot whirled around to try the door handle. It was locked. She jiggled and pushed, but it held fast. Her heart rate spiked.

"Burke?"

He added his weight to the door, but he couldn't make it open either.

Margot heard the fairies arriving on the other side of the door. She looked through the beveled glass that lined each side of the doorway. The three fairies lined up on the porch.

Sage reached for the door, but she couldn't open it either.

"Thyme. What did you do?" Sage turned her piercing gaze at the other fairy.

Thyme looked unrepentant. "It worked the first time. Trust me. It'll work again. Don't worry children. The house will be friendly to you."

Clove grabbed Thyme's arms. "You impulsive thing," she said. "Unlock it."

"I can't. Not until they're ready. So, you can yell at me all you want, but it's a done deal."

"Haven't you learned anything from me in all these years?" Clove said. "Especially now. It's a different time and place. Margot has no idea of curses and fairies and beasts. Especially of beasts. You're the one who's gone too far this time."

Margot got a sinking feeling in the pit of her stomach. Clove knew she was comfortable with Burke, even when he grew a little beast-like. Why would she be so angry at Thyme?

"Check for another door." Margot called out. "Or a window that opens?" As much as she wanted to explore this magical house, she also wanted to know how they could leave again. But while she was speaking, the fairies faded away.

"Sage? Clove? Thyme? Are you there?" Margot pounded the door.

"They're gone," Burke said. "We're on our own now."

"For how long?" Margot asked.

He shrugged. "Until it's done, I guess. One way or another I'm leaving this house a human or a beast. Shall we explore?"

"Yes! I'll start here." Margot entered the first room on the right where she'd seen a flower arrangement through the window. Burke turned to explore the room on the left.

This first room appeared to be a parlor with several cozy seating areas. The flowers that had caught her eye were a mix of the summer blooms growing in the gardens outside: gladiolas, asphodel, and sprigs of Queen Anne's lace.

Even though the room gave off a lived-in feeling, the hairs on her arm prickled. She strove for the window and tried to open it, first by pushing up, and then by sliding it sideways. She repeated this with all the remaining windows in the room. Nothing. She was about to call to Burke when she looked through the window to the outside. It was snowing. In summer. In France.

"Burke?"

"What is it?" he called out from the other room.

"Is it snowing outside your windows?" There was something odd about the way Burke spoke. She couldn't quite place her finger on it.

There was a bench near one of the windows, so Margot got up on her knees to watch the big icy flakes falling. And she thought living in a medieval walled city for the summer was surreal.

"Yes, it's snowing on this side, too." Burke's voice was louder, like he'd come into the room. Something about his speech niggled at her. She turned around and stared at the beast standing inside the doorway. It was wearing Burke's clothes, but it didn't look like Burke. It was half Burke and half something else. The something else was growing hair at a phenomenal rate, as well as muscles and claws. He leaned casually against the door frame, scratching all over, as if the only thing wrong was that he was itchy.

"Burke? You're becoming the beast."

He swung his arms forward and examined the changes taking place in his body. His hands started shaking. Reddish-brown hair now covered all his skin, and the gray claws that were his fingernails began to curl. His feet grew and busted out of his sneakers.

Pain flashed across his face. He dashed out of the room. "Stay there!"

"What's going on?"

"I thought it couldn't get worse, but I'm turning into the beast for real now?" He groaned as if in agony.

Margot's throat went dry. What if her dream had been a glimpse of the future, and Burke turned into a real beast?

"You're afraid of me," he said. "I can smell your fear." He stepped back into the doorway, and Margot automatically recoiled.

"I won't hurt you," he said, his voice deeper still. He moved out of view again.

"I know," she said, but it was hard to convince her body to ignore her initial reaction.

"I'll be across the hall while we figure out what just happened," he said. Then he gasped.

"Are you okay?"

"Sure. I will be." His voice indicated otherwise. "You need time to get used to me like this."

"I'm more used to it than you realize," she confessed. "I've seen glimpses. But only because I knew what to look for. I'm sure no one else noticed." But her words caught in her throat. That dream.

"I'll let you know when it's over." He shut her door so gently, she barely heard the click.

They remained in separate rooms while each came to grips with this latest change. Margot paced. Trapped in a castle with a beast. A kind beast, one she knew, but, *whoa*. A beast.

Windows sealed shut. Front door wouldn't open.

There might be more doors to the outside, but she instinctively felt they'd all be locked, too. No, this was another step in the curse. All they had to do was work together to figure out what to do next. Besides, even if she made it outside, she wouldn't be able to return to the walled city. She held her hand up to the glass, watching the snow fall lightly on the rose garden. Where were the fairies? Could they undo what Thyme had done to lock them in this place?

"Margot?" Burke's voice came faintly through the walls. She pictured him as the boy working on the computer in the back of the store. The boy who was teaching her to ride a horse. The red knight, strong and confident at the tournament, who used all his energy to contain himself in front of the tourists at the castle.

"Yes?" Too quiet. "Yes?" she said louder, moving closer to the door separating them.

"I think it's slowing down. The transformation."

"Good. That's good. Let me see you. I don't mind." And she

didn't. No matter what her dream was, her friend Burke was on the other side of the door. She knew him.

There was a slight bump on the door, like he'd rested his forehead on the wood. She put her hand up to where the noise had come from. "You won't let me see you?" she said.

"Not yet."

"I can hear you breathing." She tried to make her voice sound light and playful so he wouldn't think he scared her. It sounded like a wild beast caged behind the door, worse than any slobbering dog. The sounds and smells were never mentioned in the fairy tale. She'd be able to handle any triple-horror drive-in night after this.

"Sorry. I'll try to be quieter."

The sound faded as he must have gone back across the hall.

Margot continued to explore the room. There was an oversize armchair near a side table. The simple gold candelabra on the table gave the space a cozy-reading-nook kind of feel.

Before she could sit, a large shadow darkened the window and then moved past with amazing speed. Margot's heart beat hard against her chest. "Burke? Are you still inside the house?"

"Yes."

"Something's outside. And it's big."

CHAPTER 30

"What did you see out there?" Burke's voice had gotten deeper, more resonant. More growly.

She shuddered. Not at Burke's new sound, but at what was outside. She was having trouble coming up with the words to describe what she'd seen. It was more the feeling she got when she saw the shadow than the shadow itself.

A tree branch flailing in the wind might make her jump, and then she'd laugh at her own skittishness, but this was different. Her core grew cold thinking about what was out there. It was the same reaction she had in her last dream.

"I saw a dark shadow. It moved...fast." She backed away from the bank of windows, returning to the door separating herself from Burke. She couldn't look away from the window or the other door at the end of the room that she hadn't had time to open yet.

If anything came into the room, she'd run out to the foyer where Burke was. *Foyer.* French? Even when she was scared, she couldn't help but compare languages.

"This shadow. Did it move like a person or an animal?" Burke asked.

"I don't know. It was fast, and I only saw it out of the corner of my eye."

"Stay there," Burke said. "I'll check it out."

"No! Don't. You might get hurt."

Burke laughed sardonically. "Have you seen me lately? I think I'll be all right."

Margot started to open the door separating them, but Burke shut it closed.

"Not yet. Stay there and let me find out what's going on."

"Be careful."

She put her ear to the door and listened to Burke trying to get out the front exit. He rattled the handle, but it was still locked.

Thump. Thump. He must be throwing himself at the door.

"Don't break it," she called out. "I don't want what's out there to come in here. As long as it's outside, we're fine. Like when bears wander into my yard back home in Washington; we let them be, and they go away."

"You think it's a bear?"

It was way bigger than a bear. "It could be something like a grizzly. A very large grizzly." But bears, in her experience, didn't move that fast. They liked to lumber around and explore.

"You don't think it was Clove or the others?" Burke said. "They might look different in this world."

The vibe she got from outside was not that of a fairy or a curious animal. More like a wolf stalking its prey. "No. It wasn't any of the fairies."

"Check outside again. What do you see out there?" Burke asked.

"From here? Nothing. I'll get closer."

"I'll look out the windows in this room, too."

Margot slid along the wall, trying to stay hidden from view of the outside. When she reached the curtains, she draped the thick brocade material across her body like a shield before she peeked through the edge of the window.

Night was setting in while the snow continued to fall. There were no streetlights to shed light on what lurked outside. The shrubs near the window glistened with their covering of fresh snow. But beyond that was darkness. The moon and stars blocked out by the clouds. Pinpoints of light began to shine one by one, reflected in the glass.

Margot whirled around. All the candles flickered to life. The large chandelier above, the wall sconces, and several along the windows.

"Hello? Is someone there?" Her voice was barely above a whisper.

Silence.

Burke breathing. He was back.

"Burke? Is that you?" She wanted to be sure of him.

"Yes, it's me."

"All the candles have been lit." The room had a rosy glow to it as the light reflected off the burgundy furnishings.

"Same out here. I looked through the windows but didn't see anyone outside. Nothing is moving out there."

"Good." Good. But what was that shadow? And how did the candles get lit when she wasn't looking?

"I closed all my curtains," Burke said. "You should do the same."

"Right." Margot shored up her courage and raced around the room covering up the windows. The thick curtains engulfed the room with satisfying warmth. She no longer felt exposed and hoped that wasn't a false feeling.

She stood by the single door at the far side of the room. It was barely noticeable, made of the same mahogany of the surrounding wall. With her hand on the handle, Margot listened. When she heard nothing, she slowly turned the handle. It, too, was locked. It was hard to tell if it was another room or a closet.

She thought of the dream she'd had. A creature in the forest, not Burke. But now Burke was actually turning into a beast. Had she had a premonition about him? Or was the shadow something sinister?

She returned to the double doors separating them. "I meant to tell you something when I found you in the garden, but then we were pricking our fingers on the thorns and getting trapped inside fairy-tale mansions. I wish I'd taken the time, but with all the excitement I got distracted. I'm sorry, but you're not going to like it."

"Sounds serious."

"Yes. I might have been able to stop you from turning into a beast."

He was quiet for a moment. "What is it?"

"While you were at the tournament, I took a nap." She pressed her hands together. "And I had a dream. A nightmare, really, of a beast. I knew it couldn't be you, but what if it was a premonition and I dreamed of who you would become? If I had told you, we would have gone away from the garden instead of coming here."

"No," he said without hesitation. "Nothing would have stopped me. I almost didn't wait for you. This isn't on you. Tell me about the dream."

"It was creepy. I didn't see him, but he made my skin crawl."

"Well, there you go, it wasn't me. I don't make your skin crawl, do I?"

He sounded unsure.

Margot shook her head, even though he couldn't see her. No, her skin reacted to him, but by blushing and tingling. "No, you're right. Nothing about this dream could ever be you."

"Go on."

"He said, 'You aren't here, but you are coming to me.' And that 'I don't have you yet, but I will soon.' What if he's out there?"

"What did the fairies say about the dream?"

Margot bit her lip. She had wanted to tell Burke first. "I hadn't told them yet." She regretted that now.

"I'm sorry I dragged you into this. We'll just have to be careful.

If I do become...what you dreamed. A beast. Do whatever you need to do so I don't hurt you."

"I don't think—"

"We don't know. But I want to tell you now, while I'm still myself that you shouldn't worry about me. If you find a way home, and I'm not myself anymore, you need to go."

"You won't—"

"Just agree, please."

"Okay. If I find a way home, I'll take it." She didn't like agreeing, but saw his point. They didn't know what they didn't know.

"I was meant to come here," he said. "This summer, it was like someone flipped an hourglass and all the sand is running out. This is my last shot; I know it is." There was another thump on the door like he was leaning against it. "Margot, what if I brought you here to something dangerous?"

She didn't want to think about what might lurk outside for her. "I've wanted a fairy-tale adventure my whole life. You wouldn't have been able to hold me back if you tried."

"Thank you."

"What do you think it is...outside?"

"Along with the traditional story of *La Belle et la Bête*, my family tells one of a beast who stayed a beast. There was no redemption for him. I can only assume that is my fate if..." Burke became quiet.

"That won't happen to you." Margot said. "So, what should we do next?"

"Wait to see if I ever finish changing?" Burke sounded tired.

Margot cringed. "I'm sorry. This is probably scarier for you than it is for me. Talk about puberty."

She listened closely, and Burke rewarded her with a chuckle. "Yeah. It's something else. There's one thing nice about being locked inside a spooky mansion, though."

"Yeah? What's that?"

"It's just us, with no one watching. No expectations. I like that."

Margot smiled. "Me too." She sat on the floor facing the door and hugged her legs. "So, what did you want to talk about?" She wouldn't push him to let her see how he had changed, but she didn't want to be separated from him in this odd house, even if Thyme said the house was friendly.

Several minutes passed and neither spoke. Margot couldn't think of a single interesting topic to take their minds off what was happening.

Finally, Burke said, "We could talk about the weather."

She laughed. "Why is it so awkward to talk now?"

"I know. Let's pretend I call you on the phone, like a normal guy calls a normal girl. Your dad answers, and I stumble through the awkwardness of asking for you."

Margot smiled. "Then I take the phone and stretch the cord all the way to my room and shut the door. We've got one of those really long phone cords. And then I say, Hello? This is Margot."

Burke didn't answer.

"Hello?" Her voice reached out through the door. What if that thing sneaked into the house and got him? She rose up on her knees, listening.

"Hi. It's Burke. I start off kind of nervous, but then act all cool."

Margot scooted to the door and leaned with her back against it, so she would be closer to him. "Burke who? I can play the cool game, too."

"No games. I'm the Burke who keeps to himself, trying not to bother anyone, but somehow still ticking people off."

Is that how he sees himself? "You kind of stand out." How could she explain it to him?

"Not in a good way. I'm always bracing for a disapproving look. Or for one of the guys to challenge me outside the arena. I don't know what everyone's problem is."

"Someone told me you act like you're the king and want them to play the part of the peasants."

Burke was quiet.

"Is that the case?"

"Well. I do live in the castle. I'm responsible for bringing in tourists for the joust. I treat it more seriously than they do, that's all."

"You wondered. I told you."

"If that's the problem, why is it worse this summer? They should be used to it."

"That I can explain to you. Sage told me the guys in town are reacting to your, um, animal magnetism." She fanned her face. "Wrong choice of words, your heightened charisma because of the curse."

Burke sucked in a sharp breath.

"What was that? Are you okay?"

"Growing pains. Sorry." His voice was strained.

Margot didn't mask the alarm in her voice. "You're still changing?" Just how beastly was he going to get? "Let me see you."

"Not yet. I'm assuming I'll stop changing at some point, and then you can look."

"I know it's you. I don't care what you look like on the outside."

"You say that without seeing me. I can't stand to see my body mutate like this. I can't imagine how scary my face looks."

"I don't know how I can break this curse," Margot said.

"Don't feel like you have to. It's my problem, not yours."

"That's where you're wrong. It's kind of my problem now, too." The candles around the room flickered cheerily, lit by some unknown force. She and Burke were in another world now. The two of them trapped in a house with something unknown outside.

They were both quiet for a while and Margot started to get

tired. She leaned her head against the wall. "Please stay by the door. I don't want to be alone."

"I'm not going anywhere, Margot. And I won't let anything hurt you."

CHAPTER 31

*T*hey spent the night separated by the double door. After having agreed to take shifts sleeping so one could be on the lookout for anything strange, Margot tried to fall asleep first, but she couldn't.

However, she must have fallen asleep at some point, since she had a crick in her neck from where she'd been lying on a stiff pillow she'd snagged from a chair. And she'd curled up into a tight ball as the temperature dropped through the night. She could have slept on a love seat, but refused to leave her place by the door. She wanted to be as close to Burke as he would let her.

In the light of day, she wasn't so scared to look outside. She pulled back one of the curtains to let in the sun. The world outside was fresh, crisp, and clear with blinding snow coating the landscape like frosting on a wedding cake. No telltale footprints marred the smooth ground, so whatever was prowling last night was not prowling this morning. What a relief.

The kid in her wanted to run outside and build a snowman. She glanced down at her summer-weight clothes. *I'm trapped in a fairy tale wearing stirrup pants. Not the best style choice I've ever made.*

First, Margot was spending her summer in a walled city from

medieval times, walking on cobblestones and living a stone's throw from a castle. And now she was locked inside a medieval mansion with a beast on one side of the door and snow—in summer—right outside.

She went back to the double doors and called out, "Are you awake?" There was no answer, so she opened the door a crack. The hall was empty, so Margot quickly left her room and tried the front door. Still locked.

She turned around and almost ran into Burke. He'd grown a head taller and almost a person wider. Burke, in full beast form, had the face of a lion and the body of a bear. His stormy gray eyes had grown larger and were rimmed in black with a splash of white fur underneath, the way lions' eyes were made to transfix their prey in their stare. His nose had elongated into a snout with whiskers, and his hair was more of a mullet now than ever before. As for his body, well, it was big and bearlike, but...shaggy underneath his torn tunic. And he emitted a strong, strong odor. He rubbed his eyes as if he had just woken up.

Margot's body filled with adrenaline. She looked on in fright, knowing it was Burke under that beastly exterior, and that he'd never hurt her, but it was hard to turn off what she was seeing and not let her body do what the adrenaline rush wanted her to do. *Run. Run fast.*

"Good morning," she murmured as she involuntarily took a step back, brushing up against a coat stand holding a winter jacket her size.

He held up a hand in what was likely an effort to reassure her, but it only made him look about to pounce.

"Sorry. Why don't you go explore the castle while I sit in that room?" he said. "I've looked around this floor and we're alone. Call out if you need me, and I'll come."

Margot glanced inside the room opposite hers. It was filled with spindly legged furniture that wouldn't hold him and fine pottery on almost every surface. The expression *bull in a china shop* came to mind.

"That room wasn't built for you," she said, trying to lighten the mood. "We can explore together. I don't mind how you look." She said all this while staring at a dainty armchair, not at him.

More than concern for the furnishings, she was afraid to search the house on her own. She'd learned enough from horror movies to know that you don't go anywhere alone—especially upstairs or downstairs—and nowhere alone in a house you've been locked into.

She looked back at him and swallowed. "You have fangs now."

"Yes. They're uncomfortable. It's hard for me to close my mouth."

"I'm sorry. I shouldn't have blurted that out."

"Don't apologize. Just get used to me."

"I am. I will be. Why don't you show me around, and I'll follow?" It would feel less like being stalked if she was the one following. If she focused on his feet, he wasn't so scary.

"If that's what you want. Your accent has gotten better," he said. "Are you speaking French fluently, or am I understanding English?"

Margot paused and spoke purposefully in English. "You're harder to understand with your new beast accent."

He shook his head. "Go back to speaking French, please."

So, the castle turned Burke into a beast and Margot into a Francophone? "Hey," she said, "Do I look like Beauty now?" She examined her hands, but they looked the same. *Where is a mirror when a girl wants one?*

"You have always been beautiful," Burke said with a growl. Like, literally with a growl.

Her face warmed at the compliment, but her body tensed at the voice. She had better get a handle on Burke's transformation. ASAP.

"I'm ready to explore," she said. "In the fairy tale, the beast's mansion was enchanted. There must be more to this place than candles that light themselves at night."

Burke grunted noncommittally and led her down a dim hallway. The wool carpet absorbed their footsteps, and he rapidly pointed out rooms as they zipped passed them: green room, paisley room, striped room, empty closet.

"Good thing you're a knight and not a tour guide," she said. "Slow down. I'd like to see what's inside."

"What are you looking for to help us out of here? I haven't found a crowbar or a magic portal back to Chapais. I can tell you everything that's in the rooms. With my new eyesight, I don't need much light."

"I have nothing in mind." She didn't want to explain how she wanted to see everything to experience it. Her friend Amy told her to experience France, and for the first time, what was in Margot's head matched up with what she was living. She was living a fairy tale. She wanted to live it all. At least, the fun parts. "Have you found anything magical? Anything to entertain us while we figure this out?"

He grunted and then led her around several corners until he stopped at a large room. After he ducked into the doorway, she waited to give him time to get farther inside before she entered. His smell was getting worse. She was starting to get used to his wild look, at least from the back, but that smell!

He'd brought her to a theater with a dark wood stage and several rows of plush chairs.

"Oh. I didn't mean for us to be literally entertained, but interesting."

Margot sat three seats in, wondering how to signal a show to begin. When nothing happened, Burke ran up the aisle, practically giving her a heart attack, and jumped up on the stage with a loud *thump. Aisle? That has to be of French origin, too.*

Burke turned his back, which wasn't as scary as seeing his face with the fangs. Before she could ask him what he was doing, he struck an Elvis pose, with one arm up in the air. Then he started singing. In terribly accented English.

At first, Margot stared, shocked at what she was seeing. Then she started giggling. Burke was singing the lyrics from the *Summer of Love* cassette tape that she'd left in his car. Did he even know what he was saying?

Suddenly, music flooded the theater, and he sang to the actual songs. Margot *whooped* in encouragement. He looked like a beast, but he moved like Burke. Athletic and sure of himself.

By the time he'd gotten to "Walk Like an Egyptian," she was laughing so hard she was crying. He didn't seem to mind, though. He glanced over his shoulder and then kept going. Did he realize the contrast his beastly form made with the pop tunes he sang?

"This is better than a lip-syncing contest," she said, wiping at her eyes. "So funny. You're killing me."

When he finished his routine, she gave him a standing ovation, clapping as enthusiastically as if she'd been at a sold-out concert.

At that point, he turned around and his fierceness made her body react in fright. She edged out of the row of seats and walked backward up the aisle. Instinctively, she kept herself from turning and running. She didn't want to trigger a natural animal reaction in him, the way a lion would dart after a gazelle.

"I'm sorry," he said, turning around. "See? I'm too beastly even for you."

"No. No, you're not." Margot, in control again, walked toward him, embarrassed at her reaction to his new face. Beauty never seemed to have that reaction, willingly eating dinner with Beast every night. Conversing with him like he was a normal person.

"It was all you could do to keep from running away." He kept his back to her, his shoulders hunched in discouragement.

"Hey, look at me." When he didn't turn around, she kept talking. "It'll take some getting used to, but I'm not afraid. I'm not. I know who you are, and you've never done anything to hurt me."

He slowly turned, but didn't look convinced. For a beast, his face was quite expressive. His stormy gray eyes crackled with emotion.

She climbed the steps onto the stage. "Let's keep exploring." She held her hand out, but Burke didn't take it.

"Thyme, you've been fairy-headed in the past, but this takes the éclair." Sage stormed around Suzette's apartment, fists waving.

Thyme sat with her feet up on a cushion and a plate of chocolate brownies balanced on her stomach. "Me? What about Clove? There was that one princess who lived near a well. Remember her? What Clove did then was far worse."

Clove whirled her attention on Thyme. "Not helping."

Thyme shrugged and reached for her teacup.

"I don't know why you're so angry," Thyme said. "Things are finally happening. Burke has been waiting for something to change all these years. Now something has changed. You should congratulate me."

Clove stood beside Sage, creating a united front against Thyme. "You have no idea the severity of what you've done."

"No, you're angry that you never thought of it. You like to run things your way."

"I gave that prince a worthy test and second chance, and you saw how happy he and Beauty were. A romance for the fairy tale books, that one. You've no right to criticize."

"Yes, and now that I've trapped Burke and Margot together, you're annoyed you didn't think of it first."

Clove began to pace. "Margot has been an innocent in all this; her only connection was that her ancestors came from this town. Now she's trapped in that house, and we've no way to see what's going on in there. I've got to get her out."

"No!" Thyme stood, the brownies going flying.

"Why not? She'll get hurt."

"She'll be fine. It's just the old house. Nothing can happen to them in the mansion other than Burke will have time to overcome his selfish pride. He was running out of time here, and you both know it."

Clove bit her lip, like she was trying to hold something in.

Thyme cocked her head. "It is just the old house, isn't it?"

Clove walked away to the window and looked out at the ferns on the neighbor's window sill. She sighed. "I hate not being able to see what's going on."

Thyme padded over to her handbag. "You've forgotten. We've got the mirror." She pulled out an antique gold mirror with a family crest on the handle.

"You took it from the castle. Why didn't you say so?" Sage asked.

"I didn't want to interrupt Clove's tirade. She seemed to be having a grand time of it."

Clove made a face at Thyme and tried to grab the mirror. Thyme, in a rare demonstration of dexterity, moved the mirror out of reach. "It's my turn to hold it." Once Sage and Clove nodded their agreement, she held it out so all three could see, herself getting the best view.

"Show me Margot."

The mirror flickered alive and revealed a close-up of Margot in a dark room; her face lit from a distant glow. Tears flowed down her cheeks, and she wiped her hand across her face.

Sage grabbed the mirror. "Margot is crying. Burke wouldn't… If he hurts her…" Sage let the words hang in the air near Thyme.

Thyme leaned in, watching Margot's shoulders shake, her cheeks glistening in the dim light. "No. That's not right. She's supposed to be falling in love, like Beauty did. The mansion appeared for them." Thyme's voice came out stretched thin.

Sage put a hand on her hip. "Margot is not Beauty. They live in completely different time periods. There is no way to recreate the exact circumstances as before."

Thyme looked away. "I thought…" She sat on the couch. Her sharp, concentrated brow melted to a confused, lost look.

"And Clove?" Sage said. "Is there something you need to tell us about the house?"

CHAPTER 32

$\mathcal{T}$his sensitive beastly version of Burke was in no way like the beast in Margot's dream. At least that question was completely resolved in her mind.

The sooner she got used to his new look, the better. Margot forced herself to watch Burke as he exited the theater. The hunch in his shoulders, the wild, wild hair. The smell. It was hard to get past the rank odor, but she could do it for his sake.

She caught up to him and slipped her hand around his arm. He didn't pull away, so she took that as a small victory for both of them.

"What should we see next?" she said.

While everything was museum-beautiful, so far, there had been no signs of life. No talking creatures to guide them and help them figure out what to do. Thyme wanted them in here for a reason, and it would be nice to know what that was.

The torches in the wall sconces fired to life as they approached and dimmed as they passed, so the house was aware of their presence and didn't seem to mind them exploring.

Margot kept hoping one of the fairies would pop in to check

on them, but none of them had. Was Thyme barring the rest from entering, or could they really not get in?

Margot couldn't decide if she should be angry at Thyme, or thankful. Thankful, because in a way, living in a fairy tale had been a dream of hers ever since she'd made that childhood request at the wishing well.

As long as the fairies didn't let things get too far out of control, maybe Margot could enjoy her confinement in the mansion with Burke. Trouble was, in the depth of her heart, Margot didn't trust Clove. The fairy's one and only goal was to free Burke. Not Margot. Question was, would Clove throw Margot under the bus to save Burke?

"I haven't been upstairs yet," Burke said. "This staircase looks like the one that goes up to my apartment in Chapais."

"Your apartment might be a portal?"

"It's possible."

They climbed single file up the stone staircase. Burke's large feet had already busted out of his shoes and his feet—paws?— hung way out over each step.

At the top, they walked down one hallway, then another. Some doors were locked, and others led to sitting rooms of various persuasions. Blessedly, one of the rooms was a bathroom, and Margot sent Burke on ahead while she made use of the facilities. She washed her hands in a regular faucet, not a bucket or a hand pump. This place became curiouser and curiouser. If the mansion had modern plumbing, they hadn't gone back in time.

Margot found Burke exploring a music room decked out with a baby grand piano, a cello, and a violin.

"Do you think this is a parallel universe?" she asked, absently plucking a string on the cello. "A world existing beyond what we can see?"

"Does it matter where we are? I'd rather focus on getting back to Chapais."

"Do you play?" Margot asked, not commenting on Burke's insistence they find a way home when he was the one who suggested they go into the château in the first place.

Burke headed for the door. "No, I've never had lessons. You?"

"If you forced me, I could play something simple on the violin."

"I wish I knew what we were looking for," he said. "Too much has changed from my place. I can't tell where things are here."

Torch lights flickered to their left and illuminated a tower entrance.

"This way," Burke said.

The stairs ended at a small landing and a wooden door. A sign hung above the door: MARGOT'S APARTMENT.

Margot's jaw dropped. "Just like in the story!" Burke didn't seem as impressed.

He poked his head in. "Huh. Do you think I get a room, too?"

She laughed. "The whole mansion is yours. Haven't you read the story?"

She hadn't followed Burke into the room as there was only one entrance, and he was standing in it. Her fight-or-flight instincts remained high no matter what kind of running conversation she kept in her head. *It's just Burke. He's the same guy inside. He won't hurt you.*

"Excuse me." She was dying to get inside her room.

"Oh, right."

She pressed against the wall to allow Burke space to leave. He stood out of her way, disbelief etched on his expressive beastly face. *Is he jealous the house gave me a room?*

She held her breath while he passed, and he noticed.

"Do I smell?" He checked his arm pit.

Margot marveled as his expression changed to embarrassment. This beast showed every emotion. Burke was always so hard to read, but now his emotions were exposed for the world. It was endearing and helped to counteract his beastliness. How was it possible for him to be both beastly and adorable at the same time?

He cleared his throat. "Why don't you settle in while I go see what's in the kitchen. I'm...hungry."

Burke started down the stairs, and she watched as his shadow passed the curve in the tower.

His shadow didn't scare her. She was adjusting. But would her acceptance be enough?

With a conflicted heart, Margot explored her apartment. The pale-yellow room was lavishly decorated with fairy tale art painted directly onto the walls. The scene from Sleeping Beauty that she loved so much was recreated here, the young princess reaching out to touch the spindle. "Don't do it," Margot whispered.

Who was she to talk? She jabbed her finger on a thorn to follow Burke into the château.

Her room contained several heavy pieces of furniture, including a large wardrobe, two dressers, and a vanity.

The vanity was covered with more makeup and curling irons than Margot knew what to do with. "Did you think I brought Amy with me?" she asked the house.

A stack of records leaned against the wall and a record player sat on a narrow table. Beside that was...a CD player! "No way. Those are so expensive."

She turned a complete circle, feeling something was missing. "Do you have my books?" The room seemed so empty with no books. A door popped open beside the wardrobe, revealing a walk-in library.

Inside were all her childhood favorites. Every book she'd ever read. "Are there new books, too?" She waited for another door to pop open, but nothing did. "Okay, I'll keep looking."

Most of the light shone in from a large arched window near the bed. She crossed the thick area rug to arrive at the window seat, where she eagerly clambered up and looked out the window.

She expected to see more manicured gardens, but was surprised by a hedgerow maze laid out before her.

"Oh, I've always wanted to do one of those."

She tried to trace the pattern with her eye, but it was a large maze and the snow-capped hedges began to blend, so she lost sight of the path.

The rest of her view included the stables to her left and the grand causeway to the mansion to her right. The causeway was a long, elevated gravel road lined with tall yew trees, evenly spaced. If she was correct, the rose garden would be on the other side of that, viewed best from the tower where the master suite must be.

All the snow was pristine. Not a rabbit, a squirrel, person or beast had left a single track. That gave her great relief. If something was outside stalking in front of the house, she'd be able to see evidence from here.

Satisfied the house wasn't about to be imminently attacked, Margot turned her attention to her room. The canopy bed was so large, it had a stair step to help her climb up. This she did with ease and flounced on the mattress. *Ah, yes. This would do.* She stared up at the white rose pattern embroidered onto the fabric, wondering if she would sleep here tonight. Sage and Clove might have figured a way to rescue her and Burke by then. But if the fairies didn't... *What's this?*

Margot pulled out a thin book from underneath her pillow. The cover was dark brown leather embossed with stamped filigrees but no title. She opened it and read the inscription written in an old-fashioned fountain pen:

> *Welcome, Margot, banish fear,*
> *You are queen and mistress here;*
> *Speak your wishes, speak your will,*
> *Swift obedience meets them still.*

She gently traced the poem with her finger. "It's even got my name in here." She shook her head. Unbelievable. Yet here she was.

Burke cleared his throat from the hallway.

She looked up, and he was standing awkwardly in the doorway. He'd had a shower and a shave. She knew him so well she recognized the signs. But his beast nature was so strong, that all the good it had done was to tidy himself up so he looked like a groomed beast now instead of a wild thing. And he was now doused in a good amount of cologne, so that helped, too.

She smiled. "You look handsome."

Instead of giving his know-it-all Burke flip of the hair, he looked down at his feet. "Thanks. I did what I could."

Margot sat up on her bed. "Did you find your room?"

"Yes. Opposite side of the house from you. And I did a quick check of the rest of the house. The kitchen door is unlocked. It leads out to the chicken coop and then the stables beyond. Do you want to go with me, and see if we can find a way home?"

She surveyed the room one last time, the window seat in the tower, the elegant bed, the book with her name mysteriously inscribed inside. She'd only begun to explore what this house had for her. "Do we need to go home so soon?"

"I'd like to shed this beastly body as soon as I can. If we go back, I assume I'll return to normal. Getting in this house was a mistake. I was offered a choice, and I think I chose wrong."

Margot disagreed. "It's too soon to know if you chose wrong." She pointed at her name above the door. "We were expected. And the house has been welcoming."

He looked warily at her name. "I don't know if that's a good thing." He started to leave, then turned around. "Is there a long coat for you in there? I don't need one, but you will. It's snowing again."

"I never thought to look." She grinned. "Give me a minute." He backed out of the door as she closed it on him.

Fairy-tale dresses!

Margot may be comfy-all-the-way style in her regular life, but as they say, *when in Rome...*

She ran over to the standing wardrobe and flung it open. *Yes.* This was more like it. Her personalized closet had been stocked with a variety of options. From the big princess gowns like the prom dresses the Belle look-alikes wore in the costume contest, to those expensive jeans Margot would never buy for herself (could feed a hungry child for a year instead), to snow pants and boots.

"What should it be?" she murmured as she pawed through the choices. *Aha.* While normally, she'd go for the snow pants, here, she wanted to look the part. She found a long periwinkle wool gown that would have been fashionable on any Victorian teenager but with an '80s pop of color.

"Thank you," she whispered to the house. Or to the fairies. If Clove was making all this happen, she was upping her game. Clove might like her after all.

Margot quickly put on the new clothes, including a fur-trimmed coat, and then flung open the door. "Ready."

Burke looked surprised. "Are you hiding Jane Austen in there?"

"Wrong time period, but I'll forgive you this once since you seem to know who Jane Austen is. Let's find the rose garden."

CHAPTER 33

The kitchen was in the same location as the current kitchen in the castle and just as primitive. "It's strange that some things are modern, like the bathroom, but others are ancient like that hearth stove."

"The house is as messed up as I am."

Given his circumstances, she couldn't blame him for being less than thrilled. If she suddenly morphed into Big Foot, she'd be a little freaked out, too.

The door that led to the herb garden back at the castle in Chapais now led to a similar patch of garden here, covered with snow. Beyond that was the chicken coop Burke had mentioned, along with the stables and the maze.

Big fluffy flakes fell from the sky. Margot stopped not two feet out the door to lift her hands to catch them.

Burke waited for her near the chicken coop, from which muted chicken noises emerged. The snow around the small house had been cleared away and then tamped down with little chicken feet.

The château was the only thing she could see for miles, save a squat stone wall that surrounded the gardens, and beyond that were fields and a forest where the town of Chapais should be.

They couldn't walk back to the walled city because it wasn't there. What craziness was this? Did they time travel like *Back to the Future* or step into an alternate dimension like in the Narnia books?

"Burke? Even New Town is gone." He didn't comment, but continued around the house, leaving big footprints for her to follow.

The snow was almost knee deep in places, so she was thankful that he cleared a path for her. He plowed ahead and disappeared into the rose garden.

By the time she'd caught up to him, he had shaken the snow off most of the rosebushes.

"Well?" she asked. "Did you find our rosebush?"

"Take your pick. Choose any of these in the middle, here."

Disappointed, Margot looked for the bench, her point of reference, but discovered there were several benches located around the edge of the garden. Not helpful.

"What did you want to do? Prick our fingers again and see if that makes Chapais return?"

He grunted and steam came out of his nostrils.

"But nothing's changed for you yet. If we go back now, you'll be in the same place you were when we left."

"Now that I know the alternative, I'm okay with that."

Margot shook her head. "No, you aren't. Sage said you would end up becoming a beast for real." She waved her hand up and down, indicating his new form. "Like this, but in Chapais."

"Fine. Let's go for a ride, then. I'm used to going out every day."

They retraced their steps, past the hedgerow maze, and back to the stables.

Inside were two of the most beautiful horses she'd ever seen. The pretty fawn-colored one had a blond mane and gentle eyes.

The shiny black horse beside it was the largest horse Margot had ever seen, and it sported shaggy feet made for traipsing through the snow.

"Hey guys, who takes care of you?" The large one snorted and looked away, but the fawn-colored one looked at her with interest. They were impeccably groomed, the stables were warm and neat, and the horses had recently been fed. Neither seemed put off by Burke's appearance, which she found interesting.

"Hello? Is anyone out here?" She spun around, looking for any sign of life. Someone had to be caring for the animals. Was it that shadow she'd seen move so quickly last night? Clove?

Burke quietly pulled a saddle off the row of tack and began getting the horses ready for a ride. His hands were surprisingly nimble for how gangly they appeared.

"Can you ride sidesaddle?"

Flashes of every time-period TV movie she'd ever watched flashed through her mind. Women in big skirts riding gracefully with both legs on one side always looked precarious to her. "Is it hard?"

He chuckled. "I wouldn't know."

She looked down at her Victorian skirt. "Why not?" *It's a magical place. In this world, I might be a fine horsewoman.*

Soon Burke had both horses ready and brought them outside. He took the tall black draft horse while she took the reins for the fawn-colored one.

Burke plucked her out of the snow and plopped her right onto the saddle without even a hint of strain. "Steady?"

She wiggled in the saddle, then nodded.

Burke mounted his horse, and they were off.

As the beast, Burke maintained his easy way with horses. While he might lumber when he walked in the snow, he was a commanding figure on the large horse.

They started off at a walk, but when they'd cleared the yard and moved onto the causeway where much of the snow had blown off, the horses began to canter, and then broke into a run.

Margot screamed, not having ever ridden on a running horse before. She hadn't spurred hers on, but it wanted to keep up with Burke's horse.

The wind was cold and wet against her face, and the sensation was exhilarating. After they'd ridden for a while, Burke led them back to the area where the walled city should be. He stopped his horse and waited for Margot. Puffs of breath from both horse and Beast burst out in the cold.

"This is where the bookshop should be, if I figured it correctly," he said, reaching up and shaking the snow off a tree branch. He sat in the saddle surveying the land.

"Do you think it's all an illusion?" she mused aloud.

"No, this is real. The town isn't here."

Margot looked back at the mansion and the surrounding manicured landscape.

"So, this would be your family estate? All of this land?"

"Yes. Over the years they divided up the land and sold it."

"My aunt Suzette is a descendant of the original bookshop owner in the walled city."

"Yes. If she's living inside the walled city, she can prove lineage going back."

"She said something about that. What happens to the last descendant living inside the wall? Will they end up getting the whole place to themselves at night?"

Burke laughed. "I don't know. But I could live there alone as the beast. That would be some tourist attraction."

She ignored his pessimistic take. "Is that what you want? To keep living inside the walled city?"

"My parents think life inside Chapais is too constrictive. New rules say you can't build onto anything or even combine apartments. The structures must stay as they were; no more changes. And living in the castle can be awkward. There are always people around, and sometimes a tourist escapes and sneaks upstairs."

"Like groupies from America?"

He paused to smile. A sort of grimace on his lion face. It was the eyes that smiled.

"Chapais is also too small-town. Everyone knows everyone else's business. When you have a problem like mine, that is not a good thing."

"But?" she asked. It seemed like he was only giving his parent's opinion on the town.

"I like having one foot in the past. Living history. Pretending I belong in another time. Silvain is probably right to put me in my place every chance he gets. I do feel like it's my town. Just as if I were really the king. I don't mean to make everyone feel like they're my subjects."

"My aunt wants me to come work with her and eventually take over the family bookshop." She looked off into the distance, but kept him in her peripheral vision to gauge his reaction. She wanted to know his opinion, but she also didn't want to base her decision on his reaction.

"You fit in the town better than most," he said neutrally.

"Oh. Is that all?" He was hardly enthusiastic, but then again, he wasn't really listening to her anymore.

Burke turned his head and stared into the forest. His gaze pierced the air, and his nose twitched ever so slightly.

"What is it?" she whispered.

A movement in the trees caught Margot's attention. "Please be a bear," she whispered.

"Stay here. I'll go check it out."

"No way. I'm coming with you." The safest place she could be was with Burke.

"You don't understand," he said, adjusting his reins. "I smell something. I think it's blood."

"Animal?" Margot was still whispering.

Burke slowly nudged his horse forward and Margot's followed without any prompting.

They came at the woods at an angle, Burke never losing focus. Margot couldn't smell anything other than fresh, crisp air, but her horse twitched intermittently and also stayed close to the large horse.

At a small opening, Burke stopped and listened. He proceeded cautiously, brushing through branches that shook off the snow. Not far in, they came to a spot where the white snow was stained in bright red blood. Not a lot. Likely from a small animal being killed for food. The sight was a normal part of forest life, but it still sent a chill up Margot's spine.

Even Burke's horse started to get twitchy, and so Burke calmly turned them around. He kept them walking at an even pace, but Margot's heart was beating fast. Something felt off. She wanted Burke to reassure her, but he was alert and in control, watching through the trees. If he thought they needed to run the horses, he would.

When they'd cleared the trees, he relaxed his posture and let his horse take the lead. It went into a canter and returned to the stable. While Margot waited, stroking her horse, more for her comfort than its, Burke secured his horse. He came around and lifted her to the ground, barely flexing a muscle.

"Let's get you inside," he said. They were the first words either of them had spoken since the forest. He took strong, sure steps, not leaving her until she entered through the door.

"I'll see to the horses. Stay inside no matter what."

Margot wouldn't dream of going back out there. She felt safe with Burke at her side, but something he'd seen or heard or smelled had alerted him.

She closed the door, and when she turned around, saw that the kitchen table had been decked out with a spread of fruit, cheese, and a round country loaf.

Nice. When Burke returned, she'd suggest they stay inside

from now on. The creature could have the outside; they'd keep the inside. Everyone would be happy.

She couldn't even convince herself of that. No, Thyme had started them down a path to something inevitable. They had to see the story through to the end, whatever that meant.

CHAPTER 34

The snow was already filling in the tracks they'd left behind. Margot watched out the window, waiting for Burke to get safely back inside, her gaze pinned to the corner of the stables. She pictured Burke inside the shelter taking off the saddles, brushing down the horses, and then making sure they had food and water before returning.

It was taking him a long time.

"Come on, where are you?"

A chicken wandered into view, having escaped its fenced-in area. "Watch it little guy, something's in those woods." The chicken stepped gingerly on the snow as if confused about what it was walking on.

There came Burke now, and Margot's heart skipped a beat. He was okay. He also noticed the chicken and shooed it back to safety. Margot cracked up, watching a big beastly creature chasing a flapping chicken through the snow.

Chicken secured, he started returning for the house, so she ducked away from the window and found some plates for their breakfast.

"Ready to eat?" she asked.

He stomped the snow off his feet at the doorstep and came in with an armload of firewood. "Thought I'd get a fire going. It'll help you stop shivering."

"I'm not—" she started to protest, but clearly, she was cold. She kept putting her hand to her cold nose to take the chill off, and when she wasn't doing that, she was hugging herself. "A fire would be great. Thanks for noticing. There aren't any blankets around here. Don't they need blankets in the winter?"

"I don't," he said. "I barely notice the cold."

He squatted by the empty stone fireplace.

"When do you think there was a fire in there last?" Margot asked.

"Don't know." He stuck his massive head inside to look up the chimney. "The flue's open, so we should be safe to light it up." He started stacking the kindling.

"The pantry is filled with food we're used to, so we're not going to starve."

Burke sat back. "Good. I was afraid they'd want me to go hunt for our dinner."

Margot gasped. "Do you feel an urge to hunt?"

"Sorry. Poor choice of words. No. I still feel like I always have. If I don't look at myself, my hairy hands and beefy legs, I wouldn't know I had changed. Well, mostly. My senses are wacko."

"Mine, too." She wasn't joking. Her ears were constantly on alert for any sounds in the rest of the house, and her peripheral vision kept a watch on every move Burke made. Her skin prickled, and she jumped at the slightest provocation.

"Do you see any matches?"

"Up there on the mantle." Margot didn't know if the box had been there the whole time, or if it appeared when Burke had need of it.

"Could you?" he held up his beast hands.

"Sure." She struck a match and held it to some paper Burke

had scrunched up under the kindling.

Once the fire was going sufficiently, Burke held his hands—paws?—to the flames. "How's that?" he asked. "Feeling anything?"

Margot pictured Burke as the boy with the stormy gray eyes driving the convertible. The knight on the horse. The beast in front of her now, giving her a fire. He was all these things, and in all of them he was Burke, the boy who gave her fairy tales so she could learn to speak French. "I'm warming up," she said.

They sat and ate, with Burke filling out a ginormous chair that looked more like a throne. He finished off everything that Margot didn't want, then he leaned back in his chair.

"In the story, the beast asked Belle to marry him after every dinner they ate together. But, I'm not in a position to get married," Burke said apologetically. "I hope you're not expecting me to ask."

Margot tried not to smile. He was so serious. "I couldn't accept even if you asked. My dad would kill me."

"So, what would a modern-day equivalent be? It seems like we're recreating the tale here."

"Don't feel like you have to fall in love with me," Margot blurted out.

"That's not what I meant. I'm talking specifically about the marriage bit." His gaze leveled at her like he could see through her insecurities.

What was it about this house? Did it expose all their inner thoughts? She'd learned so much about the hidden parts of Burke since he took on beast form. What if he was learning just as much about her?

"I know what you meant." She got up and stood by the fire. "Not everything is the same as in the story. My dad didn't wander onto your property and pick a rose for me. I didn't swap my life for his. Your story is different. The ending might be, too."

"But that prince knew what he had to do to break the curse. That's why he kept asking."

"And you don't know how to break your curse?"

"Not specifically. Clove tells me I'm proud, and I need to learn to be less selfish."

Not fall in love? Be loved back? "Thyme implied it was more than that." *You fall in love, the curse breaks.*

"But aren't I being selfish when I try to act a certain way so I can be free of the curse? It's all in my self-interest."

"Yes. That's the risk. Whatever you do has to come from your heart." Margot didn't like the direction this conversation was taking. It was the opposite of romantic and fairy tale–like. And Burke was still wrapped up in himself. His motivations.

"Belle didn't know that the beast would turn back into a prince. She loved him as the beast," Burke said quietly.

"What are you implying?"

"Nothing. I'm only working through the logic."

Margot shook her head. "Fairy tales aren't known for their logic. They're more known for their randomness—girls turning into roses, donkeys that spit out gold, glass mountains covered in jewels." She met his gaze. "And love despite all odds."

The fire flared, shining a light on a stack of letters piled on a silver tray by the fireplace. She reached for them. They were addressed to her.

"What? We can get letters here?"

There was one from Dad. From Sage. And Amy.

"Any for me?" Burke asked.

Margot shook her head. "I'm going back to the parlor to read them."

Burke stood. "I'll build you a fire there, too."

The air grew noticeably cooler when they left the kitchen. On the way by the front door, Margot checked the lock. It held fast. "I wonder if this will unlock when we're done."

"My guess is that since we can leave the house through the kitchen door, Thyme is keeping the fairies out by locking that door."

"I'll see what Sage has to say about it."

While Burke stacked up wood, she sat on one of the love seats and tore into Sage's letter first.

Dear Margot,

Stay inside the house. Don't leave Burke's side. We're trying to get to you, but Thyme is being stubborn.

-S

"Huh."

"What is it?" Burke stood with a piece of kindling. "You look shocked."

Margot set the letter in her lap. "Sage tells me to stay inside the house and not leave your side."

He grinned. An actual grin, like he was learning to control his new muscles. And again, Margot marveled at how expressive his beast form could be.

The more humanlike he became, the more comfortable she'd gotten with him. She could look at him without her body having an adrenaline burst.

"Sounds like good advice to me," he said.

"Do you think she knows what's out there? And that's why she's so upset? When they caught us in the house, Thyme was triumphant. Sage was hard to read, as usual, but Clove was almost frantic when she couldn't get to us."

Burke shrugged. "I don't know. I'm going to look for marshmallows." He lumbered out of the room.

Margot put thoughts of Clove away for the moment and returned to the other letters. The one from her dad was filled with ball stats from the players. He seemed pretty excited about how the team was coming together.

She opened Amy's letter last. A photo fell out. Margot lifted it to the light from the window. It was a picture of Amy standing in front of the French exhibit at Expo '86 wearing an oversize navy sweatshirt with "Au Coton" printed on it. On the back of the photo, Amy had printed in neat, silver marker: *Thinking of you in France. Wearing my new Canadian sweatshirt. So comfy.*

Margot flipped the photo back around. She'd love a cozy pair of sweats right now. This house was drafty and the Victorian dress was pretty, but not ideal for a snow day. When Margot set the photo on the table, she noticed a gray sweatshirt and pants folded neatly on the love seat across from her. It was identical to Amy's in the photo.

"Did you put that there?" she asked Burke as he walked back into the room.

"Pardon?"

She shook her head. "Never mind." His hands were covered with soot. The sweatshirt was clean. *What a cool house.* "I'll be right back." She found an empty room and quickly put on the sweatshirt and pants. There was also a matching T-shirt that she layered underneath and fuzzy pink socks for her feet. *Ah, that was better.*

She returned to the parlor and curled up to read Amy's letter.

Dear Margot,

I told you this was the summer of love. How can you go to France and not be swept away? I loved reading about your chauffeur.

Margot glanced up at Burke in all his beastly glory poking at the fire, and she shook her head. *Amy has no idea.* The letter continued:

Expo 86 is incredible. I'm so glad I was able to see it. There are sixty-five pavilions and I'm going to get stamps from every one for my passport. I've been to thirty-one already! France was cool. It was decorated like the Paris airport and they talked about the fastest train in the world... Have you ridden on it? Anyway, the pavilion is number 13 in the green zone, right on the water, if you happen to make it at the end of the summer. The theme is transportation, so there's lots of that around.

Margot was still unsettled by what Burke said. She had been expecting him to turn back into handsome Burke, who she would be proud to be seen with driving in his convertible. It was almost like she was playing a fairy-tale game, and she was planning to win it.

Her heart dropped into her stomach. She had to fall in love with Burke as a beast before he could be released. That was an even higher hurdle. Of course, she could see herself loving the handsome boy who played a knight in the jousts and was a descendant of royalty. But fall in love with a beast for real?

She had assumed it was all about Burke and his motivations. This complicated things.

"So, tonight," Burke said, "meet me in the hallway before supper. Ask the house to choose something for you to wear."

Margot looked up from her letters. "Why?" *What is he up to?*

"I'll see you at sunset." He left the room.

After Burke left, Margot felt too exposed with all those windows. She gathered up her letters and returned to her room up in the tower. She stood in front of the wardrobe with its doors closed. "What should I wear tonight?" she asked it.

She waited a moment, then opened the door. A blue princess-style ball gown hung front and center. She twisted her lips and looked from the ball gown to the vanity filled with makeup and curling irons. *Oh boy.* "You don't have a makeup artist hiding behind a door, do you?"

When nothing happened, she entered her large bathroom and started to get ready.

CHAPTER 35

*T*he sunset stretched pink across the sky when Margot turned away from the window. *Burke had better be dressed up, too.* She descended the stairs and then peeked around the corner to the front hallway.

Burke stood at attention wearing a suit! He'd slicked his hair back and had an anxious look about him.

She took a breath and stepped into view. Not an expert at these sorts of things, she thought she'd done a decent job with her hair. At least, she'd back-combed it to maximum fullness.

"I knew you were a ball gown kind of guy," she said.

He met her gaze, and his eyes lit up. "For special occasions. You don't mind?"

She shook her head.

"Then follow me into the dining room."

A long table took up most of the room, but the place settings had been set at the far corner, lit by flickering candles. Crystal glasses, polished silver, and fine china plates awaited them alongside covered dishes which were giving off the most amazing smells.

"Did you cook all this?" Margot asked as Burke pulled out a chair for her to sit.

"I had a little help. What's the point of living in an enchanted house if you can't order up some fine French cuisine?"

Over chicken cordon bleu they talked about their childhoods, and later while savoring a chocolate ganache cake, they discussed their hopes for the future.

"You're easy to be with," Burke said. "Easy to talk to."

"You, too." She smiled. Amazingly, she'd gotten used to his new look. While he wouldn't win a beauty contest—maybe best beast!—he was much more relaxed in this state.

"I found another room," Burke said. He held his arm out to escort her out of the dining room.

"Oh?" Margot put her hand in the crook of his arm and followed him into a large, open room lit with candle chandeliers. The warm glow of the candles reflected off gold fixtures and gleaming hardwood floors. The entire room was surrounded with paneled walls papered with silk roses.

"A ballroom!"

Burke showed her the sound system and stack of CDs.

Margot flipped through the stack. "Classical? Not what I expected from you."

"Believe it or not, I took three years of ballroom dancing."

"You joust and you ballroom dance?"

"My parents wanted me to be a Renaissance man. Jean Robert took lessons, too. That's why he tolerates me. We both took a lot of ribbing over the years."

"I've never danced to music like this."

Burke pressed play and then gentle piano music came out of some hidden speakers. "Follow my lead." He opened his arms.

"Go slow," she said, stepping into his embrace.

MARGOT LAY in bed staring up at the roses on the canopy bed. She'd gotten the best sleep she'd had since Sage put her under with the sipping chocolate. With sweet dreams of Burke and their time together last night, she woke up happy and content. Thyme might have done the right thing in locking them into the house.

She was ready to give the beast a chance. Not Burke the cute boy from France. But Burke as the beast, who built her a fire and taught her to ballroom dance. The beast who wanted to go home. He didn't ask for a fairy tale. She did. And last night, he proved to her that he was trying. He'd romanced her like she'd only read about.

Now it was her turn. She'd fully opened her heart to whatever came next.

Margot remembered the photo of her mom that Suzette had given her. She pulled it out and studied that hopeful little girl. "I got my wish," she said. "It's somewhat frightening, but exciting at the same time."

After she changed into a pair of jeans and V-necked sweater, layered with a white T-shirt, she stuck the photo into her back pocket in case they had to make a hasty departure.

By the time she'd gotten to the kitchen, she became a little worried about Burke. She'd poked her nose into several empty rooms along the way, but the house was eerily silent and empty.

Finding an icebox filled with eggs, bacon, and orange juice, she set out to make breakfast. The smell might draw him in. She took a quick look out the window, wondering if the bacon would tempt another creature.

There'd been no sign of the shadow she'd seen when they first arrived, but she still felt like she was being watched. By more than whatever was filling their icebox and delivering letters.

A wood stove now sat beside a farm sink in the kitchen. A happy upgrade from the hearth stove, and hopefully easy enough to use. It had already been heated, so it didn't take long for

Margot to cook everything. Just as she put the last of the scrambled eggs onto a plate for Burke, a big form, dark against the snow, rushed by the window. Her heart leaped into her throat. *It's back.*

Before Margot could panic, the creature stopped and rose up on two legs. She sighed in relief. Dressed in track pants and a muscle shirt, it was Burke. When he walked in, she was about to comment on his new wardrobe when she noticed he held a black rose in his mouth. He quickly transferred the rose to his hand, looking sheepish, if that were possible.

"Sorry, I didn't mean to startle you. I thought you were still sleeping."

She warmed with memories of being in his arms, dancing last night. "I haven't been up long." She held up their breakfast. "Have you eaten yet?" By his reaction, she knew he had.

"But I can eat again. Seems I'm always hungry."

Margot put the plates on the little table in the kitchen. She sat with her back to the wall and where she could see out the window into the snow-covered yard.

"So, super speed, huh? I think you're enjoying being a beast."

Burke clumsily downed his food. "There are some advantages, but that doesn't mean I want to stay this way." His gaze fixed on hers.

She met his challenge and didn't look away.

He held up the black flower that lay beside his plate. "I checked on the rose garden this morning, and it's not good." He handed her the dead rose. "All the plants have been torn up and spread all over the snow."

The creature wanted them to see what he did. Why? "Show me."

"Sage doesn't want you going outside."

Margot bit her lip. "She also told me to stay near you. The daytime seems to be fine. And you'll be there. I know how fast you can run."

He stood and offered her his arm. That was an improvement over yesterday when he wouldn't take her hand. "So, you're giving me a chance?" she asked.

"I shouldn't make the decision for you. You decide what you can handle and what you can't. I need you to see if you can handle a beast."

She slipped on the jacket hanging on the coat rack and then grabbed hold of Burke's beefy, hairy arm. She didn't imagine him as his old self, but accepted him as he was now.

Along the snowy path they came across first a twig, then a branch, and another, and another. Bits and pieces of rosebushes lying torn apart on the white snow. When they walked into the garden, Margot's knees buckled. It looked like a tornado had gone through and destroyed everything. Not a rosebush was left in the ground. It had been a violent attack, clumps of dirt mingling with the snow, all trampled by huge footprints.

Margot examined a footprint that extended past Burke's own large feet.

"It's bigger than you," she said.

"Much."

"What do you think it is? And what does it want?"

Burke locked eyes with her. No matter if he was Beast or Burke, his stormy gray eyes were always pure Burke. "We need to be careful."

"But we also need to save this garden," Margot said, practically. "It must be the way back or the creature wouldn't have torn it up like this."

"We could replant the root balls and hope that's enough."

"But won't he come back and dig them up again? Only worse so we can't fix it. We need to bring them into the house. If the rosebush is the key to getting home, we have to save it."

"There's a greenhouse on the other side of the house," Burke said. "I can see it from the master suite."

"Let's do it."

A quick trip to the stables yielded a shovel and a wheelbarrow.

Burke brought the wheelbarrow over to Margot. "Hop in." His growly voice had an edge of fun attached to it.

"Excuse me?"

"Haven't you ever had a wheelbarrow ride?"

"Yes, but not since I was a kid." She hesitated for only a moment before climbing in.

Burke started walking, and the wheelbarrow rocked side to side. Margot had forgotten the sensation was not like a wagon, but had a subtle swaying movement added in.

"Hold on." Burke started to run.

Margot jerked back and grabbed onto the sides. She laughed out loud as the frozen wind burned her cheeks. They hit a bump, and she almost fell out. Burke slowed down.

"Sorry. You okay?"

Margot stopped laughing. "Yes, I'm fine. Don't stop."

As they zipped by the trees, Margot got a chill. Not from the wind, but from a dark part of the woods.

"Is there something there?" she asked Burke. "Try your super smell." She couldn't tell what was paranoia and what was real fear anymore.

He slowed down and sniffed the wind. Then he sped up to the rose garden. "I smell lots of things. The evergreens are overpowering, but I think there's a rabbit, a deer, and maybe a snowy owl hiding out in that part of the forest.

"Nothing...bigger?"

"Farther away, there might be a moose. I'm not sure. This is all new to me. I didn't sense anything yesterday when we went into the woods."

Margot couldn't tell if he was keeping something from her or not. Didn't matter at this point. They couldn't hide out in the mansion when the rosebushes were dying. The roses might be the very thing that would get them back to Chapais.

With as much speed as possible, they rounded up all the root balls. Most were in large clumps of soil, so they had a good probability of surviving the attack. The creature had acted out of instinct or malice, not an awareness of biology.

With a wheelbarrow full of roots and broken stems, they made their way to the greenhouse. Margot hadn't seen this side of the house and marveled at the domed roof covering the circular greenhouse attached to the house with a short, enclosed walkway.

"This is a solarium," Margot said. "A sunroom."

The door was unlocked, and she opened it wide for Burke to wheel in the rescued plants.

Warm air welcomed them; the sun having done its job. A variety of plants grew inside and the high humidity led to moisture dripping on the glass panels. Several chairs and small drink tables were scattered among the healthy plants.

"Seems like there's a gardener." Margot said. "Perhaps it's someone who knows how to fix the second chance?"

"You really think this is the second chance?" Burke asked.

"The fairies spoke of a second chance, and roses play an important role in the Beauty and the Beast story. There's some kind of symbolism tied to it, don't you agree?"

"Yes, and I wish we knew how that fits into our story."

Our story. Margot turned around and smiled. "Here are some buckets we can use to plant them in." She pulled out a stack from under a table and brought them to the potting bench near the door.

Burke found barrels of soil and soon they had all the roses tucked into their own containers, twelve in all. Hopefully, one of them was the special bush that would bring them back to Chapais.

With their task complete, Burke paced in front of the bank of windows.

"Why don't you see if there's a game cupboard in the house?"

Margot suggested. He needed something to do, or he'd wear a hole in the floor where he paced in front of the roses.

"Really? You want to play games?"

Margot nodded. "You have a better idea?"

He started to grin, but then looked at his beastly hands. "I'll see what I can find."

Watching Burke pace so protectively worried her. She didn't want to think about what he might do if the creature returned to dig them up a second time.

Burke might be a trained knight, practiced in combat, but that was in a jousting arena meant for show. This creature was huge, if his footprints were any indication of his size, and didn't seem like someone to be reasoned with.

When Burke didn't come back right away, Margot began to feel vulnerable sitting in a glass enclosure. It wasn't hard to break glass. She dashed into the house after Burke.

She followed some odd sounds that led her back to the parlor, but he wasn't there.

"Burke?" she called out.

"In here."

The single door on the far side of the parlor was ajar.

"I found something I think you'll like," he called from inside. He sounded as excited as if he'd found a treasure trove of jousting equipment.

Curious, Margot followed him into the mysterious room.

"I don't believe it," she said. Books from floor to ceiling. Shelves upon shelves of books. Burke was halfway up one of those ladders that slides on tracks and was pushing himself around the room.

"Hop on," he called.

"*Whoa.* Now this is a library! I'll be in here for the rest of my days," Margot said.

"There're some games over there, too. Not many two player, but there is this new one called Jenga. Have you heard of it?"

"Sounds good," she said distractedly.

Burke walked over to the doorway, keeping a watch out the window.

"Go ahead and check on the roses. I'll pick out a few hundred books and meet you there." Margot thought working in a bookshop was amazing. She could live here for years and not get to the end of the library. "Although, fairies, if you can hear me, I don't want to live here for years. This is fun, but I want to see my family again."

Margot slid her hands along the leather spines, stopping at a burgundy one with gold letters that stood out to her. *Belle's Diary*.

She pulled it out and much to her delight discovered it was a handwritten journal filled with entries. She'd never been so faithful with her own diary. Mostly because she wrote boring things like about the weather. Who cared what the weather was?

The diary was written in French, of course. But now she could speak it, so, *huzzah!*

She brought the book back into the solarium with her.

He'd already dumped out a bunch of wood blocks onto the potting bench and was creating a tower. Burke looked pointedly at the book in her hand. "Just one?"

"This one is special. Give me a few minutes to flip through it."

She settled in an Adirondack chair and randomly cracked open the book, eager to read.

I never knew I could love like this. Flesh of my flesh, I would do anything for this sweet child we've been given.

Margot sucked in a breath with the realization. *Belle's diary*. This entry was from *after* she married the prince. She was writing about their baby. This could cast some light on what was happening with Burke and why.

"Well?" Burke's voice was near.

She jumped. He was right beside her.

"Sorry," he said. "you're kind of into that book. What's it about?"

"Belle's diary."

He looked at her sideways. "Should you be reading that?"

"Yes! I'm looking for clues about what's happening to you."

"Oh." He continued to watch her read.

Finally, she put the book down. His watchfulness was making her jumpy. "Do you mind if I take this upstairs to read? It might be important."

He glanced at the game he'd set up. "I could get a snack and read the rules. Meet back here in an hour? Is that long enough?"

"Perfect." She held up the book. "I might have some answers by then."

CHAPTER 36

*M*argot brought the diary up to her tower room and curled up in the window seat. She skimmed through page after page of cute baby girl antics, but she kept looking out the window for signs of the creature. What would he do when he noticed the bushes were gone? Would he even notice?

There were several time gaps in the diary as their daughters were suddenly older and then leaving the house to start their own families.

When Margot sensed that the account was leading toward the prince's death in old age, she stopped reading. Sometimes you didn't want to know how the story ended. It was better to imagine it for yourself.

At first glance, it appeared the diary would be no help. So, why had the house given it to her? To satisfy her curiosity? She'd have to go back and read each page carefully and see if she missed something.

Margot looked out the window to do a quick scan for the creature. Everything was still except for a figure walking across the snow-covered yard to the maze. *Clove?*

Quickly, Margot unlatched the window and pushed it open with a jerk. "Clove! Is that you?" she yelled. "We're in the house."

Margot beat on the window frame, but Clove didn't hear her. Rather, she glanced around furtively, then stepped into the hedgerow maze. After Clove entered, she turned right and disappeared.

"Burke!" Margot dashed down the stairs as fast as she could take the little steps. "Burke! Clove is in the maze. Let's go."

She ran to the solarium, but he wasn't there. The roses, however, were still tucked into their pots as they'd left them.

Where did he go? The kitchen.

No. He wasn't there either. The fire in the fireplace had gone down to embers. She looked out the kitchen window and noticed the footprints leading out the back door toward the stables.

You could have told me you were visiting the horses.

With a passing thought about the creature, Margot darted outside without her jacket. They had to find Clove before the creature did. And, just as importantly, find out why Clove went into the maze instead of the mansion.

First, Margot stopped by the stables, but Burke wasn't there either, and the black horse was missing. What a time to go for a ride!

If this were a horror movie and not a fairy tale, the two of them would play right into the creature's hands. Separating. Going outside.

In Burke's new beastly form, he thought himself even more invincible than when he was in the jousting arena. She hoped he hadn't gone to find the creature.

Meanwhile, Margot plowed a path to the maze where she met up with Clove's footprints. Good, that should make finding her easier.

"Clove? Wait up."

Margot reached the first turn and looked around the corner of the hedgerow. The footprints kept going. "Clove?" Margot didn't want to go too far into the maze in case they got lost. The sun set early here, and they'd risk the creature coming out. One more turn and then she'd go back to the house.

"Go back, Margot." Clove's voice came from deeper in the maze. "You shouldn't be out here."

"Clove? It's dangerous when the sun goes down. Come to the house with me."

There was a rustling noise and Margot said, "Clove, can you hear me?" Margot stopped. She refused to go farther into the maze. If Clove kept going, that was her business. "I'll be back at the château fixing hot chocolate for everyone. Meet me there."

Margot turned around and was immediately disoriented. She thought for sure the path was shorter than the one she was looking at. She thought she could follow the tracks in the snow, but now they scattered in all directions.

Left. I go left because I turned right last.

There was a thumping. Crashing. Something was coming toward her and fast. Forward or back? Margot didn't know where to turn. It was coming. *Do I call out for help or hide?*

"Run Margot!" Clove's voice was near, like that time she spoke to her from high up in the bleachers at the jousting tournament.

The creature's footsteps pounded with each beat of her heart.

Margot ran. Ran harder than she'd ever run in her life, turning and winding her way blindly through the maze, with ice crystals stinging her cheeks.

But the creature kept getting closer. The snow crunched underfoot and dry branches scratched at her body as she turned sharp corners.

Suddenly everything went silent. *Where is he?* The hedges weren't that thick. He could be on a parallel path and reach out to get her. She stopped and listened, slowly moving forward, hoping to get to safety before the creature found her. Her breath came out in panicked puffs. A sound came from behind, like someone had jumped over the hedge and landed hard.

Margot sprinted for the next gap in the hedge, but then the creature bounded over her head and landed hard in front of her. At a height of about seven feet tall, he was covered in hair, a muscular body like a bear with a face like a boar. A few shreds of torn trousers were all that was left to reveal he'd ever been a man.

He roared.

She froze, watching and waiting to see what he would do next. If she ran, he would pursue.

He stood, mouth in a snarl, watching her. The snow fell gently around them, so disquieting compared to the tension crackling in the space between them.

"Hello," she said meekly. *Do I speak to him as a man or as an animal?*

He roared back in response.

Margot swallowed. He was too far gone to talk as a man. She took a small step back, trying not to trigger any chase instinct. *Nice creature. Stay right there.* She took another step away.

He cocked his head, as if his animal brain were trying to figure out what she was doing. His lip curled. Then he pounced.

Arms outstretched with sharp claws pointed directly at her.

Margot turned to run, flinching in anticipation at the same time. She got three steps away when there was a loud *thud* behind her.

She turned to see beast thrashing on the ground with beast.

"Burke! No!"

Burke was smaller than the creature. It would kill him. The creature's roar tore through the air. He was mad.

Red blood soaked into the snow. Whose blood was it?

"Margot, this way. Now." Clove's voice came from behind. Margot turned to see the fairy waving her away from the fight.

"But Burke? I can't leave him."

"Yes, you can. This fight is not meant for you. Come with me now. You're distracting Burke. It'll be better for him if you leave."

"Can't you do something?" Margot went to Clove. "Protect him?"

Clove hesitated. "I've not been able to help either of them. But I can help you. I'm sorry we pulled you into this. It's time to get you out." She grabbed Margot's hand and pulled her farther away.

Margot balled her hands into fists. "We can't leave him. He'll die." She tried to look behind her but Clove pulled her attention back.

"I can only bring one of you back each time the portal opens. If you stay now, you'll both be killed. Is that how you want this to end? Come now while Sage holds the portal open."

There was a crunch of bone behind her and Margot automatically turned to see what happened.

The creature stood, howling in victory, blood covering its face. It started walking toward them, sneering at Clove.

"He hates me," Clove said putting herself in front of Margot, "but I'm also the only thing he fears here."

"Who is he?"

"Someone I couldn't help." Leveling her eyes at the creature, she commanded, "Leave us."

The creature roared at them before it turned around and limped off into the maze.

Margot ran to Burke's mangled body and checked his breathing. "He's alive, Clove. Take him back and get him help."

"I can only take one of you. I'll come back for him when we can get the portal open again."

"He'll die if you leave him here. You have to take him. You can come back for me. I'll be safe in the house until you do."

"I don't know about that. Burke was in the house with you. Now that he's not, I don't know if the creature will stay away."

"What else can we do? Burke needs the help more than I do right now."

Clove's expression pinched. "Sage is going to kill me. Kill us both."

"I'll explain when I see her. Which will be soon, right?" Margot spoke with more confidence than she felt.

"Get in the house, first. It's the safest place for you. Wave out the window when you're in. I'll not leave a moment sooner."

Margot took one last look at Burke. "Hurry. Please."

CHAPTER 37

*M*argot waved wildly from the parlor window. "Go," she whispered. "Save Burke."

The mansion was so quiet Margot heard the wind blowing forlornly in the trees outside. Her ears were tuned to every twist of wind circling around the tower.

At first, Margot sat in a chair in the corner, her eyes fixed to the door waiting for the beast to come get her. But after a while, it appeared that he was not immediately coming for her. Maybe he was too hurt. Good. That gave her time to figure a way out. She didn't fancy waiting for the fairies to come get her.

She remembered the poem in the book by her bed.

> *Welcome, Margot, banish fear,*
> *You are queen and mistress here;*
> *Speak your wishes, speak your will,*
> *Swift obedience meets them still.*

Could it be that easy?
"I wish for a way home."

She waited, slowly circling the room looking for a magic portal. A shimmer. Anything.

"I thought I was queen here?" she asked the house.

Nothing.

"I could use some of that sipping chocolate—minus the fairy dust—to help me think…"

She turned around and there, on a tea cart was a steaming mug of chocolate.

"Really? You'll feed me, but not help me leave? Seems like I'm more a prisoner than a queen."

She took the drink and picked up Belle's diary. There must be a clue in the story. How did Belle leave the castle? There was the mirror that showed her how poorly her father was doing. But Margot had seen no mirrors in the house.

She had seen a fancy mirror in Burke's apartment in the castle in Chapais. That wouldn't be any help to her, though Burke, when he got better, might be able to see her.

Wait. What is this?

Margot reread the section describing Belle's visit to her father.

Before I left to see my father, Beast said "you need only lay your ring on the table before you go to bed, when you have a mind to come back." He said it in such a hopeful way it near breaks my heart when I think back on it.

Margot scanned the text until she found the next reference.

I can't believe I waited so long to return to my beast. I didn't know if I'd be able to sleep; I was so excited to go home. I put my ring on the bedside table and lay down. Next thing, I was waking up in my room in the château.

That was it. The ring brought Belle home to the beast. It could bring her back to her beast. To Burke.

She immediately dug through the jewelry box on the vanity. The tall cabinet made of little drawers was loaded with bracelets and broaches, but no rings. *Oh, come on.*

"Where is Beauty's ring?" She held her breath, waiting for an answer from the house.

Her gaze landed on the flowered pillows on the window seat and she rushed over to it. She thrust her hands between all the cushions, hoping to find the ring had fallen and been forgotten there all these years. Empty-handed and frustrated, she lay on the bed.

What if the magic ring was also in the castle in Chapais? She traced a rose on the bedspread and thought about all the places a girl would hide a ring.

She flipped open the diary again and read the final account listed. This time she pushed through the sadness and read about the prince dying.

Even though I know his soul has gone to God, I wanted him close to us so we can visit his grave. Everyone agreed it was best for him to be buried where we met. In the place we both loved so much.

Every day I sit near the rosebush that grew from the one the fairy gave him as a second chance and remember him. He always took special care of that rose, putting it in a place of prominence in the garden. It bloomed a beautiful snowy white every summer, and he called it Beauty's Rose.

We will meet again one day, only this time I won't need the ring to return to him. I buried it with the rose.

Margot stopped reading and tossed the diary aside.
She wouldn't need the ring. But I do.

Margot bit her lip as she ran to the window. No sign of the beast or any of the fairies. Belle was a romantic through and through. It was so like her to bury the ring as a final symbolic gesture. *Bless you, Belle.*

Next, Margot ran to the master suite. It was strange walking through here without Burke. He'd been sleeping here, as evidenced by the unmade bed. The furniture in this room was sturdy enough to support a beast.

From the window, Margot studied the grounds on this side of the house. The rose garden looked cold and barren and still torn apart. If Margot could find a headstone or other grave marker, she might find where Beauty's Rose had been planted.

Shallow divots revealed where the bushes had been before the creature yanked them out. That would narrow the search.

"But the beast is out there," she told the house. "You really want me to risk my life to check in the garden?"

She turned away from the window. "I'll take the silence to mean yes."

She headed for the door and noticed a small spade leaning against it.

"Thank you," she said. "Now, is there any way you could keep the beast occupied while I try to dig up the frozen ground?"

Before she could lose her nerve, Margot grabbed her jacket and ran for the nearest door to the rose garden. The front door. It opened. "Now you let me out the front?"

She left the door wide open in case it somehow locked behind her. She needed a fast entrance as she anticipated having to make a run for it. Already her heart was beating fast, and she kept her ears focused on any unusual noises.

The torn-up condition of the garden made it extra hard for her to find the specific location where the bush used to be buried. Did the beast know, and is that why he attacked the garden? Maybe it wasn't the rosebush itself, but the ring buried with it.

She started in the middle of the garden, her best guess as to where the bush Burke pricked his finger on was located. She kneeled in the snow and began to prod at the dirt with her spade. Her fingers burned with the cold, and despite her best efforts, she could barely scratch the surface of the frozen dirt.

A soft swish caught her attention. Not waiting to see if it was friend or foe, Margot shot up and ran for the house. A shadow moved pace with her in her peripheral vision. It was lurching, like it was injured—thank you Burke—but was still as fast as she was.

It was aiming for the front door of the house, trying to cut her off. Margot veered to the side and sprinted to the solarium door. She berated herself for leaving the front door open. The creature would have access to the house.

Safely inside the solarium, Margot pressed her back up against the potting bench and glanced around the room looking for something to defend herself with.

Her gaze landed on the potted root balls. What if?

She lunged for them and began pulling them, shaking their roots free of dirt. She hoped it was there. If the creature had pulled up enough of the dirt around the roots, the ring might have gotten caught up *en masse.*

Three pots in, and she'd made a mess of the floor, but no ring. She could hear the creature in the house, now, tearing things apart. The thuds and crashes grew louder as the creature made his way through the building. Margot's hands trembled as she searched through the roots.

"Come on. Where is it?"

Finally, a glint of gold sparkled in the dirt. Margot pulled and broke off the roots that locked the ring in their grasp.

This was her second chance. A roar emanated from the house, and she jumped.

... lay your ring on the table before you go to bed, when you have a mind to come back.

Margot had a mind to come back immediately. She lay on the ground and put the ring eye level with her. *Please work.*

She closed her eyes and tried to calm herself into a sleepy state. A nearby roar pierced the quiet of the solarium. The creature would soon be on her, but Margot forced herself to keep her eyes closed. If this didn't work, she'd fight back as best she could.

Breathe in. Breath out. Let yourself be carried away.

Come on.

Try to let go. He's getting closer. Drift off...

The door burst open, and Margot leaped up with a gasp, ready to run.

She stood in her bedroom at Suzette's, the fairies crowding into the doorway.

"We thought we heard something," Sage said. "Well done, Margot. How did you do it?"

She held out her hand, and the ring lay in her palm. It was a plain gold band with a small gold rose at the top.

Burke lay on the daybed, back in regular Burke form, only extra hairy. Eyes closed, he lay so still he could have been one of the mannequins in the Torture Museum.

"Is he dead?" she asked. Several cuts had been stitched, and someone had applied iodine, staining his skin.

"No. We've done the best we can for him, but—" Sage started to explain when Clove interrupted.

"Kiss him."

Margot looked askance at the fairies.

"You love him?" Thyme asked.

"He saved my life. I want to save his." *Of course, I love him.* Margot stared at his tattered and barely breathing form. Their feelings should be expressed to each other first, not the fairies.

"Then kiss him," Clove said. "Why the hesitation? Does his look repulse you?" Her voice held derision.

"No, it's not that." Margot's gaze dropped to his lips. She'd thought of kissing him plenty of times. When he carried her to the bookshop after the horse stepped on her foot. When they shared a horseback ride. At his apartment when he was adorably sleeping. Anytime there was a *moment*.

Sage cocked her head and studied Margot for a second before leaving the room. She signaled for the others to follow her lead.

"Make it quick," Clove said. "He's not doing well."

Margot needed no other prompting. "Come back to me, Burke," she whispered. Margot closed her eyes before placing a gentle kiss on his lips. She kneeled on the floor, waiting.

In unison, the fairies turned around and came over, watching, waiting with her.

After a moment, Thyme whispered, "Let's go have tea. Margot will tell us of any changes."

Margot glanced up and smiled her gratitude before reaching for Burke's hand. "This is the time," she told him. "I've done all I know to do. It's your move." With her other hand, she stroked his long hair away from his face. A clump of it came away in her hand.

Her heart skipped a beat. "I hope that's a good sign," she said. "You'll probably be happier with less hair." She looked down at the hand she was holding and saw that his fingernails were short again. She dared to hope. "Keep going," she whispered. She squeezed his hand, willing him to know she was there.

His eyelids fluttered and finally opened. His gaze darted around the room until his searching eyes finally honed in on her. "Margot," he said.

Oh, the way he said her name. She leaned closer. "How are you? We're all worried about you." The question she wanted to ask went unsaid. Are you still beastly or is it reversing and gone for good?

"I'm not sure. I ache everywhere." His voice was still deeper than normal, but the growl behind it was gone.

"Can you sit up?"

He nodded, and she helped him lean back against the pillows. Wherever he moved, he left a trail of hair. Margot laughed. She couldn't help herself. Now his arms had patches of regular skin. "You're shedding."

"So I am. I feel different, too. Tingly, like when water evaporates off your skin when you've been swimming. What happened?"

She blushed. Was she supposed to tell him about the kiss? Shouldn't he already know?

He continued. "I remember attacking the beast in the maze." He gave her a quick once-over, looking concerned. "Because I didn't want him to hurt you. He didn't, did he?"

She thought back to the heart-pounding moment. "You hurt each other. Pretty badly."

"And how did we get here? I remember Clove being there and saying there was room for only one." He rubbed his head and more hair fell out. "But you wouldn't go."

"If you had stayed, you would have died. Beastly form or not, you needed modern medicine." She grabbed a clean towel from the dresser and while she rubbed Burke's skin free, she filled him in on what he'd missed.

"And that was it? That broke the curse? Us sacrificing ourselves for each other? Because I can tell something's changed. Never mind how I look." He reached for her hand and held it. "I was glad to save you from the creature and would do it again to keep you safe." He swallowed. "Margot. I think I love you."

His stormy eyes were less volatile, now. She took a deep breath before saying the words she'd never said to anyone before. "I love you, too."

He grinned, then leaned forward and kissed her this time.

"They're kissing," hissed Clove from the doorway. "Can I go in now and check on him?"

Embarrassed, Margot sat back and made room for the fairies to cluster around, talking all at once.

"Are you sure?" Clove asked Burke. "I can't leave Chapais until I know it's over."

"Yes. For the first time in my life I feel... I don't know, normal?"

"Excellent." Clove beamed so wide dimples dug into her cheeks.

"Well done." Sage put her arm around Clove.

"I hope you learned your lesson," Thyme said. "But please, keep baking. You've got a knack."

As the tension released from the room, Margot fully realized that they were in Suzette's apartment. What did her aunt think of Burke landing here in such condition?

"Where is Suzette?" Margot asked.

Sage answered. "Don't worry. No time has passed here. She's next door visiting the good doctor. Thyme thinks an old romance has been rekindled."

"I hope she likes ferns," Thyme said with a smile.

"I don't need to see any more," said Clove, looking at the wild creature roaming the maze. He was no longer bleeding, but he would have a limp the rest of his days. She put the mirror face down on the kitchen counter.

"Why didn't you tell us the last one turned into a beast, and that you hid him in the maze?" Thyme said. "I wouldn't have locked Burke and Margot into the house had I known."

Thyme slid a pan into the oven while Clove set the timer on the stove.

Clove crossed her arms and leaned against the counter. "In the future, I won't try to hide my failures."

Sage shook her head. "Ultimately, he chose his own path. You tried to help him, but he refused it. Surely, Burke reminded you of that."

Clove nodded, still contemplative.

"And look at you two, working together so well and not bickering." Sage extended her arms to them.

Thyme and Clove looked critically at each other.

Then Thyme let out a giggle. Clove followed suit, and it

bubbled out of her. Soon they were all laughing and Clove and Thyme embraced.

When Sage tried to join them, they shut her out, but then, heads shaking, included her.

"All is well that ends well," Thyme quipped. "Now, who's having fudge?"

CHAPTER 38

*A*ll of Margot's new friends stopped by the bookshop on her last day. Tanvi came with Silvain and Jean Robert, and they made plans with Burke to go to the beach one last time before summer was over.

"Here's my address," Tanvi said, slipping her a piece of paper. "Write often."

"I will."

"See ya, Burke," Silvain slugged him on the arm.

Since returning from the château, Burke had let Silvain win a few jousting matches, and that was all it took for the two to make peace.

Tanvi and Margot rolled their eyes. *Guys.*

When it was time for Burke to drive her to the airport, Margot gathered her luggage. She didn't want to go, so much of her heart was now in France.

Suzette hugged her. "I'm sorry I didn't get as much time to spend with you as I'd like. But you will talk to your father about the bookshop?"

Margot nodded. "Not the first day home, but soon after. He's already agreed to come with me next summer, so I only have to wait for the right moment to let him know I want to move here permanently."

The fairies stood around Burke's convertible, saying their goodbyes.

"Thank you," Clove said to Margot. "I had my doubts at the beginning, but you came through."

Margot shared a look with Burke. "Happy to exceed your expectations."

Thyme was next, pulling her off to the side while Burke packed the luggage. "What did you think of your wish coming true?" she asked, a mischievous glint in her eye.

"My wish?"

"When you were a child at the well. You wanted to live a fairy-tale life. A tall order for me, I tell you. A fairy-tale princess needs a kind heart, a strong work ethic, and a great deal of love and selflessness to survive the tale."

Margot cocked her head. "You were in that garden in Victoria?"

Thyme just smiled and patted her hand. "You can keep the magic going by writing your own story." She slipped Margot a slim journal. "You might find it gives you the 'more' that you're looking for. Oh, look at that cute cat. Excuse me." Thyme set off. "Here, kitty, kitty."

Sage was last.

"Will I see you again?" Margot asked.

"You shouldn't. One fairy tale per prince." She glanced at Burke. "Off you go. Quick goodbyes are best."

Margot slid into Burke's convertible. She was hoping for a long, drawn out goodbye with him. He had the top down, and when he started the car, the *Summer of Love* tape blasted out of the speakers. They grinned at each other.

They left early enough to take a trip down to the beach where Burke bought her a hot dog and they walked along the shore.

Margot eyed his hairline to make sure it hadn't changed from their morning horseback ride.

"It's over," he said. "You can quit studying me."

She shook her head. "Never."

He grinned and bumped her shoulder.

They spent some time leaning against the log on the beach, holding hands and not saying much. The beach was crowded with families, but as the clouds rolled in, people started leaving.

"I can't imagine what my life would be like if you hadn't visited this summer," Burke said.

"Silvain would have killed you by now," she joked. She was glad that Burke had made peace with the other guys in town. "We should probably go, too. It looks like rain, and the roof on your convertible is down."

As she spoke, the rain began to spatter, and they ran for it. Off the beach and through the trees where Burke pulled her under a protective branch. "I don't know if we'll have time for a proper goodbye at the airport, so do you mind if I say goodbye here?" he asked, his arms already around her.

"Not at all." She lifted her face to meet his kiss.

<hr />

THE RETURN TRIP home was the reverse of the beginning of Margot's summer. Except, instead of wondering what Chapais would be like, she relived fond memories of the best summer of her life.

Back at home, Margot stood near her wall and examined the photo collage she'd made of the photos she'd brought back with her. *Collage. Another French word I'd already known.* The pictures were of her mom as a little girl, the castle, tournament scenes, her friends, the fairies, and Burke. Lots of pictures of Burke.

She and Burke would exchange letters, and if they splurged,

they could even talk on the phone. It would be one long year until they saw each other again.

Margot continued to unpack her suitcase.

The flower headdress that Tanvi had given her lay on the very top. Margot had dried the flowers and carefully wrapped them in tissue. They'd survived the trip fairly well. Before unpacking anything else, she draped them on the edge of her mirror, letting the red and gold ribbons hang down.

Next, she brought out Dad's tacky tourist gift. Also wrapped in paper to protect it. She'd almost forgotten to buy him something, but luckily the gift shop at the airport had the tackiest set of salt and pepper shakers. The pepper was a Frenchman in a beret and the salt was a plump Frenchwoman wearing an apron. They could sit on the kitchen table and remind them of France and how next summer they'd both go.

Next summer was a long time away. She went back to her suitcase.

Wait, what's this?

Underneath her jeans, she found a thin box wrapped in blue glitter paper with a note attached:

Dear Margot,

I hope you enjoyed your fairy-tale summer. You were a good sport about it, and if I'm correct, things worked out well for everyone. Please accept this token of our appreciation. We've connected it to Burke's family mirror, and he knows how to use it. We've also given it an upgrade. Instructions are carved on the back. Keep it a secret or it disappears. For real.

—Clove

Margot tore open the paper and opened the box. Inside, she found an ornate hand mirror similar to the one in Burke's apartment. *No way.* She was right? It was the mirror that lets you see someone. She'd be able to check up on Burke whenever she wanted to.

She sat on her bean bag chair and read the instructions. Easy enough. She positioned her hands on either side of the mirror and said, "I wish to see and talk with Burke."

The mirror turned dark. The angle changed, and then there was some bumping around. Finally, Burke's face appeared. "Salut. I've been waiting."

"Burke! This is amazing. Imagine we can see and talk to each other across thousands of miles. It's like the Jetsons."

Dad knocked. "Everything okay?"

Margot tossed a T-shirt over the mirror. "Yeah. Just daydreaming about my summer."

Dad poked his head into the room. He immediately noticed the new photo collage on the wall.

"Can you stop daydreaming long enough to join me for supper? Amy said she'd be over for dessert. Said something about wanting to show you her new Swatch. Doesn't she already have three? How many watches does one girl need?"

"You'd be surprised."

"I heard you speaking French there. Sounded good to me. Does this mean you are set on going to school in France next year?"

"I'm pretty fluent now." *Thanks to my time in the enchanted château.* "But my plans have shifted a little."

"Oh?"

"We can talk about it later."

"Something tells me you found more than you expected."

She only raised her eyebrows. Let him sit with the idea of change before she forced the issue.

"Amazing what can happen in a summer."

After Dad left, Margot returned to Burke.

"Are you still there?"

Burke grinned. "I've told you in the château. I'm not going anywhere."

Dear Reader,

Did you know that the *Beauty and the Beast* story from 1756 included a fairy? Since I have a predilection for fairies, I zeroed in on her and expanded her world to include two friends.

To see how they were involved with Beauty and the prince in my version of the tale, you can download a prequel for free on my website.

The download also includes a translation of "La Belle et la Bête" by French novelist Jeanne-Marie Leprince de Beaumont, published in 1756.

It might explain some other aspects of the story you don't recognize from recent movies.

ShonnaSlayton.com/beautys-rose-prequel/

HISTORICAL NOTES

The town of Chapais does not exist, but was inspired by Carcassonne, a real medieval city in France, complete with castle. Carcassonne is a real tourist destination that you can visit.

Another confession: I didn't stick to the historical line of French royalty, but choose instead to embrace fairy tale "royalty" for Burke's lineage.

The '80s were a fun decade for exploring pop culture and new technology. Some things that are every-day to us now were still in their infancy in the '80s, like personal home computers (now I carry a computer in my purse!) And it was an interesting decade for music with records, cassettes, and CDs all coexisting. Communication back then seems near the dark ages compared with how easy it is to call people around the world, practically anytime, anywhere on our cell phones.

Finally, a note about 80s hair. I could have spent pages on hair alone. My editor pulled me back from the brink and suggested I tone it down. Like, totally. '80s hair was awesome.

ACKNOWLEDGMENTS

Faith K. Moore's developmental edit saved this book. It was just not coming together the way I envisioned, and she pushed me off the rabbit trail and back onto the main story. Thank you!

Jenny Zemanek's cover would make any Belle proud.

Kristi Bledsoe, fellow author and critique partner. Thanks for persevering through the early drafts (!)

To those who beta read this round: Stephanie Shackelford, Marci Mathers, LynnDell Watson, Shawna Shade, Kassie Lamoreaux, Andrea Huelsenbeck, and Rebekah Slayton. I appreciate your feedback more than you know.

Lisa Knapp, as a proofreader, you're like that friend who sees you coming out of the bathroom with your skirt accidentally tucked into your pantyhose and fixes it before anyone else notices. Thank you!

Fairy Tale Forum members: Your enthusiasm for fairy tales inspires me and your depth of knowledge pushes me to dig deeper into the genre.

Above all, I thank God for creating this world where we can use our imaginations to craft story worlds that reflect the mysterious and magical parts of our own fantastical world.

ALSO BY SHONNA SLAYTON

Which one will you read next?

Fairy-tale Inheritance Series

Cinderella's Dress

Cinderella's Shoes

Cinderella's Legacy

Snow White's Mirror

Beauty's Rose

The Little Mermaid (coming next)

Lost Fairy Tales

The Tower Princess

Historical Women

Liz and Nellie: Nellie Bly and Elisabeth Bisland's Race Around the World
in Eighty Days

With Entangled Teen Publishing

Spindle

CPSIA information can be obtained
at www.ICGtesting.com
Printed in the USA
FSHW011735010621
81955FS